CATCHING BUTTERFLIES

BOOK 2 ESCAPE SERIES

SANDRA J. JACKSON

For my mom

ACKNOWLEDGMENTS

As always, a big thank you to my family for putting up with my "disappearance" when I was still physically in the room.

Thanks to my readers who have waited patiently for this second book of the trilogy. The third is already written so should follow shortly.

Thank you to my beta readers Leslie and Denis Brown; I value your opinion.

To my Creative Editor, Ron Bagliere, whose 30 years of writing and editing knowledge helped me to see where my story needed improvement.

Thank you to Creativia; I continue to look forward to this and other published works.

1

CROSSROADS

THE TINY CREATURE FILLED ITS BELLY, GORGING ON BLOOD. It swelled red and then after a moment lifted off, swaying under the burden of an engorged body. The bug flew toward a patch of undergrowth and landed on a stick. I squinted and sought to recall the name of the insect. *Mosquito!* The word popped into my brain. While my memory had improved, some words and events of the last five years still eluded me.

"You're welcome!" I called before it disappeared into the brush.

"April, who are you talking to?" Beth opened her pale blue eyes and yawned. We had stopped for yet another break, the fourth since escaping our confines despite having not travelled very far. And while we'd filled our stomachs with as much food as possible before leaving, our bodies remained weak. A fallen tree at the side of the roadway made for a perfect rest-stop.

"The mosquito I fed." I waved in the direction where the overstuffed bug landed, a proud smile on my face for having helped a fellow living creature.

Beth wrinkled her nose and shook her head. Tangled

brown waves swept the top of her shoulders. "Probably sh-shouldn't have done that."

"After being half-starved yourself, I thought you'd appreciate my generosity."

"Oh, I do, it's just that there's s-something about them. I can't quite—"

"Crap!" There was a flutter in my stomach and my heart quickened its pace. The information Jasper had shared sprang to mind. "Those pests carry the virus." A slow breath escaped between my lips as I worked to calm the rising anxiety.

"Yes, but that's not what I was th-thinking, there's s-something else. Anyway, he also said close contact with anyone infected and we have been—"

"Oh!" I interrupted, and with a frenzied motion, scratched the spot where the bug had fed. "This is so itchy!" Red scratch marks covered my forearm, and a small bump appeared.

"That's it!" Beth's eyes widened, and she grinned. "Mosquitoes cause great itching."

"Wish you would've remembered that sooner." For the moment my itchy arm erased any concern for contracting a virus.

Beth shrugged, and a more serious expression replaced her cocky smile. "We sh-should have s-stayed." She cast her gaze ahead of her.

"What? Where?" I rubbed at the deep creases in my brow with my fingertips.

"At the house, we sh-should have s-stayed there."

"With two dead bodies? And it wasn't a house, it was a prison." The mention of our former living arrangements conjured images of our attic room. Rough wood walls, rusted cots, buckets used as toilets, the tall wooden wardrobe filled with the belongings of the unfortunate, and the dirty round window played in my head like a strange movie. The echo of Jasper's raspy last breath and the buzzing flies provided the cinematic sound. We had prepared to die in that room, had given up hope. *Stop, it's over,* I rebuked, *we're free.* The memory faded, and I gulped in fresh air, relaxing my clenched fists. *But are we safe?* My eyes scanned the trees, leaves rustled; the faint smell of death, an odour I knew well, tainted the breeze

"At least, there was sh-shelter, running water, and electricity." Beth didn't hide her irritation.

"A dilapidated old shack, drippy faucets, and solar generated power from panels that looked outdated and unreliable." I reminded Beth. The much older style of power generation was in the back yard. Granted they supplied electricity, we'd had a working lamp, but that meant nothing. It was odd I remembered technical things such as solar panels but couldn't put a name to biting insects that caused itching and the potential for disease.

"Still..."

"And. Dead. Bodies," I repeated, emphasizing each word. Visions of Cecil's fly-covered, rotting body flashed in my head; the overpowering odour was one I would never forget. And then there was Jasper. My breath hitched as I thought of poor Jasper, the pain and anguish he must have suffered.

"We could have removed th-them." Beth picked at the decomposing wood with a jagged fingernail. Small chunks flaked off and fell.

"Hmph! Don't you mean I would have removed the bodies? You could barely stand the sight let alone the smell."

Beth shrugged and dropped her gaze; her foot pushed around a large piece of bark and disrupted a small and slimy, legless creature. The squirming body slunk under a pile of rotting leaves. A tuft of red fur clung to a nearby shrub, and I pulled my gaze away, worried the animal's remains lay hidden beneath the twigs and leaves.

We sat in silence. Insects hummed and buzzed; birds sang in the treetops while I shut my eyes and absorbed the sounds of the world. Nature overwhelmed my senses. My lungs expanded, and the action filled my nose with the smells of the trees, the air, the earth, and even the rotting timber. I bent forward until my face hovered above the surface of the downed tree. The strange scent of musty, decaying wood was unlike the boards on the floor and walls that had encased us for... *How long were we there?* The scratches carved into the floorboards appeared in my head, and I counted the envisioned lines, adding extra for the days I missed.

"What are you doing?"

Beth's voice interrupted my thoughts and caused me to jump. "Thinking." Green moss brushed against my skin, soft, wet, and cool. The heel of my hand wiped across my nose.

"Looks more like you're s-smelling."

Another mosquito prepared to dine right next to the growing welt left behind by the previous customer, and I swatted it away. "This is not a buffet!" I held out my itching limb and stood, stretching my arms to the sky. Tiny cracks and pops rippled up my spine. "Time to go."

"Where?" Beth looked up at me from her spot on the downed tree. Her eyebrows rose high and hid under wavy locks. "Can we search for the t-trail?" There was excitement in her voice.

Confused by her strange question I pressed my fingertips against my brow. I turned in a slow circle and immersed myself in the surroundings. Tall trees met with the cloudy sky, its leaf covered limbs reached upward like outstretched arms trying to sweep away the grey puffs. Occasionally the sun broke through, and I swore the leaves sighed as they bathed in the warmth.

The dirt road weaved through the forest and disappeared, swallowed by the trees. Branches hung with ominous intent, reaching out to grab at whoever dared to walk close enough. The house of our imprisonment was no longer visible when I looked back at the path we'd travelled, but it was easy to imagine.

Goosebumps rose, and I trembled. "Keep following the road." I shrugged.

"To where?"

"To wherever it leads." I bent over and picked up my pack. The green bag bulged, silver zippers stretched out to their limit, and I worried they'd split open under the pressure.

We packed the backpacks with whatever things we deemed necessary and useful. Unable to stuff in any more items we tied our bedding to the bottom of the full packs.

"Probably sh-should have grabbed more food," Beth said. She stood and hauled up the black bag. The weight and sudden movement caused her to stumble, but she regained her balance.

I helped her place the heavy pack over her shoulders. My eyes fixed on a small hole in her grey t-shirt as I straightened the straps. Rolled blankets hung below the backpack and hit just above the backs of her knees.

The snap and click of the buckle on Beth's pack pricked my ears and assured me she'd secured the backpack. "This bag is too heavy as it is; you'd never been able to carry it." I turned away from Beth, swung my load over a shoulder, and waited for her to help with the other strap.

With the other shoulder strap secured, I clicked in the front belt and then tugged on the hem of my bright blue t-shirt; the material straightened out from beneath the harness. There had been many articles of clothing in various sizes in one of several huge boxes, and we each grabbed two t-shirts and two pairs of sweatpants. The soft, grey material of the slightly large pants felt strange yet comforting as it rubbed against my legs when I walked.

I turned and faced the old tree, placed my foot on top, and reached to secure a blue shoelace. The shoes, found in a separate box, were a size or two larger than my feet. "Your turn," I said and finished tying the lace of the other shoe.

Beth raised her foot and rested it on the tree as I stood behind and steadied her. "We really need to remember to tighten sh-shoelaces before we put these packs on," she huffed and tightened the black shoelace of one runner.

"Next time." I clutched Beth's pack as she worked on the bright pink lace of the other.

We discovered footwear in several boxes but none had laces. After searching more cartons we found a small tangled and tattered roll, most on the verge of breaking. Several minutes of untangling and two pairs emerged from the mess. Beth had grumbled that the laces did not match. Finding four intact shoelaces had been hard enough let alone matching ones.

A bright blue lace secured my right shoe while a green one kept my left one in place. The fact they weren't a match was of no concern. "Let's go," I said, hooking a thumb under each strap.

Beth heaved a loud sigh but uttered no other complaint as we continued walking away from a horrendous past into an uncertain future.

The scuffing of dirt drowned out the sounds of nature as we plodded. My feet slid inside my shoes with every step. *Tie them tighter next time*, I thought as my attention focused on the ground. A rock bounced off the end of one runner as my toe kicked it aside. A yellow and black caterpillar wriggled across the path right before my foot landed, and I stepped over the critter in time.

"We sh-should have looked harder." Beth's voice shifted my awareness back to her.

"We did."

My sister shook her head. "No, there was one place we didn't ch-check."

There *was* one place we hadn't checked. There was no way I would poke my fingers into a dead man's pockets in search for a set of keys to his truck. "You didn't want to do it either," I called out to Beth who continued walking after I stopped.

She came to a halt and turned her icy stare on me. "No, but st-still..."

"Still what?"

Beth waited for me as I caught up to her. She shrugged, and we walked together. "Nothing, just still..."

We trudged along; floppy shoes scraped the ground and caused a mini dust storm.

"Even if we found the keys, we don't remember if we know how to drive." I booted a rock and watched as it bounced and tumbled out of the way.

"Don't you think we would have remembered once the t-truck started?"

Procedural memory, I hadn't wanted to take the chance. "Maybe." Silence fell between us again as every step took us closer toward the unknown.

The pack jostled. The weight of it pushed into my body, and I could sense everything it held. But the journal, Jasper's journal, was the most bothersome. We had taken no time to read it before we left, and my anxiety grew at the thought of reading the secrets within its pages.

Stop, I told myself and returned my attention to my feet. It was easier than looking at the trees standing sentry, like they were watching us. I half expected to see a camera, its bloodshot eye peeking out from between the branches of a foreboding tree. My thoughts flickered to the watchful lens in the corner of our room at the compound.

"Do you th-think anyone else got out?" Beth's voice once again broke my concentration.

My gaze narrowed. "What about our brother?" A tingling sensation spread up the back of neck to the top of my head as I spoke the word brother out loud. Jasper's strangled whisper of the truth echoed in my ear. Knowing we had a younger sibling that neither of us remembered having was still weird.

"Not from the house," Beth jutted her thumb behind her, "from C.E.C.I.L."

Images of the compound flashed in front of me, cameras, white hallways, injections—each memory a snippet of a strange existence. *Who else had escaped?* Workers were the only ones I recalled ever seeing though only a few memories of my life at C.E.C.I.L. had surfaced. Even the closest rooms to our own were vacant. *Was it possible we had been the last ones?* The thought disturbed me. "I don't know." I smacked and squished a mosquito that tried to dine on me again. My finger flicked its crushed body from my arm and it left behind a tiny streak of blood. I licked my thumb and washed the stain away.

"This forest looks nothing like the one at C.E.C.I.L." Beth waved a hand at the woods surrounding us.

Once again, my mind filled with memories of tall plastic trees and meandering trails. "Of course not," I snickered, "these are real. And you mean the forest at C.E.C.I.L. looked nothing like this." A large rock standing alongside the road caught my attention. It reminded me of a similar one placed by the winding path within C.E.C.I.L. and the day I had planned on touching it. But at the last second I pulled my hand away, afraid they'd see and learn of my awareness.

I moved closer to the side as we approached and stretched out my left hand. Beads of sweat broke out on my forehead as I neared the huge rock. *What if someone is watching?* "Who?" I questioned back aloud and laughed. The skin on my face tightened, and I wiped my palm across my damp brow.

"What are you doing?"

"I'm going to touch that." I pointed and moved towards it. My feet stopped in front of the large, grey boulder. Small fissures ran over the surface branching off in every direction. A black bug with red legs disappeared into a deep crevice that almost split the stone.

My left hand trembled. A loud buzz filled my ears as my palm neared the rock. I snapped it back then laughed when I saw an insect buzzing above me. I inhaled and let the air escape through pursed lips; my heart slowed. With much caution, I extended my hand again; my fingers quivered.

"Just touch it already." Beth's slim digits wrapped around my wrist, and before I could resist the sharp tug, my palm rested on the rock. Its rough surface scratched my skin. Coldness travelled up my arm, and I shivered. Beth's warm hand patted the top of mine. "There, now let's go."

I shook my head and laughed as I trailed behind my sister with my eyes fixed on the ground. Neither of us spoke as we followed the road to wherever it led.

"Now what?" Beth said after several minutes, her voice sounded defeated.

"What?" I halted and stared ahead. The road we'd been travelling on had ended, and another crossed its path. We needed to make a decision at our crossroad.

2

AWAY

"So, which way do we go?" Beth's head swivelled.

I stepped up next to her and contemplated each direction of the crossroad. There were no signs, and it resembled the road we'd travelled—dusty, long, and deserted. Left or right, neither promised help.

"Let me know when you've figured it out." Beth released the buckle on the backpack and allowed the heavy load to drop. She sank to the ground, pulled her legs up and rested her chin on the top of her knees.

Unable to decide, I sighed and did the same. Moments later my sister laid flat on her back, with ankles crossed, hands folded on her chest, and her eyes closed. Shallow breaths produced a slight rise and fall of her belly, the only part of her body that moved. Even an ant crawling along her forearm, did not cause her to flinch.

My fingers plucked at the green leaves from various tiny plants around me. The broken stem released a sharp woody scent as I rolled it between thumb and index finger. Each leaf's subtle differences amazed me, their shape, colour—different yet the same. Every one designed to capture energy from the sun and turn it into nourishment for the plant. *Photosynthesis,* another remembered word.

Paying no attention, I pulled out a weed with three leaves fixed to a dark green stem. Two leaves reminded me of arms and the single leaf at the end, a pointy head. The greenery was familiar, but I didn't know how. The little 'body' twirled between my fingers as *leaves of three,* chanted in my ear.

"Let it be!" The plant dropped from my hand.

"What?" Beth spoke but didn't stir.

"Leaves of three let it be. Stand up!" I said louder than planned and scrambled to my feet.

"Why?" Beth moved to a seated position.

"Poison Ivy." Whether it was the name of the plant or the word 'poison', I couldn't be sure, but it caused Beth to jump to her feet.

My eyes scanned the forest edge and spotted the offending plants. The weeds crept from the forest and gathered in patches along the roadside. I investigated where we rested; our weight had flattened everything underneath us. I crouched lower and inspected the ground; a loud sigh of relief escaped my lips.

"What?" Beth said.

"It's okay. There isn't much here, just the odd plant, but I had to go and pick the closest one."

"What is it?"

"A weed that can leave an itchy rash." I wiped my palms on my pants and smiled but behind my grin I worried. Not because I'd touched it, I had a vague feeling I'd done so before without consequence. But while my memory grew stronger daily, Beth remembered little. I only hoped it was because I had been off the drug given to us at C.E.C.I.L. for longer.

"What's with you and itchy th-things?" Beth's eyes rolled, and her lips pulled into a half-smile.

I laughed and shook my head. The question made me think of my mosquito bite, and I scratched my arm.

A sudden gust of cool air whipped a lock of my light brown hair against my cheek. I lifted my chin and stared up at the sky. Grey clouds edged with white swirled against a steel blue backdrop. In the distance the sky darkened.

"Definitely going to rain soon; we better decide."

Beth glanced up before turning her gaze on me. Blue eyes brightened as though a beam of light shone across her face. "Heads or tails?" she said.

"You remember that?"

"A game, sort of, helps with deciding. Now, heads or tails?" She repeated.

"We don't have a coin."

Beth's brow furrowed. After a few seconds she squatted and dug a small rock from the ground. She held it out in her palm. "Heads or tails?"

"Which is which?" I poked at the flat, round stone in her hand.

Beth sighed as though I'd asked a stupid question. "This side is clean." She pointed to the rock. "This side," she pushed the stone over, "is dirty. Clean is heads, dirty is tails."

"Okay. Heads, left, tails, right?" My eyebrows rose to meet my hairline.

"Fine. Now heads or tails?"

"Heads."

Beth tossed the small rock up into the air. It tumbled in perceived slow motion, flipping and rolling as gravity pulled it back to earth. The flat stone landed in her outstretched palm and she closed her hand. She uncurled her fingers one at a time to show the dirty side. "Guess we're going right," she said and reached for her pack.

No longer intimidated or fearful that cameras watched our every move, I observed the trees as we walked. The branches swayed and squeaked as they rubbed against each other in the wind. The leaves rattled. Part of me wanted to climb and ride the rocking limbs, wanted to experience the motion, the freedom. But I kept my feet on the earth.

A bird flew in front of us, its flapping wings the only sound other than the hushing breeze.

"No bugs either," I said, noting the surrounding stillness.

"What?"

"Since the wind picked up, the birds stopped singing, and I haven't swatted away any buzzing insect."

"Yup, I noticed. What do we do if it rains?"

The bottom of my t-shirt once again rode up under the strap secured around my middle, and I had to straighten it out. While it had been enjoyable to play in the rain earlier that morning, it had left us soaked. Much to our relief we'd found the clothing we now wore. And though we each had one other change of clothes in our packs, I did not intend to wear mine right away. The aim was to stay clean and dry.

"We should look for shelter."

Beth stopped and waved her hand at the surroundings. "And where do you suppose we'll find th-that?" She crossed her flailing arms.

If it didn't storm the surrounding thicket offered protection in any downpour. If it involved lightening, hiding among trees was an unsafe idea. "It's not raining yet. Let's continue walking. When it does, the bush is thick and should keep us dry." I walked past Beth, the sound of her grumpy sigh in my ears.

With my thumbs hooked under the straps, I adjusted the heavy backpack; my lower back ached under the weight. We'd stopped again for a brief rest but the threat of rain kept it short and my body complained with every step.

"How's your back?" I yelled to Beth who was several feet ahead of me.

"Fine." The gusting wind and rustling leaves muffled her voice. "Yours?"

"Hurts."

"Want to st-stop again?"

Yes, my body yelled. I wanted to stop, lie on the grass, curl up into a ball, and go to sleep. The wind blew through my hair, and my skin rose into tiny bumps. "No." A distant roll of thunder spurred me forward. A loud snap from the forest beside me quickened my pace and pulse. "Keep moving."

"Sh-shit! Did you hear th-that?" Beth stopped and waited for me.

"The thunder or the snap?" I said as I reached Beth.

"Both."

We marched in unison, our strides long and steps hurried. Another thunderous boom and Beth clutched my hand.

"Sorry," she mumbled, and released her grip.

My lips parted to speak, but I changed my mind. Though Beth hadn't regained her full memory her personality had returned. She'd always been the tough and the stubborn one, but underneath was a caring, and sometimes scared young woman who rarely showed her vulnerable side. When she did, she liked no one to notice.

We continued our silent walk, our steps slowed. Ever vigilant, I looked back from where we came. I needed to know how far we'd walked and a small part of me wondered if something followed.

"How long do you th-think it's been?" There was a nervous edge to Beth's voice brought on by the impending storm.

"What do you mean?"

"Since we left."

Time made no sense; the effect of having lived in a room with a sealed window. Until I saw a setting sun and a rising moon, hours and minutes meant nothing. I couldn't estimate any moment without a reference. While the growing weariness in my body suggested we'd travelled a distance, my brain told me we hadn't gone far; the house was closer than we thought. Several times I had checked to be sure it was nowhere in sight. I looked at the sky, hoping to catch a glimpse of the sun but it had long since disappeared. "Not sure. Could be minutes, hours."

"Oh," Beth muttered.

We slogged on, the grinding of rocks and dirt under our feet not loud enough to drown out the creaking trees. The fresh scents and rotting odours of the outdoors blended and drifted to us on the constant breeze. Black clouds covered the sky; the storm was in our near future.

"Maybe we should have gone the other way," she huffed and stopped.

"Too late for that now."

"I know." Beth held out her arm, and I steadied her as she raised her left foot and pulled off her shoe; the bright pink bow bounced with the movement. She turned it over and shook out several small pebbles. "Can't help wonder th-though," she said as she wiggled her foot back inside the runner.

"If this leads nowhere, then we'll head back."

Beth turned. "At least it'll be downhill." She adjusted her pack and continued. Unlike the level, first leg of our journey, this second route had more hills, and we climbed higher.

"Are you hungry?" Beth said as we rested atop a small, yet noticeable incline.

"No." My stomach rumbled in loud contradiction.

"How far have we walked?" Before I could respond Beth continued. "We've walked a lot, but st-stopped as much too. I don't th-think we've travelled th-that far."

"It's hard to—" The dark sky lit up with a flash of lighting and interrupted me.

Beth squeezed her eyelids and counted in the manner she had whenever there was thunder and lightning.

From the top of the small mound I could see the two other hills we'd climbed. But the intersection where we'd flipped the rock was not in sight. And it wasn't because we'd travelled a great distance but because a slight bend in the road altered our point of view. The intersection wasn't so far away but hidden behind the trees. I shut my eyes. In my head I mapped out our entire route from the house to the incline where we rested. My stomach sank.

Beth's eyelids remained closed, and her lips moved in silence. Thunder rumbled and stopped her counting. "The storm is... I th-think."

I nodded, only hearing half of what she said, preoccupied with keeping my sight focused on the foreground. But the need to look beyond overwhelmed me, and I conceded. My eyes narrowed and scanned the forest behind Beth. Seconds later I found what I'd surmised was there. The faint red roofline visible through the trees was the proof. We hadn't travelled far, our breaks longer than our walks, our progress hindered by weakness, our minds stunted by *his* hunger for power.

"You were right, Beth." The ghost of the house floated in front of my eyes, and I blinked it away. "We should have waited until we were stronger." I pointed behind her.

Beth turned, and a moment later her small sharp intake of

air showed me she saw what I indicated. "No, you were right. We had to leave, st-staying—" A crack of thunder interrupted her, and she sprang toward me and wrapped an arm around my waist. "Sorry." She drew away.

"It's okay, Beth." I didn't stop myself this time. It was okay after what we'd suffered.

Beth's eyes glared at me for a moment but softened as she nodded.

We rose to our weary feet; the storm drew closer and resting would not find us shelter. I reached out and took Beth's hand as we sauntered up the road. Eventually, our steps would take us further away.

3

THE RETURN

It was an odd thing to find a concrete wall crossing the road, a solid door in its middle. And yet there it was. It towered in front of us, its length undetermined as it stretched in opposite directions from the entrance until the forest on each side swallowed it. Its hard and unyielding form a stark contrast to the living trees that ran along beside the barrier. Wind rustled the leaves and limbs swayed and creaked. Apart from the branches bumping into it, the gusts had no effect on the obstacle.

The dirt road passed underneath the large and sturdy entry, and I could see no other passage through the barricade. I pushed on the heavy, steel door, the metal cool and rough beneath my hands, but it was as strong as the rest of the rampart.

"What do you s-suppose is behind it?" Beth said.

"Who knows, but whoever built it didn't want just anyone on the other side. Anyway, we can't climb over it." The smooth concrete offered no footholds, and it was far too tall to scale with no equipment.

A drop of water splashed on my forehead and trickled down my nose. Whether we found a way through or turned back, we needed to decide soon; the weather worsened by the second.

"There's a panel up there." Beth pointed to a small solar panel sitting on the top of the wall several feet away from the entrance. Below it a camera pointed at us.

"Do you think that camera works?" The thought it might, made my stomach roll.

Beth picked up a large stone from the side of the road. She approached the surveillance system, brought her arm back, and released the rock. It sailed past and hit a tree with a solid knock. Before I could say a thing, Beth scooped up another rock and tried again. This time the projectile connected with a loud crack. "Maybe that will get someone's attention." She brushed her hands on her pants and smiled.

"And you think that was a good idea? Maybe we don't want attention from the other side."

My sister seemed to think over what I said and shrugged. "Too late now." While she sounded indifferent concern flashed in her eyes.

Beth paced while I worked at slowing my pounding heart. After several minutes and no one arriving at the gate, the fear eased. We were both disappointed and relieved.

The solar panel gave me an idea, and I ran my hands along the edge where the concrete wall and the steel door met. "There!" A narrow, metal plate slid open, behind it a black screen, like that on a cell phone and like the one outside the rooms at C.E.C.I.L. I pressed my fingers onto the smooth, tempered surface, remembering the day I found myself unescorted in the white corridor. The overhead lights had flickered, and the cameras were still, their red lights extinguished. My thoughts returned to the present.

"Maybe it's for an eye," Beth whispered beside me.

I unfastened the harness from my pack and let the straps slide from my shoulders as I recalled the hazy memory of Jasper pressing a card to a scanner. The darkened sky lit up with a blue flash, and my sister began her ritual counting as I rummaged through my green sack. About halfway down, under a large flashlight, was the leather-bound journal, wrapped in the spare orange t-shirt. Inside the front cover was a pocket and inserted into that was Jasper's identification badge. I had found it tucked inside the journal earlier when looking for the portrait I'd drawn at C.E.C.I.L. The picture of Jasper on the white plastic card knotted my stomach.

"Is that Jasper?"

As words would only get caught in my throat, I nodded instead.

A bar code marked the backside of the ID, and I pressed it to the screen. Nothing happened. After wiping it on my t-shirt, I tried again.

My heart skipped. A small, green light in the top corner blinked. Some mechanical instrument whirred, and the door slid back then halted. The space was just wide enough.

"Looks like we're squeezing through," I said.

Beth unbuckled her backpack and shifted it from her shoulders. I tucked the journal inside my bag and the ID into my pocket. A heavy drop of rain landed on my head and it tickled as it trickled through my hair.

I bent over and retied the green lace. "Put the bags through first and then—" Squeaking metal interrupted me. When I looked at the gate, a blue runner with a pink shoelace disappeared behind the door.

Beth's smiling face poked through from the other side. "Not much of a s-squeeze."

I shoved my bag through the opening and followed it. A

loud rumble in the sky made me jump and Beth yelped as we hurried. The other side looked much like what we left behind, a dirt road sandwiched between trees. Whatever else hid behind the steel door and concrete wall had yet to show itself, but I hoped for shelter from the storm.

"Stop!" Beth called. With her hands resting on her knees she leaned forward; her shoulders pumped with her heavy breaths.

"Why?" Another lone rain drop fell on my arm.

"So tired," she huffed.

A sudden wave of dizziness came over me, and my body swayed. I stared at the steel entrance well beyond my sister and at the barely visible opening we'd crossed through moments ago. The skin on the back of my neck prickled as I peered at the eerie narrow space. My imagination was on over-drive, and I pictured Cecil climbing through to catch us. "Me too, but we must keep going."

Beth removed her backpack and let it drop to the ground, her body did the same. She leaned up against the pack and closed her eyes. "No."

The only way to convince her to keep moving was to join her, arguing made her more stubborn. I strode forward, my feet aching with each step, and joined Beth.

The wind whipped up a small funnel of dirt; it spun across the road and disintegrated as it hit a clump of wildflowers. The scattered dust floated then settled on the ground. With the entertainment over, I focused on my bag and drew it close. My fingers pulled the metal tab on one of the side pockets. The resulting *zip* broke the silence of the humid air. *It's the calm before the storm*, my father's voice whispered in my ear.

I dug my hand into the pocket and pulled the lid from a plastic container. "Here, eat these." A few hard macaroni pieces sprinkled my palm. We'd found the container in a kitchen cupboard, and I packed it inside the pocket before leaving. The food wasn't the tastiest choice, but it was light and edible.

Beth took the raw pasta from my hand and ate one. "These are gross."

I popped one into my mouth and nodded in agreement. "But it's food—sort of."

The sky filled with a flash of lightening, and I tilted my head back in time to see the white-hot light streak through the black clouds.

Beth groaned beside me. "Come on," she said standing up and pulling her pack with her.

The forest looked inviting. I fought every part of my aching body that wanted to leave the path and lie amongst the plants and bushes under the cover of trees. When the clouds burst, I decided that's where we'd go.

The road took a sharp turn to the left, and Beth and I followed with agonising steps. Several paces later, the route curved to the right. As we rounded the corner we halted, and my mouth fell open. Further ahead of us, the forest that had followed along both sides came to a sudden end. In its place, acres of deep green grass spread out on either side of the laneway and where it stopped stood an enormous building.

A loud clap of thunder jolted me from my stupor. "Come on!" I said as I adjusted the pack and willed my heavy feet to move once more. Large rain drops fell.

My eyes narrowed as I focused my thoughts on the concrete building ahead. While the lawns suggested a stately home, the structure looked like an old, abandoned factory. The closer we got the larger and more sprawling it became.

"What is it?" Beth called out above a loud rumble.

I didn't answer; I needed every bit of energy I had to propel me and motivate Beth to keep moving forward to shelter. The air smelled of rain, electricity, and another odour I could not place. I wrinkled my nose as we closed the gap.

On closer inspection, the great structure ahead of us was not old but damaged. As we drew nearer, we could see some destruction, though most of the building remained intact. I sniffed the air again. The odour I could not distinguish before was now unmistakable and the scent of burned wood and wet ashes evoked a memory as voices from the past echoed.

"Don't forget to douse the campfire." Mom leaned forward and kissed Dad on the cheek. Beth rested against Mom's legs and rubbed at her sleep-filled eyes.

"I won't." Dad smiled. "Remind me, okay Av?" Dad looked at me. I nodded and yawned.

"I think you should come with us." The orange glow of the firelight lit up Mom's face and showed me her raised eyebrows.

I shook my head. "No, I'm not tired."

Mom patted Beth with her free hand. "Okay, but not too late."

"Night Beth, night Caleb," I said to my siblings.

Caleb's eyes popped open, and he lifted his head from Mom's shoulder and smiled. "Night Av," he said, "night B..."

"Av, did you hear me?" Beth used my nickname.

I closed my eyes for a moment and shook the memory away. "Sorry, what did you say?"

Beth's face paled. "It's... It's..." she stammered.

"What?" I placed my hands on her shoulders and stared into her wide, icy gaze.

"It's...," she started again. She squeezed her eyelids shut for a moment, her lips pressed together. "Cecil!" she cried.

My eyes darted back and forth as I searched the edge of the forest and the path behind her. My heart thumped in my ears.

How is it possible, he's dead! My mind yelled through my dizzying thoughts.

"No," Beth said, stepping out from under my hands still on her shoulders, she took my arm and led me around.

My eyes tracked along her arm, past her pointing finger. Just underneath the roofline that protected the front entrance and above the door were silver toned letters as cold and as hard as its namesake. We had found C.E.C.I.L.

4

CONTAGION ERADICATION CENTRE
FOR INTELLIGENT LIFE

I WRAPPED MY ARMS AROUND MY DRAWN LEGS AND watched as the rain poured, beating a rhythm on the metal roof above our heads. The hypnotic sound lulled Beth into a deep sleep. She sat beside me on the threshold, the weight of her body supported by the doorjamb. She looked much younger than her barely sixteen years. And though I had three years on her, I wondered if I too looked younger.

My eyelids grew heavy, and I blinked many times as I fought to stay conscious. Only when I had a clear plan, would I allow myself to rest. I focused on the rain and picked out individual streams of water as they sliced through the air and splattered on the ground. I stretched out an arm and leaned forward, pressing my hand to the earth. The vibrations of the driving rain travelled up to my elbow. Lightning flashed, and I counted under my breath until the low rumble of thunder followed. The storm was crawling away.

I reclined against the door and stared up at the undersides of the metal letters fastened to the wall. We had returned to where our nightmare began; one we didn't remember. A vague shadow of a memory niggled much like the lingering sensation of a dream that dissolved upon waking. Small remaining fragments left a sense of dread deep in the gut but not enough information completed the vision.

A sudden strong gust blew through the covered entry. Dirt and leaves rolled across the step. The steel roof clanged as a shard of glass bounced off it and smashed onto a glass-covered shrub. The wind died and returned me to my reflections.

Was it necessary to know the whole nightmare? An involuntary shudder rocked my body for a moment. *Yes, I* answered. A loud sigh followed my relinquishment, and my muscles relaxed as I pressed my weight against the doorjamb. We had to find out, too many questions needed answers. The misfortune of our return to C.E.C.I.L. had to be a sign.

The sky lightened, and the rain slowed into a gentle rhythm. A small sparrow flew under the cover of the porch and rested on the step. His eyes met mine for a second before he tucked his head under his wing. Exhausted from the storm he cared little of our presence and went to sleep. We would explore C.E.C.I.L.; I decided and closed my eyes. Beth snored quietly beside me as my consciousness faded. The sudden flutter of wings interrupted my descent into sleep and I peeked to see the bird had gone. Rain soothed me back toward oblivion as thunder rumbled in the distance.

Swallows flew back and forth in front of the window; they entertained and impressed with their show of aerial acrobatics. They frolicked as they hunted their breakfast and dove for insects, snatching them from the air with their beaks. The birds' antics kept a smile on my face and the hope in my heart to experience such freedom.

Bright sunlight streamed in through the round window and warmed my cheek. I closed my eyes and imagined a light breeze blowing through my hair. The red inside my eyelids brightened when I tilted my head back and allowed the sun to bathe my entire face. A shadow moved over my closed lids, and my first thought was of a cloud. I opened my eyes and gasped, startled by his maniacal grin as he placed a board over part of the round window and screwed it into place. Laughter reverberated off the glass as he covered another part. With each piece of wood his smile broadened.

My hand slammed against the hard glass, and I screamed; his laughter grew louder. The room darkened into a black abyss as he sealed us into our coffin.

Closed eyelids squeezed tighter as my semi-conscious mind sorted out reality. Warm air grazed my cheek, a light feathery kiss. A soft flutter tickled against my nose, and I raised my hand and brushed it away with tingling, sleepy fingers. My eyes fluttered open to a brighter scene than when I'd closed them, and sunlight bathed the sprawling lawns.

I sat upright and stretched my arms above my head; fingertips brushed the door behind me. *C.E.C.I.L.!* My sleep induced amnesia cleared as I woke, and my stomach knotted.

"Beth!" My hand rested on my sister's shoulder, and I nudged her awake.

"S-sleeping," she grumbled.

"The storm's over."

Beth sat up and yawned before opening her eyes. "Where are we?"

"C.E.C.I.L.," I pointed upward.

Beth nodded and twisted a piece of hair around her finger. "Oh yeah, I forgot." She rose and stretched. "Look! A butterfly!" she squealed and crouched. The insect fluttered its large yellow wings edged in black as it rested on a plant with pink flowers growing beside the stone walk. Thick black bands ran through the yellow from the top of the forewings, and yellow, orange, and blue spots dotted the jagged hindwings.

The memory of light fluttering against my nose came back to mind. "I think we've already met."

Beth narrowed her eyes; the corner of her top lip drew up in confusion.

"Never mind. Let's explore." I rose and left the porch.

Warmth washed over my face as I pointed my chin toward the sky. White puffy clouds replaced the grey ones. And while the rain delighted upon our escape, so too did the sun.

"Are we going or not!" My sister stood with her hands on her hips, and her foot tapped on the ground, the pink bow bounced with the movement.

"Where?"

Beth blew out an exasperated breath and rolled her icy-blue eyes. "You said we were exploring." She reached up and tucked a lock of hair behind her ear.

"Yes, let's go!" I walked past Beth and toward the entrance. Before I reached the porch, I turned to the left, stepping over the small plants that lined the walk and onto the lawn.

"Aren't we going inside?" Beth called from behind me.

I shook my head and called out over my shoulder. "Let's walk around outside first and assess the damage." The inside could wait; I was in no hurry to face whatever memories might return.

A row of nine windows on either side of the entryway marked out the first floor. A line of twenty-one panes stretched across the second level, the middle three above the covered porch. Thirty-nine in total covered the façade.

The panes on the main floor were intact, but the second level suffered damage, many shattered with a few bits clinging to the frame. Two of three windows above the entrance were unbroken; the third had a large diagonal crack with a missing piece. And I suspected the earlier gust had knocked that chunk to the ground. Three others to the left remained whole.

Large pieces of glass impaled the ground while smaller bits dusted the lawn, glinting like diamonds in the sunlight. I stepped with caution closer to the building. Waist high, overgrown shrubs grew next to the grey brick exterior. The bushes cradled shards of glass in its mass of tangled branches and leaves. With great care I manoeuvred myself between two of the shrubs. Beth followed, and we sandwiched ourselves between the unruly hedges and one of the tinted, main floor windows. We pressed our foreheads against the window.

My warm skin rested against the hard pane as I cupped my hands and placed them on either side of my face. Blocking out the sunlight, I caught my first glimpse of the interior.

The office was stark. Positioned below the window was a small dark coloured couch with two matching pillows. To the right sat a desk. I guessed it was white as the tint cast everything in varying shades of grey. The top of the desk was bare except for a book. It lay open waiting for whoever read it to return.

A closed door stood opposite the window. I imagined it swinging open and had to blink to erase the image. The space offered little else, not even a picture on the wall.

"Come on." I dropped my hands and moved away, squeezing myself through another opening between two glass-covered shrubs.

"Do you th-think that was his office?" Beth said.

"Whose?" Jasper's face flashed in my mind, though I doubted she was speaking of him.

"Cecil's."

We were several strides from rounding the first corner. I clasped my hands and looked back toward the window. "Maybe." The second-floor windows caught my attention. "This place doesn't look burned out, does it? Jasper said there was a fire."

SANDRA J. JACKSON

"No, not here anyway."

We walked the remaining steps and turned. The side of the building extended further than I expected. The featureless wall resembled a concrete barrier, reminding me of the barricade out by the road. Constructed with grey blocks, it was in good condition and looked untouched by fire. Though high, it was not the same height as the main entrance. If it was a part that housed rooms they were not as lofty as the offices at the front. As we rounded the second corner we halted. Small angular buildings arrayed five across by ten deep in a large open field. Each concrete and panelled structure had one door and was windowless. Atop the roof sat an enormous solar panel tilted southward. This was C.E.C.I.L.'s solar farm.

"PV power station." The words tumbled from my mouth without thought.

"What?"

"Photovoltaic power station, converts sunlight into electricity."

"And you just remembered that?"

"Yes, I guess."

"Wow! On both counts. Wonder if they work," Beth said.

I shrugged, and we trudged along the back of the building. Upper and lower windows confirmed my suspicion that there were two separate floors. The wall showed no sign of any burning. But ahead of us a larger construction jutted out beyond the partition we followed. Fire had ravaged this charred and windowless structure with its cracked concrete walls.

A faint whiff of smoke and ash hovered in the air as we trailed along the blackened wall. We stopped at a darkened steel door at the centre, the metal warped and pitted. I ran a finger over the exit, leaving behind a rust coloured path through the black residue. *It has all gone awry*, Jasper's voice whispered inside my head.

Beth and I continued our investigation of the perimeter until we made our way back to where we started.

"Now what?" Beth's eyes widened.

"I need to rest." A yawn punctuated my words.

"Me too, but not out here."

"Then where?"

Beth walked towards me, her hand dipped with the quick agility of a pick-pocket. She grinned as she held Jasper's ID between her fingers. "There's a scanner at the front." She spun around and skipped toward the entrance.

"I don't think it's safe." I rubbed the back of my neck.

Beth yelled back, "It'll be fine." Dark knotted waves bounced on her shoulders; pink and black laces flopped from her shoes.

I sighed; Beth had decided, and I moved forward with reluctance.

The tall, grey door was flat, devoid of any features—unyielding and solid. Beth's steady hand placed the card against the screen, while my own curled into fists in my pockets. The display of the scanner remained black. She tapped the ID against the glass again, a dim green light blinked.

"There's probably not enough power stored in the battery." I turned and lowered myself to the step, sitting in the same place I had when I'd fallen asleep earlier.

"There are solar panels everywhere." She tried the card once more.

There *were* solar panels everywhere. They covered every rooftop, including the porch, and the field out back. The compound had its own power supply.

"Maybe the storage batteries are damaged." I leaned against the entrance.

"Aargh!" Beth yelled and kicked the steel slab. "St-stupid door!" She plunked herself beside me.

Every muscle in my body relaxed as the rest of my energy drained away. My stomach rumbled. "We should eat." I sat forward and grabbed my pack.

"If we eat every time our stomachs rumble, we'll have no food left."

I ignored her comment and unzipped a pocket on my green backpack. She said the same thing whenever we had a handful of food. But she never complained or refused when I handed them to her.

An inside pocket held some foodstuffs we had scrounged. I pushed aside a bag of beef jerky and a ration pouch and pulled out crackers.

"These won't get fresher with time." I held out three saltines, and my mouth dried at the sight. There was nothing nutritional about them except for the salt, and they did little to quell the rumbling in my stomach, but it was something.

Beth reached out and took the offering. "These suck!" she said, and she placed one between her lips.

I did the same and allowed the cracker to rest on my tongue for as long as possible before chewing whatever bits hadn't dissolved. It was as flavourful as eating paper, something I had tried once as a child. The last two biscuits were no better.

Out across the yard the surrounding trees shaded much of the lawn as the sun dipped lower to the west. Darkness would fall soon, the impending night caused a wave of fear, and I imagined pairs of glowing eyes staring out at us from the forest. I shut mine on the thought and rested.

Perhaps it was because my head leaned against the door and the sound had travelled through the steel and echoed in my ear. Whatever the reason, the click was loud, and I sat up straight. I hadn't been asleep, just in that in-between phase, where muscles relaxed, but the mind teetered on the edge between conscious thought and when dreams start.

The stale crackers had dried out my mouth, and my tongue ran across my lips. "Did you hear that?" Cracker crumbs sprinkled my lap; I picked them up and licked them off my finger. "Beth!" I shook my sleeping sister's arm.

"I heard you, nothing else."

"Stand up," I said, my curiosity surpassed any reluctance I had.

Beth grumbled but rose to her feet with arms folded over her chest.

The door looked solid. My hands clenched as I raised my foot and kicked it hard. Hinges squeaked, but the steel slab swung open with ease, and I stumbled over the threshold. The acrid smell of ash burned in my nose.

Beth followed behind me and closed the door with a resounding thud, plunging us into darkness.

In an instant, I was back in our attic prison. "OPEN IT!" My hands groped in the dark for Beth, quadriceps tightened, ready to launch me out the door, but the blackness pressed against me, keeping me in place. The closeness of the room drew the air from my lungs like a vacuum, and I struggled to breathe. Despite the panic that took charge of my mind, I heard the faint shuffling of Beth's feet. The steel door squeaked open, and the entry filled with light once again. Oxygen returned to my lungs; my body trembled.

"Sorry." Beth's wide eyes and ashen face showed me she hadn't enjoyed the brief period of darkness we endured either.

I nodded and exhaled a relaxing breath. "Just hold it open for now."

"Sure." Beth shrugged one shoulder and leaned against the open door.

The room was as big as the office we'd peered into through

the tinted window. In the corners closest to the exit were two large pots containing small, dead trees. A few, brown leaves hung from the branches while the rest lay scattered on the floor and inside the planters.

I stepped up to a bare wall and traced a fingertip along the painted surface. A streak of white trailed behind, and I wiped my soot covered finger on my pant leg. My mind flashed to the period of my awakening as Jasper reduced the hypno-drug. The sterile environment I remembered no longer existed.

There were no other furnishings within the vestibule, no reception desk to greet visitors, or chairs for guests. C.E.C.I.L. was not a place people visited, of that I was sure.

5

BEN

"I'd like to explore too." Beth's impatient voice drifted in the air behind me.

A camera in the far corner of the room held my attention. Unable to tear my gaze away, my pulse raced, and my stomach knotted. *Is someone watching us right now?* My paranoid self questioned.

"Are you listening to me?" Beth spoke again.

No one is watching. No one is here, I reassured myself. My breath escaped through pursed lips in a slow and controlled way, quieting my heart to a near normal rhythm. I stepped to the side. The camera remained immobile, silent. Another exhale released the tension in my shoulders. Apparently, my reassuring thoughts hadn't convinced me.

"I s-said—" Beth's voice echoed in the empty chamber.

"I heard you," I muttered.

Beth had her arms crossed, and she tapped her foot, the pink bow bounced. Ignoring my sister, I strode back out through the exit.

"I thought we were going to explore." Beth's footsteps followed me.

The sun had dipped just below the tops of the trees. Golden fingers of light highlighted the highest branches and danced among the leaves. Soon there wouldn't be enough daylight to shine in through the windows and illuminate the interior.

A deep inhale brought with it the aroma of the earth and every bit of vegetation my eyes could see. It was fresh unlike the warm stuffy air of our attic prison or the sterile atmosphere of the compound, turned acidic from the fire. The fresh air filled my lungs, expanding my chest, each intake deeper than the last until I sated myself. If we were spending the night inside, I wanted my lungs to breathe in as much goodness as possible.

I crouched and unzipped my pack. Hands sifted through contents, shoving and moving things aside until they found what they sought and drew it from the bag.

The black flashlight was heavy. Its stippled, rubber surface was course but secure in my grip. My thumb pressed the red button, and intense blue-white light shone from the lens. Seconds later, I turned it off. There was no telling how much charge remained, and I would not waste it.

The light in one hand and the strap of my pack in the other, I crossed the threshold. Beth followed as my feet carried me back inside C.E.C.I.L.

"Shut it." The moment I heard the click of the latch, I pushed the red button, and the vacant room brightened under the glow. The flashlight's beam emphasized the sealed door leading out of the vestibule and into the rest of the compound.

"How are we going to open th-that?" Beth whispered beside me.

"No need to whisper." The inanimate camera pointed in

our direction from the corner of the ceiling. Even with its extinguished red eye its presence was eerie. "Hold this." I handed the flashlight to my sister and let go of the backpack.

The door was the same that had confined us in our cell inside the compound, a sliding, solid, electrical gate. If Cecil had achieved entry and egress during his forages, we would too.

My mind recalled a power interruption in the corridor outside our room. The surveillance equipment malfunctioned and overhead lighting flickered and buzzed. My cheek tingled at the recollection of the cool door beneath it as I listened for sounds of movement on the other side. I shook away the memory and waved my hand in front of the ID panel and waited. But the passage remained silent and closed.

"Why would you think that would work?"

"It did once before." The vision flickered again and faded. "Or at least, I think that's what made it open."

"When?"

"It doesn't matter. It doesn't work now. Point the light here." I dug into my pocket, pulled out Jasper's ID, and swiped it over the scanner. After several tries the door remained closed.

"Now what?"

I placed my fingers along the sealed edge of the pocket door and tried to slide it back, but my fingers slipped. "If I can widen this gap a little more, the door will slide open. Sort of like an elevator door. It's heavy but should glide once we get it started."

"The knife!" Beth cried out, her tone filled with either hope or desperation.

"What?"

"Use the knife."

The tool I overlooked, rested in the front compartment of my green bag, and it was easy to find. I removed the rust-spotted, pearl handled implement from the pouch and flipped out the blade.

The cutting edge was no longer sharp, dulled by the picking and slicing of rubbery goo and the prying and sawing of wooden floorboards. The tip, I tested on my thumb, careful not to pierce my skin, remained pointed and strong.

I inserted the point into the narrow gap between the door and the jamb. With slight pressure I pushed on the handle and pried.

After a few minutes of prying the gap widened enough to allow for fingertips; the acrid odour of soot wafted in through the opening. I folded the blade and placed the knife in my pocket.

Beth bounced the beam of light between the ceiling and floor. Particles of dust undulated and swirled like dancers in a spotlight.

"Help me!"

She laid the flashlight on the floor, its bright arc of light rolled back and forth across the door then stopped as the flashlight stilled. She moved in beside me, our shadows loomed in front and darkened the door. Beth wedged the fingers of both her hands closer to the bottom while mine were near the top and together we pulled. The door squeaked and slid with a little resistance in its track. The space widened enough for us to squeeze through.

"Ready!" I gasped, wiping fresh sweat from my face and a few locks of damp hair that hung in my eyes.

Beth panted behind me, "Ya."

The beam of light lit up a long hallway that ran perpendicular to the doorway. Smoke had stained the once white walls. I angled my body sideways and stepped into the dark hall and waited for Beth. Once she was through, she reached back and tugged on a backpack. After a moment of effort she wiggled and manoeuvred the packs into the corridor.

"Which way?" Beth's voice echoed.

"That office first, I guess." As the only room we'd peered into from outside it was the best place to start. And if it was Cecil's office, I hoped to find answers.

We halted at the first door, and I pulled the knife from my pocket, flipping open the blade.

"Think it'll work?" Beth tapped the dark tempered glass of the card scanner mounted on the wall beside the door.

"Doubt it." I pushed on the door with my free hand and it swung into the room.

"How did you..." Beth yawned.

I bent down and picked up the small piece of card someone wedged in the door and showed Beth. "This was sticking out so it wouldn't lock properly."

The office was untouched by soot and the smell of smoke. It was stark and sterile. Beth wandered the perimeter while I focused on the centre of the room. A pristine, white desk sat midway between the windows and the door, a large book on its tabletop. Grey tubular legs didn't look strong enough to support much more than the tabletop and the book that sat on it. Pushed against the wall was a black leather chair.

I moved closer and brushed my fingers over the smooth surface until they collided with the open book. My eyes widened in recognition, but I had no idea if this text had belonged to me. I had no desire to flip through its pages to find out or have it remind me of this place any more than I needed. Instead, I ran the blade across the desk and marred its unblemished surface.

"Let's get out of here." I rubbed a finger over the scratches, ignoring the inner voice that told me to look at the book. "Beth?"

A low groan came from the curled-up figure on the couch in front of the two tinted windows. Beth shook her head. She wasn't going anywhere.

"Great." My pack hit the floor, and I folded up the knife, putting it in the pocket of my pants, its weight a comfort. I stomped toward the couch and sat at the other end. My sister snorted and rolled to face the back of the sofa. I leaned over and rested against the large arm rest, its grey material soft on my cheek. Within minutes I drifted off to sleep.

I shook my head. "No, I'm not tired."

Mom patted Beth with her free hand. "Okay, but not too late."

"Night Beth, night Caleb," I said to my siblings.

Caleb's eyes popped open, and he lifted his head from Mom's shoulder and smiled. "Night Av," he said, "night Ben."

A yellow, crescent moon met my sleepy eyes as it hung above the tree tops. The stars lit up the sky. "Ben," I whispered, staring at the dark shape of my sister at the other end of the couch.

The dream solved the mystery of why so many of my memories had us referring to Beth as Ben. It was the name our little brother Caleb called her because he couldn't say Bethany when he was little. It always came out sounding more like Benny and with time he shortened it to Ben.

6

OVER HIS DEAD BODY

ONE DAY. WE HAD BEEN FREE FOR ONE DAY. WE'D experienced the setting of the sun as it disappeared behind the trees. Later, awakened by a dream, I saw a luminous, crescent-shaped moon. But the dream about my brother prevented me from sinking back into blissful sleep, and I needed to clear my thoughts.

I tiptoed out of C.E.C.I.L. and breathed in the cool, pre-dawn air. The heavy stillness weighed on me while I watched for daybreak. Seated on the front step, I leaned against a support post and waited for life to begin again.

When it started, my back straightened, my senses piqued. A bird warbled a morning greeting and others followed. A cacophony of songs shattered the silence. The sky brightened, and I rose to my feet. Blacks and deep blues faded to purples and violets as night shifted into day. Time returned with the birth of dawn. The trees obscured the sun, but it was there. And soon it would rise higher and touch everything in its path with warmth and light.

Caleb was out there, and I sensed his presence. It was like

feeling someone's eyes as their glare pierced into your skull. A gnawing in my gut told me it had to be true. And I quickly dismissed any doubt that told me otherwise.

A smile spread across my face, evoked by a new memory of the past. Caleb hid better than anyone in our family, better than our friends. During a lengthy game of hide and seek, no one could find him. Beth and I had enlisted the help of our parents, and after several minutes of searching, even they grew worried. A more aggressive search and a half-hour later, they found him sound asleep on the upper shelf of a storage closet. Caleb had climbed to the top of the unit and tucked-in behind the vacuum-sealed bags of food and other emergency supplies. Had it not been for his tendency to talk in his sleep, discovering him might have taken longer. His sleepy, nonsensical voice had alerted our father to his whereabouts. When the tense search ended, we laughed with relief. But afterward, Mom and Dad told Caleb to never hide there again.

Worry replaced my grin. Caleb was hiding, waiting for us to find him, I only hoped he remembered who 'us' were.

A wide yawn interrupted my thoughts and exhaustion returned. I dragged my weary body back inside the compound, glancing over my shoulder as I stepped inside the foyer. "We'll find you, Caleb," I whispered.

The tinted windows had not allowed the beginnings of daylight to seep inside, and the office looked much like when I first woke. In the dim light I could just make out Beth's form on her half of the couch as I settled on mine and curled into the fetal position. The return to sleep was moments away.

"Was this yours?" Beth's voice roused me from what remained of my slumber, and sleep-filled eyes saw her standing by the desk holding up a book.

Bold silver letters shimmered from the centre of the tome —*History*, the shiny word prominent against the matt black cover. Yesterday, fear kept me from wanting to know if the book was mine. It was different now. I walked over to Beth, took the text from her outstretched hand, laid it on the desk, and flipped it open.

The print, while it appeared old, had events dating back only as far as the late twentieth century. And from what I gleaned, as I thumbed through the pages, it was not in line with any education I remembered pre-C.E.C.I.L. I committed the thought to investigate later.

My breath caught. Highlighted words and sentences floated out from the pages. Midway through the textbook, I stopped. Deep, yellow scribbling of a highlighter traced back and forth several times over one word attracted my attention. The bright ink had nearly obliterated the term. Yellow highlighter had bled through and stained the other side. I flipped the page back over and stared at it, *escape* etched into my pupils. "This was mine." The overuse of the highlighter had buckled the paper.

A faint pencil line underlined the emphasized word and continued toward the outside margin. I followed the mark with my finger as it travelled out from the paragraph, along the outer edge, across the bottom of the page, and ended at the gutter. With a hand on opposite sides, I flattened the book, stretching it open. I turned the book horizontally and read the words *over my dead body* written in the fold.

"He figured it out." I shoved the textbook away and looked into Beth's surprised eyes. "Cecil knew I was becoming aware. That I wanted to escape."

The backpack sat by the desk. An object inside willed me to it, and my hands rummaged among the various items until they grabbed what they sought. I drew Jasper's journal from my pack. It was time to read the secrets it held.

"What are you doing?"

"Reading." I sat on the couch. The cushions jostled as Beth plunked beside me.

Fingers flipped through the pages, eyes scanned for information. When entries fascinated me I paused long enough to read the writing. After each interval Beth inquired to its importance. The journal offered more than I wanted to understand. When I had the nerve, I would delve further.

"Here!" I tapped the page. The handwriting was neat, and I noted the date on which Jasper had written the entry: May 16, 2029.

Beth leaned forward. "It has been discovered," she began, her voice trailed off but her mouth moved as she read the rest of the entry to herself. A loud sigh escaped her lips when she finished, and she ran a hand through her tangled, dirty waves. "I don't know about you," she said, "but I don't understand what Cecil wanted. Why would he th-think we would have knowledge about any micro SD cards? I mean I know what they are but..."

I shook my head and closed the diary. Reading one passage was enough to cause a headache. And now I understood it was Jasper who allowed me to access the neighbouring rooms. That his bruised face was because Cecil found out and had him beaten. I rested and listened to the silence, interrupted occasionally by our breaths and the screaming in my brain.

"What now?" Beth whispered after several minutes had passed.

"I guess we search."

"For what?"

"Answers."

Daylight filtered into the office despite its tinted windows. Before any searching began we planned to open every east facing door on the first level and allow the sunshine to light the way. And we started with the one where we'd slept.

The dark hallway brightened with each door we opened. We'd found that just like the first office door, the others also had pieces of card preventing them from being locked. By the time we finished we had opened four offices and slid the pocket door of the vestibule centred between them, all the way back. Pure, unhindered sunlight beamed in through the front entrance, filled the foyer, and spilled into the hall. At both ends of the corridor stairwells led to the second floor, and along the soot-stained back wall were three sealed doors. The middle one, across from the main entry, was blacker than the others. I imagined smoke rolling out from under it and staining the white paint. Neither of us had any intention of opening that door.

"Where do we begin?"

"How about where we spent the night?" We returned to our sleeping quarters and though it was unclear what we searched for it was a start.

The room would be easy to search; apart from the single desk drawer and the bookcase there were no other storage units. Unless there were secret compartments, it was inconspicuous. And that made it a perfect hiding place.

The knife jimmied the locked desk drawer with relative ease. When I pulled it free, I tipped it out onto the table top. A few pens, pencils, and several miscellaneous pieces rolled around, but nothing of great importance. Disappointed by the insignificant items I swept them off the desk and back into their home.

"Maybe you sh-should put that back?" Beth gestured with her chin toward the drawer.

"Fine." The drawer balanced on my palm, and my fingertips brushed over an unusual bulge on the underside.

Objects spilled over the desk, pens rolled and clattered on the white tiles as I dumped it.

"What is it?"

"I'm not sure." The shiny metal object taped underneath was strange. It was cylindrical and no longer than my thumb. Welded to one end and perpendicular to the shaft appeared to be an infinity symbol. "But it must be important." I tore it free and dropped it into Beth's waiting palm.

She bounced it in her hand, weighing the solid metal item. She pressed the infinity symbol into the pad of her thumb; a small impression remained for a second then faded. "Some kind of... stamp?"

I took the piece from her hand and dropped it into the front pouch of my pack where the knife usually sat. My hand rubbed over the pocket of my grey, sweat pants feeling the bulge of the knife as it pressed against my thigh. I regarded the bookshelf with interest. "Let's pull those out."

We yanked books from the shelves, flipped through their pages, and tossed them on the floor.

"Why so many?"

I stopped and looked at Beth, a volume clenched in my fingers.

"At home we didn't have th-that many."

"You remember?"

Beth nodded. "We had four, I think."

"Three. And one was *Charlotte's Web*." I thought of my favourite childhood story.

"You notice..." Beth pulled a black book from the shelf. Printed in silver on the spine was the word history, much like mine on the desk. She dropped the volume on the floor; the resulting thump caused me to jump. "No tablets, no devices of any kind in this office. Not even a cell."

"Yes, I did, and it is strange. But remember Jasper wrote

that Cecil locked the doors and cut communications the past two years. This place remained self-sufficient despite being sealed and off the grid. Maybe books made more sense. Anyway, I'm sure we will find electronics somewhere else."

We worked without speaking, the silence broken only when the volumes thumped to the ground.

"Well, one th-thing is for sure—we did." Beth dropped another text to the floor.

"Did what?" Deep creases settled in my brow.

"Escaped over his dead body."

7

ANOTHER DOOR OPENS

EVERYDAY MORE MEMORIES FLOODED MY BRAIN, MEMORIES of C.E.C.I.L. and of home. Sometimes I recalled ordinary childhood moments. Other times strange thoughts filled my head like random, highlighted words in a history book from the compound. The sudden deluge of returned knowledge made me wonder if my recollections were real or part of an active imagination.

"By the way," I grunted as my sister helped me to open a door at the far end of the lower level hallway. "Ben is what Caleb used to call you." The vision replayed again as I solved the mystery of one of the few memories she recalled. The memory wasn't important, but I hoped it would spark more.

Beth stopped working and wrinkled her nose. "How do you know?" Sweat covered her red cheeks.

"A dream reminded me. Caleb couldn't say Bethany when he was little, so he said Benny instead. Later it became Ben, and we all called you that." The recollection caused a proud smile.

"Hmph! Something tells me I don't like that name. Anyway th-that's one of a th-thousand mysteries s-solved."

"You really don't remember much, do you?"

Beth sighed, pressed her hands against the door, and we both shoved on it again. "Not like you, no," she grunted, "but sometimes I have emotions about s-stuff I don't remember. Th-that's what I have to work with, gut instinct, I guess. But some things are coming back... a little." With a final push the panel slid all the way open.

The corridor was dark. Stale, warm air tinged with the faint smell of smoke wafted up the black tunnel and tickled our noses. My thumb pressed on the flashlight's red button. With a click, blue-white light shot out from the flashlight and stretched down the long hall as far as it could go.

"Ready!" My heart thumped in my ears.

Beth rubbed her nose with the back of her hand and stepped over the threshold. I took a deep breath and exhaled through pursed lips as I followed my sister.

The spastic beam of light flashed around the corridor, bouncing from wall to wall and ceiling to floor. It lit up inert cameras, doors, and random objects strewn on the white tiles. A shoe here, a book there, pieces of someone's life left behind in a hurry as the occupants made their escape. The light exposed everything but never rested long enough for the eye to pick out any fine detail.

"Av!" Beth's warm hand wrapped around my wrist and stopped me.

"What?" My pulse quickened.

"St-stop bouncing the light all over the place. It's making me s-sick." In the dim lighting I could see Beth's furrowed brow and pressed lips.

"Here," I said as her words registered and handed her the flashlight. "I don't think I can."

Beth seized it from my hands and shone a steady beam in front of us as we walked. The light showed more of the chaos left behind and more recent things.

"Ew!" Beth stopped and shone the light at the object that caused her disgust.

In the middle of the corridor was a dead mouse. The long tail stretched away from the body with only the tip curled. Pink feet stuck out as though reaching for something, and black beady eyes stared up at the ceiling. The stink of death rose from the small corpse. There looked to be nothing wrong with the mouse apart from being dead.

Beth covered her mouth and nose with her hand. "What killed it?" she whispered.

"Hopefully nothing that's still here," I said beneath my hand.

Beth searched the hallway with the flashlight. The sudden scuffle of feet and high-pitched squeak made us jump as another, larger furry lump scurried away from us. Its long tail dragged behind.

"Th-that mouse was still alive." Beth placed her hand on her chest.

"That was a rat." I shook my shoulders in disgust.

"Sh-shit!" "Why don't we ch-check in here before we go any further?" Beth shined the light on the first door in the corridor.

We were proficient with the knife, working it into the small gap until a larger crack enabled our fingers to grab hold. In less than two minutes we had the barrier open. The room was as I expected, an exact copy of the one we'd occupied months ago. The memory having returned seconds before we unsealed it.

"Is this ours?" Beth said as she walked around and inspected every corner with the flashlight.

I remained in the entrance. Memories of sight and sound

filled my head. I envisioned the camera's red eye, bright overhead lights, and white-garbed visitors. The ghostly echo of whooshing doors, hissing steam, and the warning buzz deafened. It was enough to keep me rooted in place. "No." I cleared my throat.

"How do you know? It feels like it's ours." She spun, a streak of blinding light flashed across my eyes, and I covered them with my forearm. "S-sorry!" she said. "But it does. Somehow. In here." Beth rested her hand on her stomach.

"Because our door had a small scratch." The mark had caught my attention as I stood outside my room on the day I'd been unescorted to the forest simulation chamber.

"So! Any door can have a scratch. This looks a lot like the one we sh-shared."

I shook my head. "Does it have a black dot on the ceiling over the dresser?"

Beth pointed the light above her head. "No," she said.

"Then it's not ours. Besides our room was half-way down the corridor." I stepped back out into the dark, warm passage and waited for Beth.

"Keep going?" Beth pointed the light down the hallway made more ominous by the rat that lurked in the darkness.

Every part of me said no, except that bit that needed to find answers. "Yes."

The hallway was long. Our flashlight showed us several doors many of them closed, though a few were partly open and fewer still opened all the way. We stopped at the odd one of those and with trepidation shined the light inside, hoping we wouldn't find any more critters or worse. But there was no point in inspecting them further, the rooms had belonged to other occupants, and I doubted we'd find anything useful inside them. As we moved further down, the smell of smoke and ash grew stronger. By the time we reached the end of the hallway we'd counted thirty rooms, fifteen on each side of the corridor.

"Well, it's either turn left, or go back." Beth shined the light in both directions showing our choices.

"Left, I guess."

A thick dusting of black soot covered every part of the corridor. Indistinct footprints tracked through the residue and trailed between rooms. And though nothing appeared burned out, the odour of smoke was heavy.

Four doors marked the entrance to the apartments in this shorter wing. Apart from the larger spaces there was a more noticeable characteristic. They were homier. Art decorated the walls, area rugs covered the tile floors, there were personal effects, and each of these rooms had a small window.

"These must have belonged to sp-special people," Beth said as we explored one of the more ornate suites with great care. A crystal suncatcher hung in the window and she poked it with her finger. The prism spun on its delicate nylon thread. The diminished lighting outside caused no effect, but I imagined the glorious rainbows it cast when the sun made its way to this western side of the building.

A black dresser with three drawers decorated by silver knobs stood in a corner. The top came almost to my hip and on it rested a box of blue rubber gloves. The fingertips of the next pair peaked out from a slot, waiting for its owner to pull them free.

I tugged open a drawer. Shirts lined the inside, each one folded into a neat square and stacked in three piles of three and every pile speckled with rodent droppings. Pants creased and bundled in the same manner filled the second along with more droppings. The last contained several pairs of socks, underclothes, and an item that confirmed the tenant.

"They belonged to the people that helped Cecil keep us

captive." I turned around and held up the mask I'd found. "These are the rooms we should search."

"Now what?" Beth said after we finished searching the last room. She pointed the flashlight at the end of the hall. The light reflected off a blackened and warped glass door.

"Lunch." Hungry and disappointed by our fruitless investigation I trudged up the dark hallway, tiny feet scurried behind us, and a stream of light led the way out.

The front walk was hot and uncomfortable, but the grass was far too tall. I shifted again on the hard surface while sunlight warmed the top of my head. We gulped the fresh air and shared a package of rations under a blue sky with cotton ball clouds. We'd found the rations in the kitchen of the old house. While Cecil fed us expired cans of food, he'd dined on vacuum packed foodstuffs and fresher canned goods. Before we left, we'd filled our packs with as much as it would hold along with the other tasteless morsels. The rations we would eat once a day.

"So," Beth smacked her lips and swallowed. "Do you th-think we need to explore everywhere?" She jutted her thumb over her shoulder toward the compound. "With the rats and all?"

I looked up at the broken glass windows of the second floor and shrugged. "No, but as much as we can." Re-entering the compound was unappealing; stalling seemed a much better idea. I lay on the cement walk, my arm as a pillow, and stared up at the sky. Fluffy white puffs morphed from one form into another. In seconds a cloud resembled a rabbit then shifted into a cat as bits drifted away.

My fingers absently plucked at the cool blades of grass beside me. A steady stream of memories flowed through my head. I closed my eyes and tried to sort through them. But the sudden influx of information overwhelmed me, and I needed a distraction.

"Let's go!" I sat upright, and my head spun from the quick movement. I took a moment and waited for the dizziness to go away before rising to my feet.

"Now?" Beth picked up the empty packages.

"Yes." Bits of grass clung to my grey sweat pants, and I brushed them away. I bent forward and rolled my pant legs to my knees. It was hot.

"What's your hurry?" Beth called out from behind me as I stepped across the threshold and entered C.E.C.I.L.

"We need to leave this place," I said as memories of home pushed their way into my brain. I wiped my burning eyes. "We're going home."

"Really? Now?" The look of surprise on Beth's face made me chuckle.

I composed myself and looked out the door toward the green lawns and beyond that to the road. My heart thumped with anticipation. "No, tomorrow. We finish searching today."

We swept through the other offices on the first floor, finding them emptier than the office we'd slept in. It seemed they were only for show. Our search led us to the second level where we discovered six tiny apartments instead of more work spaces. Their doors were wide open; someone had ransacked them. Furnishings were strewn about, cushions ripped apart, clothing and personal effects littered the floors. They had destroyed tablets and laptops, items which didn't exist on the first level. Whoever vandalized the suites had been looking for something.

Cecil's dead face flashed in front of me, and I jumped back as though he were there.

One apartment remained intact, and we knew whose it was the moment we stepped through the open door. The faint scent of his cologne permeated and clung to everything in the room, even weeks or perhaps months later, and it made me gag. I still didn't understand how much time had passed between Jasper getting us out of the compound and our escape from the house.

"This was his," Beth said as we stood at the entrance.

I nodded and stepped further inside the room.

The apartment was neat, a modern space with clean lines and little décor. It was cold and impersonal and offered only the essentials of living, much like Cecil.

I opened a door and stepped into the bedroom. It was plain. The closest things resembling any ornamentation were two framed illustrations on the wall across from the foot of the bed.

The glass covered images were the same apart from a few descriptive words: *first floor, second floor, offices, apartments.* Everything else was identical. They were the floor plans to C.E.C.I.L., and they mapped out every area of the building.

There were three offices on each side of the main entrance. Above each office was an apartment. The largest of which also occupied the space above the foyer, the room we were in now. Cecil's bedroom. The rest of his suite was above his office.

I swallowed. I could no longer deny what the floor plans confirmed, we slept in Cecil's office. My skin crawled and bile burned in my throat.

Branching off the hallways behind the offices and the apartments were three wings, two outer and one in the middle. Three doors on each level accessed these corridors. According to the plan the outside wings contained thirty rooms on both the upper and lower levels.

I studied the plans. The wings on the south and north sides of the compound had the word children printed on the blueprint. In total there were enough quarters to house one hundred and twenty children at one per room. The middle wing had sixteen chambers on each level, and the plans labeled these as sleeping accommodations for staff. Two large greenhouses filled in the spaces between the outside and the middle wing, Garden A on the left and Garden B on the right. At the end of the central corridor was an enormous building which according to the blueprints stretched up higher than the second level of the three wings. The only entry and egress to this huge space was from a short hallway on the first level that branched off from the ends of the outside wings.

"Simulation room," I whispered as my finger tapped on the glass.

"Th-that big steel door we saw outside must've led into th-there."

I closed my eyes and pictured the large forest room. The image so clear I was certain when I opened them again, I would find myself standing in the entrance.

In my head I followed the path to my right through the fake forest, along the length of the building. I passed the large rock and turned left around the first corner. My memory took me along the width of the building to the second left turn. When I rounded the third and walked the breadth again, I imagined where the steel door would be and I stepped off the trail. My imagination carried me through the trees; hands pushed away plastic branches dressed in cloth leaves. Forest murals covered the walls, painted in such detail the landscape appeared to go on forever. I envisioned the metal door layered in paint and blending into the background. An exit I never knew existed, for if I had...

"Guess it doesn't matter now," I whispered.

"What do you mean?"

"Nothing." I shrugged my thoughts away. "Anyway, we were right about these rooms," I pointed to the two small hallways that ran parallel to the front of the building and connected the wings at the back. The blueprint labeled the small suites for staff. "That's the room with the suncatcher." My fingernail tapped on the glass covering.

"The glass door we saw here," Beth touched the spot on the floor plan. "It was black."

"And warped," I added.

My finger traced along the illustrated corridor and my mind once again flashed to the day I found myself unaccompanied outside our room. "Here." I pointed to the wing on the far left. "This was where we were." Another flash and I saw myself making a right-hand turn at the end of our corridor.

"First or second floor?" Beth said.

"First, I never had to go up or down stairs." I took a deep breath. "Let's go take a look."

"Ready?" I whispered though not sure why.

Beth nodded.

The knife tip ran along the seam of the entrance to the south side corridor and stopped half way. I gripped the pearl handle and pried the door with gentle pressure, but it remained sealed.

"What's the matter?"

"It's stuck." I tried again.

"Let me try."

"Careful!"

Beth took the knife and wiggled it into place.

"Don't break it!" The knife blade bent a little with her effort. From the corner of my eye a red light flashed, and I turned toward the camera in the corner. "Did you see that?"

Beth panted and wiped her hand over her sweaty forehead.

"What?" She closed the blade and dropped it back into my pocket. The weight against my right thigh comforted me.

"I saw something blink."

Beth looked toward the camera for a second. "You have that card in your pocket?"

My brow creased as I stuck my hand into my left pocket and gripped the plastic card. Jasper came to mind. "Why?"

Beth pointed to the scanner on the wall beside the door. A red light blinked. "Probably won't need that." She pointed to the flashlight clipped to the waist band of my sweat pants.

I pulled the ID from my pocket and passed it over the scanner. The light flashed green, and the door slid open.

8

DUST TO DUST

The South corridor was not dark like its twin on the other side. Flashing overhead lights created the illusion that the white walls of the hallway moved. It was as though it breathed. As though it lived. My heart thrummed in my ears.

Beth gasped. "How is this happening?" she whispered, her fingers wrapped around my wrist and held me in place.

"Power surge?" A brief thought to run crossed my mind, but it faded. It was better to not draw attention. "We should be quiet. Just in case."

"You th-think s-someone's here?" A rapid flickering of the overhead light punctuated her question.

"No. But still..." A hint of concern tinged my voice but Beth did not react. My sense of reason believed we were alone, my imagination thought different.

The colourless tunnel stretched out ahead as our feet echoed down the hall. My pulse raced as lifeless cameras stared, and I closed my eyes for a second against my creative power which conjured up a figure in white walking toward us.

"Which one?" Beth's voice echoed.

"Middle, left." I glanced back over my shoulder.

We stopped, and I inspected the two closest doors. "Here." The small scratch made my stomach knot, my pulse hammered. Etched into the door was the mark where I said it would be— where I remembered.

Beth raised an eyebrow and held out her hand for the ID. The sliding panel unnerved me as it opened.

The organized room was now in disarray. Unlike the others we'd inspected someone had turned it upside down. Mattresses on the floor, naked, stripped of their bedding, which lay in heaps beside them. The drawers from the single dresser pulled free, emptied of what little contents they held, and thrown on the tile.

"What the hell was he looking for?" Beth stomped over the threshold and placed the drawers back into the dresser. My wish to be inconspicuous was no longer her concern.

I watched her from the doorway, my feet unable to move me any further. My throat tightened as a vision played in my head.

My fists pounded on the door that had sealed me into a white room. "Where's Beth? Caleb?" I'd remembered seeing them when my eyes had fluttered open during a brief period of consciousness. Beth lay beside me on the floor of some vehicle, and Caleb slept curled up on the seat behind her. Tucked under his arm, his small, one-eyed teddy winked at me. Despite Beth's body heat, I shivered and pulled my hands into the sleeves of my orange and yellow pyjamas. Mumbled voices came to my ears. I tried to force myself to stay awake and hear what they said but my eyelids had another idea and slammed shut.

"Well, are you?"

I blinked. Beth stared at me, arms folded over her chest and she tapped out a rhythm on the tile floor.

"What?"

"Are you going to help?"

Tears burned and my legs crumbled. The expression on Beth's face went from frustration to concern and she rushed to my side, threw her arms around me and kept me upright.

"Sh, it's okay," she whispered and patted my back. "I take it you remembered s-something?"

A shaky breath blew out between my lips; I cleared my throat and pulled away. My hand brushed the remaining tears and wiped my nose. I nodded. "I remember that night."

Beth's eyebrows rose high on her forehead and disappeared behind her dark, overgrown bangs. "Do you mean–"

"Yes."

"Like when we were taken?"

"Yes."

"Like even–"

"Yes, Beth!"

Beth startled. I'd said it louder than intended. "Sorry." It seemed being quiet was no longer my concern either.

"It's okay, I get it." She turned away and picked up the few packages of clothing and placed them inside the drawers.

I inhaled and stepped further into the room. We replaced the mattresses and the bedding. When we finished, it looked as I last remembered.

The door to the laundry chute in the corner was wide open. I pulled the flashlight from my waist and lit up the interior.

"That's how we got out." My voice echoed down the dark shaft. Images replayed in my head. Jasper's masked face, my slurred speech, his drive to get me out, my cries for Beth, and the injection that led to darkness.

"How?"

"Jasper drugged us and put us inside."

"So, there must be a basement. How did he get us out of there?"

I turned around and looked at Beth. The floor plans in Cecil's apartment showed no such level existed.

"Come on!" I grabbed my sister's wrist and pulled her along behind me.

"Where are we going?" Beth freed her arm from my grasp.

"To find the basement."

We hurried through the corridor, toward the simulation room, a journey we'd walked many times during our imprisonment at C.E.C.I.L. but only I remembered. An echo from the past replayed, *Yes, sir. Subject in sight, sir. She's about to enter the Simulation Room, sir.* We made a right turn at the end and halted as the stronger smell of smoke and stale air wafted toward us.

Unlike at the front of the compound where broken windows let in the breeze no air flowed at the back. Sweat beaded on my forehead, and I wiped it away before it dripped into my eyes. We tiptoed past open doors of staff accommodations, taking seconds to stop and have a peek. Every suite ransacked like our room.

As we neared the passageway to the simulation room and the stairwell, I saw a shoe wedged in the gap of a partly open door of the last apartment. A putrid odour hung in the air. Curiosity made me stop and glance, and I regretted it; the image forever imprinted in my mind. The white-clad remains lay just inside the room, his foot, or what remained, caught in the door.

"Don't look." I held my hand up at Beth.

"Why?"

I covered my mouth and nose. "Dead guy." Bile rose in my throat, and I swallowed. "And it's not pretty."

Beth covered her nose, scurried past, and waited for me at the stairwell entrance.

The door was black; the glass cracked in several places but still intact. I reached out and grabbed the handle.

"So, other than th-that guy," Beth jutted her thumb over her shoulder, "it looks like everyone else got out, right? I mean he's the only one we've found."

I shrugged. *So far,* I thought and tugged on the handle.

The door creaked open, the odour of soot and smoke escaped. My throat tickled, and I coughed; the scent irritated my senses. Beth cleared her through behind me, and when I finished hacking, we entered.

The stairwell inside the glass entry and to our right was as I remembered. One set of stairs ascended to the second-level corridor, and another led to what I assumed was the basement. Straight ahead of us a doorway had shattered in its frame. Ignoring the staircase, I stepped forward, and stared into the skeletal remains of the forest simulation room.

"Wait there," I said, my steps ground bits of glass into the concrete.

"What about the basement?"

"In a minute," I called back and stepped through the steel frame.

The real sky replaced the blue-painted ceiling and anything that remained littered the floor inside the four walls. Blackened, melted plastic covered the floor. Steel beams from the ceiling crushed and mangled other structures, some warped and twisted, some intact, the coating on them darkened by heat. Several metal skeletons of trees stood erect, defiant to the fire that ravaged them though their leaves and smaller branches succumbed and turned into puddles of hardened plastic. An intense heat cracked the walls and left no sign of the murals that once covered them. The flames had destroyed everything in the eighteen by sixty-one metre room, according to the dimensions printed on the floor plan.

Mounds of liquefied and re-hardened fake vegetation dotted the ground in varying sizes, and I took great care stepping over and around them. Small clouds of ash billowed around my feet and reminded me of the dirt road we'd followed that led us back to C.E.C.I.L.

The rock was bigger than I remembered though towering trees no longer dwarfed it, and it was now the largest thing in the room apart from the beams. The forest reduced to melted piles and random twigs of standing steel.

I picked out careful steps, counting each one like I had in the attic room as I paced out its dimensions. Like I had in the simulation room every time I walked the path though now, I had to climb and step over debris. Numbers rolled through my head and landed at two hundred and ninety, the number of strides it had taken to walk around the trail through the artificial woods. When I cleared my thoughts, the boulder was within reach.

Blackened by smoke and splattered with hardened, melted plastic, the rock drew me toward it like metal to a magnet. I reached over and brushed off unknown burned residue from the top and rested the palm of my hand on its surface. *It's real!* The revelation surprised me. I removed my soot-stained palm. Birds chirped and warbled in the distance. That too was real; recorded bird songs would no longer fill this room.

Whatever had dragged me into these remnants pushed me away, and I turned back toward the entrance and to Beth. I stepped over burned debris, melted piles, and twisted fragments—the mangled flora indistinguishable.

A gnarled piece of steel poked out from a pile of ash, the remains of an artificial branch I presumed. I gasped and my hands flew to my mouth.

"What's the matter?" Beth called from the doorway.

"Nothing, just stifling a cough." My hand fell back to my side as I stepped around, unable to pull my attention away. The misshapen and blackened limb belonged to no tree. It was human. Its charred fingers reached for the sky.

My eyes focused ahead as I dashed the last couple of steps toward the exit. I did not want to discover further surprises. I did not want to learn that not everyone had escaped.

9

THE JOURNAL'S SECRETS

THE BASEMENT WAS HUGE, AND IT WAS WHERE THE WORK within C.E.C.I.L. took place. It was the heart of the compound. Ceiling lights flickered at half-power in several rooms while our flashlight lit up the rest. In the centre of the lower level a stairwell ascended to the two greenhouses on the main floor. To the left were accommodations for staff, examination rooms, labs, offices, infirmary, and an operating theatre. Signs in black lettering pointed out these facilities and included more dismal ones such as *Quarantine* and *Morgue*. On the right a large cafeteria, kitchen, and laundry facility filled the space. A corridor ran around the perimeter. And below the first level chambers of the north and south wings, laundry chutes opened into bins waiting for soiled linens and clothing. The hallway behind the central staircase branched left and right, and each side mirrored the other with staff suites and a stairwell leading back to the first floor. Ahead of the stairwell a hall led to more offices, labs, and four storage areas. There was also a communication and security room—everything inside destroyed.

Apart from a bed, four of the sleeping quarters were empty and appeared as though no one ever used them. Someone vandalized five other rooms, everything inside turned into piles of rubble. Fire burned the contents piled in the centre of three remaining suites, and smoke blackened the walls. The items suffered varying degrees of destruction from charred to ash. Near the doorway of each room sat an empty container of charcoal starter fluid. The fires were deliberate.

Beth and I searched the gardens but found nothing more than rotted or dried out produce. The smell of rotting food inside one of four storage rooms made my stomach turn. A few damaged cans remained on the shelves, their contents leaked out into puddles of rot and mould.

Glass crunched under our feet as we entered a lab, its thick door propped open by a large desk. A stop sign on the inside of the door reminded people they could not exit from the room through that entry. At the end of the lab was a closed door with a small glass window.

Broken and useless pieces of equipment scattered across the top of a counter area along one wall. Cupboard doors above the counter hung open; the shelves inside empty except for an unopen box of rubber gloves sitting on one shelf. In the middle of the room were four workstations. Along the opposite wall was a metal cabinet with a slanted glass top. Attached to the front of it were two pairs of blue rubber sleeves. I'd never seen a containment cabinet before, but as scientists, our parents had described the equipment they used on many occasions.

While Beth went to explore the counter area, I headed toward the work tables. I righted a microscope tipped over on its side and peered through the dual eyepiece. It was nothing like the ones used in the biology lab in high school but some parts were the same. The nosepiece turned with ease but each objective lens appeared scratched.

"Centrifuge," Beth said from behind me.

"What?" I pulled my eyes away from the damaged microscope and turned around. Beth stood at the counter.

"It's a centrifuge," she said again.

I moved toward her. "How do you know?"

She pointed to the bottom corner of the box-like piece of equipment sitting on the counter surrounded by broken test tubes. Printed in black was the word centrifuge.

"Oh. You haven't touched anything, have you?" My eyes scanned over the broken glass tubes.

"No, I'm not st-stupid. Who knows what was in those th-things. So, sh-should I open it?"

"Hang on." I reached up and pulled down the box of rubber gloves I'd seen sitting inside the cupboard. "Put these on first." We each pulled out a pair of white gloves and put them on.

Beth lifted the cover of the centrifuge. Inside were several small stained test tubes. She dropped the lid. "Well I am not investigating th-that any further. Do you th-think it works? It doesn't look broken."

I pulled out the power cord tucked in behind the machinery and held it up. "No." Someone had cut off the plug. "Have you checked these lower drawers and cabinets?"

Beth shook her head. "Not yet." She bent down and pulled open a door. "Shit!" She yelled and jumped out of the way, her hand on her chest. A white mouse scurried out from inside and ran from the room.

I giggled, not knowing who the rodent startled more, and went back to work. Much like everything else in the room I found numerous broken items inside the drawers. A soldering gun with a damaged cord made me wrinkle my brow as I thought it a strange piece of equipment for a laboratory. "Anything?" I said as I closed the last drawer.

"Yup!" Beth stood and held up a small animal cage. Inside was a nest of paper, shredded bits of what appeared to be cloth, and some fur.

"Well, I guess we now know for sure we weren't the only lab rats at C.E.C.I.L."

We found the examining room, infirmary, and another smaller lab to hold not much more than broken equipment, empty boxes and vials. There was nothing of value anywhere, not even a first aid kit. We would have to make do with the limited supplies we'd taken from the house including a small first aid kit. At least we had one. The heart of C.E.C.I.L. was as empty as its namesake.

Fading sunlight filtered in through the tinted windows of Cecil's office. Morning couldn't come sooner. We would rise with the sun and leave. There was nothing for us here—no answers to our questions, no guidance for our journey.

I removed the journal from my green pack and clicked on the flashlight; Beth slept at her end of the couch. Jasper's first entry was on September 23, 2023, and my brain absorbed the writings I skimmed over in the first several pages. Whatever entered through my pupils ingrained in my memory. I promised myself to return to those first few pages as I flipped through the diary. For now I searched for entries referring to us. *Where did Beth and I fit in Cecil's plan?*

Silent words slipped from my lips as I perused the entry dated June 25, 2027. I reached toward my neck and plucked the delicate gold chain from under my t-shirt, rubbing the heart pendant between my thumb and fingers. Despite memorizing the passage on the first read through I studied it twice more, engrossed by every word. I closed my eyes, and the paragraphs appeared in front of me as though I'd taken a picture. Every

sentence remembered in perfect detail, including the way
Jasper looped the tail of his Gs and crossed his Ts.

Friday, June 25, 2027

*The compound is nearly at capacity. Another group was brought
in tonight. Why in the middle of the night? I do not understand,
and I hope my surprise did not show to the others. Meeting these
families upon their arrival is rare, however, tonight it was
different. They needed me to sedate one child, a teenager, who
was in a panic. I was quite surprised when I saw her as I never
hear of any difficulties. After her sedation, I collected her
personal effects. A female staff member accompanying me had
been instructed to dress her in nightclothes supplied at the
compound after I left. The girl, introduced to me only as A2
(which I found a little strange) was wearing a gold chain. I
waited out in the hall until the other staff member came out and
she handed me the pyjamas the girl wore into the compound. I
found a button in the pocket of the bottoms and placed it with
the necklace in a small safe in my room. These items will be kept
secure until I know what to do with them, and I am sure they
mean something to the girl. The pyjamas were taken to the
laundry facility.*
*I've learned Cecil ordered that all non-staff residents are to be
given ID numbers, which now I understand the girl being
introduced as A2 (though I still think this is strange). Tomorrow,
A2 will begin the new vaccine regimen. Many questions fill my
head, but I will not question Cecil's motives.*
*More arrivals are expected tomorrow, and we should be at
capacity by the weekend. The outside world still continues as
normally as possible, but it will not be long. It is my
understanding that more and more centres (of one sort or
another) are cropping up every day.*

Canned food is purchased in vast quantities though I suspect that some families have brought in whatever stores they had. The vaccine continues to be administered, and the virus has shown no further mutation. No ill effects have been reported and so all residents have received their correct dose. It is only a matter of a few more weeks before we know its complete effectiveness.

Cecil is a brilliant man, albeit his ego sometimes impedes his brilliance. I was definitely surprised that he had named the compound after himself—though I have yet to be told, despite my asking, the exact acronym. It appears the rest of the staff are not too sure either. Contagion Eradication Centre, however seems to be the only part that everyone agrees with. The meaning of the I and the L are not clear. I must remember to ask Cecil himself the next time I see him though it has been at least a week since the last time. We have been working carefully with the new vaccine, the virus having remained unchanged for the last three weeks. We hope that this will be the key before this horrible illness wipes out the planet.

Jasper's entry faded from my recall and the memory of our abduction returned, and the event was as clear as if it had happened in recent days.

I had drifted in and out of consciousness after they'd invaded my bedroom, and I felt that first poke in my arm. During one episode of brief awareness I found myself in the back of a vehicle, Beth and Caleb asleep and oblivious. Later, I awoke again in a strange white room. My fist pounded on the sealed door as I demanded to see my family

I rubbed the side of my hand along my pinky. It ached as the memory became more vivid.

The door slid open, and I jumped back. Through blurred vision, two people dressed from top to bottom in white suits stepped into the room. I rushed them trying to escape, but my groggy effort was futile. One of my captors grabbed me and held my arms. And though weakened, I landed a backward kick to her shin. The quick suck of air through her teeth and the groan that followed was my proof. Her grip loosened. I made another attempt for the exit, but distracted by my struggle to get free I had forgotten there was another person. Forgotten until a sharp jab in my shoulder made me stop, and I stared into the goggle-covered, dark brown eyes of my other assailant. I stared until my lids had slammed shut. The last memory I had from that night was the sudden crumbling of my legs as though the floor had fallen out from underneath me.

I turned the page; a part of me hoped the action would erase the memory. Unlike earlier entries, the next one referenced the following day. No pattern existed with Jasper's journaling; his writings occurred at random, sometimes several months apart.

The entry was short, a small paragraph, but it held a clue I didn't expect to find and confirmed another of my memories. My finger traced over the name Linden. Distant voices swirled and echoed in my ears.

"April Linden!" The voice called.
I sat at a table, my hand rose in the air. My lips parted and the word 'Here' escaped—roll call in school.

"Linden." I'd remembered our surname; the L at the end of our alphanumeric identifiers. The identification number floated in front of my eyes, A20100315L, a combination of my first and last initial along with my birthdate.

The IDs marked everything we had at C.E.C.I.L. from clothing to the covers on our food tray. These identification labels became our new monikers, and they shortened mine to A2.

The words in the diary levitated from the page as I focused my attention on Jasper's entry regarding his conversation with the Lindens. Once again, he kept it brief, and he did not allude to what they discussed. It was as if the lack of detail was because he feared someone might find his journal.

My skin prickled and rose into tiny bumps on my arm as a thought occurred. *Were our parents involved with Cecil's scientific team? Had I been right? Were we the 'things' being kept in exchange for something else?* I searched my memory for any visions of seeing them. Many questions swirled in my head. I buried my face in my hands as a wave of nausea washed over me.

The dizziness eased, and I scanned over more passages, searching for mentions of my family. Two entries later, almost a month after our arrival, they appeared again. The vaccine they had worked on and believed would work, had failed, and they started again. The Lindens played a vital role in the effort and lived in the quarters near the labs.

"Beth!" I slammed the journal shut.

She groaned unintelligible words, rolled over, and faced the back of the couch.

"Beth! Wake up!" I reached over and shook her leg.

Beth sat up. Even in the dim light, her stare pierced through the dark. "What!" she grumbled.

"We've got to go!"

"What! It's too dark."

I pointed the flashlight in my sister's direction.

"Aargh!" She raised her hand and shielded her face.

"Sorry." I pulled the beam toward the floor and took a deep breath. "Just come with me."

"Where are you going?" Beth's voice called from behind me as I stepped out into the hallway.

I turned and looked at her. "To find out what happened to Mom and Dad."

10

THE BOX

Cecil's apartment looked more ominous in the dark. Dust particles swirled in the eerie glow from the flashlight as we stepped through the doorway. The faint scent of his cologne still hung in the air and made me wrinkle my nose.

"Do you smell that?" I said, wondering if it was real or something I imagined.

"What?"

"Never mind." I pointed the light toward the bedroom. "Didn't we leave that door open?" The sealed entry triggered my imagination.

Beth sighed behind me and sharp words followed. "No, I closed it."

Her impatient sigh did not go unnoticed. "What's the matter?"

"Aren't we going to the basement?"

There was no need to turn around, Beth's tone evoked an image of her standing with folded arms and pressed lips. Her glare penetrated the back of my skull.

This time I ignored her statement. Goosebumps rose on my

skin, and the nape of my neck tingled. Beth's foot tapped on the floor behind me as my hand reached for the doorknob and turned.

I stepped into the bedroom; the flashlight beam hit a mirror and shined back temporarily blinding me. Bright purple spots floated in my way. With cautious steps I moved to the pictures hanging across from Cecil's bed. The frames rattled against the wall. I narrowed my eyes, catching for a moment their sudden and almost undetectable movement. Beth's foot tapped louder.

"Take this." I removed the first frame off its hook, held it out behind me, and waited for Beth to free it from my hands before taking down the second. "Let's take these back to the office. I don't want to stay in this room any longer than we have to."

Back in Cecil's office, we set the framed plans on the desk, and I tore the paper backing from the one labelled as the first level.

"What are you looking for?"

"This." Behind the diagram was another drawing, and I lifted it from its mount. Though not as colourful, the depiction showed the layout of the basement. The labelled rooms included the names of some occupants staying in the living quarters. "This was Mom and Dad's room." My voice cracked. Printed across the representation of one suite was the name Linden.

"Linden?"

"Our last name." Poor Beth, I hoped she would remember soon.

Beth touched the name on the drawing. "Do you remember them being here?"

"No, I don't. I'll explain later. Trust me, it's true."

"But–"

"Beth."

"Fine, but what made you th-think this was here?"

I shrugged. "A guess. Cecil was proud of this place. This plan might not be as ornate, but he wouldn't have thrown it away."

"Hmph!" Beth folded her arms.

"Come on." I tugged on her elbow. She yawned; eyes glistened.

There's something about the night that brings out the creepiness of a basement and C.E.C.I.L.'s was no different. There were strange noises and rodents scurried from dark corners and crossed our path making us squeal and grab on to each other more than once. And to make it worse the room we searched for was in an area of the basement where the lighting failed. We stood in the back hall behind the central stairwell, and I held the flashlight for Beth as she studied the layout. Despite my assurance that I remembered where the suite was my sister insisted on taking another look.

"Th-that way." Beth pointed to the left. I nodded; my feet prepared to lead us in that direction before she spoke.

The echo from our footsteps was louder than on our earlier visit as we trudged past the open doors of rooms we'd investigated that afternoon.

We stopped, and I shined the light through the entrance. The bright beam swept over partially blackened walls and other items, highlighting a cobweb in the corner of the room. Our parent's quarters had been one of the three suites set on fire.

"Do you th-think they..." Beth's voice trailed.

"No, they didn't."

"How do you know?"

"Because." Something under my shoe crunched as I

stepped through the doorway, and I shined the light on a crushed starter fluid container. "Someone lit this later—after everyone left." I pushed away debris with my foot; the dirty, green lace bow flopped. "The blaze didn't last long. Whoever set it put it out soon after." I aimed the flashlight beam on a fire extinguisher lying on the floor. "Just the stuff on top burned." The light brightened the items I poked at, and I showed her the things that remained unaffected by fire.

Beth stepped inside the small suite and together we sifted through the stuff piled in the middle of the room.

She shoved an unidentifiable item out of the way with her foot. "What are we looking for?"

"Something, I don't know—just keep searching."

Charred pieces of furniture rested on the top of the heap and we moved them after the careful inspection of each piece. There was a large bureau, its drawers removed and emptied and though blackened much of it was still intact. Tattered and melted blue fabric clung to the remains of a small couch comprising the frame and metal springs. There was also what remained of a burned mattress. As we cleared it from the pile, and dug deeper, the damage lessened, even bits of paper had survived. We combed through the rubble but found no evidence explaining our abduction or whatever involvement our parents had.

I sighed and sat on a dirty area rug with my legs outstretched in front of me.

Beth looked away from the mound of ruins she inspected and refocused her attention onto me. "What are you doing?"

"There's nothing here." I lifted my hands from my lap let them go limp. They fell back to my thighs with a slap.

"I did not come down here s-so you could give up!".

"But there's nothing here," I repeated louder. The sound of my voice reverberated in the desolate space in confirmation.

"URGH!" Beth growled. A charred chair leg rattled against the tile floor. The sudden and strange disturbance brought about a new memory.

"Is Beth going to be like me?"

Mom shrugged. "Maybe," she said, "or she'll be special in another way." She patted the top of my hand and rose from the side of my bed. The faint aroma of roses wafted through the air with her movement.

The cool blue sheets soothed as I slid underneath them, and mom helped rearrange the pillow under my head.

"What about Caleb?" A wide yawn caused my eyes to tear.

"I'm sure he will have his talents, too. Now, off to sleep, we have company tomorrow."

Mom left my room and closed the door a little. A shard of light shined in through the crack. I rolled over onto my side and yawned again. My conversation with my mother played in my head bringing with it an assortment of thoughts. It would be nice to have someone share and understand my burden. Mom and Dad were great to talk to, but they didn't know how it felt to remember everything. They may have been members of MENSA, but neither had a memory like mine. Hyperthymesia, they'd called it, the ability to recall every personal experience, or nearly. Gifted, Mom and Dad called it, that and my creativity. A curse, was my definition. Sure, it was useful sometimes, but most often it drove me nuts. A sibling with a 'gift' was my hope.

"APRIL!"

My heart skipped. "What?"

An object sailed toward me, and I caught it with both hands.

"Beth!" I warned.

"What? You caught it!"

The metal trinket box sat in my palm and it measured the length of my hand from the heel to the tip of my middle finger.

Its width was about as wide as my palm and it was five or six centimetres deep. As for its weight I couldn't help think it was about as heavy as two Granny Smith apples. "Where did you find this?" I held up the soot covered container.

Beth shrugged. "Found it wedged inside the couch spring." She thrust her chin toward the couch remnants. "I thought it was a part of the couch until it fell out."

"Did you open it?"

"No, it's locked."

I turned the dirty box over in my hands. "Give me that!" I pointed to a piece of torn cloth lying on the floor.

Beth handed me the cloth, and I used it to shine the silver-toned exterior. "Look." I touched an etching on the top.

She moved closer, shining the flashlight beam onto the box. "It looks like..." she hesitated for a moment, "a butterfly."

"We have to open this."

"How? We don't have a key."

A grin spread across my face as I pointed out the infinity-shaped slot on the front. "Yes, I think we do."

11

THE PUZZLE

When I'd placed the strange object we'd found taped to the underside of the desk drawer into my backpack, I'd had no idea what it was. Now my fingertips caressed the smooth cylinder nestled in an inside pouch of the pack. I hoped the thought that occurred to me in our parent's suite was correct. I pulled the object from its hiding place and curled my fingers around the small metal shaft; my thumb covered over the flat infinity-shaped end.

Beth sat next to me on the grey couch. The blackened silver-tone box perched on my lap. Hundreds of thoughts and images flipped through my mind as I traced a finger over the butterfly etching. I turned my head and looked out the darkened window of Cecil's office. Outside the moon rose high above the treetops. The light barely penetrated the tinted windows.

"Are you going to open it?" Beth pointed the flashlight on the case.

"Try to, but I'm not sure it will work." I pulled my soot-coated fingertip away from the butterfly etching and added the black smudge to a dirty, grey pant leg. The tubular key shook as I brought it closer to the matching depression. When the infinity symbols joined, there was an audible click and the top of the box unlocked. My heart fluttered as I raised the lid and peeked inside.

The box was empty. A fixed metal insert with curious recessed shapes sat just below the edge of the box. The top depression had a slit along one edge as though the metal had split. I traced a fingertip over the two indentations, homes for whatever small items had once sat in the spaces.

"Th-this looks like a butterfly." Beth pointed to the shape in the centre.

"Or two hearts joined at the points." I set the box on the couch between us. Below the butterfly/heart impression was the other indentation.

"Kind of looks like a..." Beth's voice trailed, her nose crinkled, and she squinted. "I don't know," she said.

I turned the trinket box horizontal so she could get a better view. "Like another infinity symbol or a figure eight?"

Beth nodded. "The key... please." She held out her hand, and I pulled the cylinder from the lock and dropped it into her palm. Beth picked it up and held the metal object in front of my eyes. "Like an infinity s-symbol." She stood the key on its flat end inside the indent in the tray. "Bigger than this one, though."

What is this box? Why was it in our parent's room? Why–

"Why was this key in HIS office?" Beth interrupted the ramblings in my brain.

I shook my head and rubbed the creases in my forehead. "I've been wondering the same thing."

"Maybe Mom and Dad stole the butterfly box." Wide eyes punctuated her statement.

I plucked the heart pendant from underneath my soot

stained t-shirt. My thumb and finger rubbed over the gold surface; the tiny butterfly engraving came to mind.

A quick yank on the necklace and the chain snapped. The golden tether tickled as it slid from my neck. Beth gasped. I pulled the chain from the charm and dropped it inside the box's lid. The gold heart lay in my palm, the weight and warmth, a comfort. I closed my hand and squeezed as though giving it a hug. My fingers loosened, and I stroked the flattened surface of the pendant, the butterfly image more striking than ever. My gaze wandered to the silver-toned container, and I closed the lid. The butterfly etchings looked almost the same.

With my focus turned back to the insert and the indentations, I placed the heart charm inside half of the depression and snapped it into place—a perfect fit.

"Give me yours." Excitement heightened my voice, and I held out my hand; fingers wiggled in anticipation.

"Hang on! I'm not about to frigging break it like you did." Beth reached up and worked at unclasping her necklace from behind her neck.

Under my watchful eyes, her movements couldn't have been any slower. Her actions were painstaking as she pulled her intact chain from the heart. The moment it was free I snatched it from her hand.

"Hey!" Beth protested.

The pendant sat opposite mine and I pressed it into place. The points of the hearts touched in the centre and looked like a golden butterfly.

"What does it mean?" Beth said.

"This box belonged to Mom and Dad. They didn't steal it."

"How can you be sure?"

"This heart was a gift from them for my thirteenth birthday."

"And mine?" Beth rubbed her bare neck.

"There was one for you, but it was a secret, until you turned thirteen." The memory came back.

"So, you knew when you found it tucked inside the journal?"

I nodded.

"Pretty sure I'm not thirteen now."

"Yes, but I forgot to tell you, I've been a little preoccupied."

Beth's gaze softened. "So how did it get inside the journal?"

"Mom and Dad must have had the locket with them and gave it to Jasper." It was the only explanation I had.

"Never let anyone say you can't keep a s-secret." Beth dropped the chain into my palm, and I placed it inside the box with my broken one.

I studied the remaining empty indentation before closing the lid and locking the container. I returned the key to the front compartment of the backpack; the old knife brushed against my hand. Then I nestled the box inside the pack between the t-shirt wrapped journal and extra sweat pants.

I closed my eyes; Mom and Dad's faces appeared behind my lids as clear as though I'd just seen them.

My lids fluttered open, and I gazed into Beth's icy-blues. "You look just like Mom."

A grin spread across my sister's face. "I do?" she said, somewhat surprised.

I nodded and smiled. Reaching out, I took both of her hands in mine and squeezed. "We will find them, Beth."

"How?"

"I don't know, but we will—and Caleb, too."

Beth nodded. "And Caleb, too," she whispered.

12

SURVIVAL

WE LEFT THE MOMENT THE SKY BRIGHTENED WITH THE first hint of sunlight. We walked out of C.E.C.I.L. with everything we'd brought in and only the box and key hidden in the green pack. There was nothing else worth taking. There was nothing we needed to remind us of the compound. We left hoping to find our family and with the resolve we'd never return.

Rested and strengthened legs carried us through the gate and away from our nightmare. Neither of us turned to look back. Neither of us gave C.E.C.I.L. another thought.

We walked in rhythm as our feet scuffed the dirt and kicked away stones with a purpose. Our shoes drummed a steady beat while bird songs filled the air. Coloured shoelace bows bounced and danced to the music.

We passed the intersection and the path that led back to the house. My eyes focused on the road, and my thoughts raced with worries for the journey ahead.

"Do you have any idea why the key was in Cecil's office?"

A black crow darted across the trail, its loud squawk in great contrast to the more peaceful sounds of nature. A smaller brown bird followed close behind and chased it into the trees. The fleeting distraction was a welcome respite from the memories and concerns that rolled through my head. But the moment ended, and Beth's question urged for an answer. It was one I had pondered then dismissed seconds after it crossed my mind, that, and a million others. Along with the influx of returning visions, *the who, what, when, and why* of everything, overwhelmed my brain. I feared it would drive me insane. I tried to switch off my thoughts as much as it would allow and concentrate on one thing—finding a way home. And from the writings scanned in Jasper's journal, I concluded the entries held the answers to our questions. Sweat dampened my brow, and my heart skipped at the thought of the diary and the mysteries it kept.

I shrugged and tugged at the bottom of my stained, blue t-shirt. "I don't know." My gaze shifted from one side of the road to the other. The feeling that cameras watched our every move returned.

"I have a th-theory," Beth said.

"Okay."

"Actually, maybe a couple."

"Are you going to tell me?"

"I'm s-still working out the details, but I'll let you know."

"You do that."

The road was a straight and continuous route of dirt and stones of which we had to free from our shoes on many occasions. There were no junctions or turns to break the monotony. Every so often we stopped and rested, ate stale crackers or raw pasta and sipped water. At the compound we'd drank our fill. Though the battery stores supplied reduced power, it was enough to make lights flicker and operate groundwater pumps at a limited capacity. And while the pressure wasn't sufficient to run a shower, we could coax water from the taps for sponge baths and to fill our canteen and bottles. But now we had to be careful with our supply.

"Will probably run out of food." Beth's distant voice interrupted my thoughts.

I stopped walking. Beth was no longer at my side but stood along the edge of the road with her back turned. Waves of dark brown locks sat on the tops of her shoulders; copper highlights glistened in the sunlight. Our hair was no longer the greasy, limp and odorous mats that framed our faces. In the last few days the healthy shine of clean hair had returned despite having been at least two months since we'd used shampoo. An old brush found in a box at the house painfully fixed the problem of tangles.

"What are you doing?" I waved away a mosquito and its high-pitched whine from my ear.

Beth turned around and held out her hand. "Want one? They're good!" Tiny, deep purple-blue berries filled her palm. Streaks of magenta stained her skin where a berry had burst.

"Beth!"

"What?"

"They could be poisonous!"

Beth rolled her eyes. "Oh jeez! They're not effing poisonous."

I raised my eyebrows and pointed at the feathered carcass beside the bush. "Really? Maybe that bird ate one. What makes you an expert now on flora and fauna?" I folded my arms.

Beth popped the handful of berries into her mouth and wiped her stained hand on the leg of her sweat pants which she'd turned up to her knees. With hands resting on her thighs she peered at the dead bird. "Doubt it," she said and unclipped the front buckles of the black backpack and let the heavy burden fall to the ground. After unzipping it, she plunged both of her hands inside and rummaged through the contents. She removed several items including a small clear fishing tackle box with a rusted hook, a container of matches, and a magnifying glass. "Aha! She said and pulled out a tattered book. One I did not recognize.

"Didn't we decide on taking only the box from the compound?"

"You decided, and I decided th-that this old field guide might be useful."

I snatched the book from her hand. A chunk missing from the front cover made the title difficult to read but not impossible.

"Hey!" Beth protested and snatched it back.

I pointed to the worn manual. "That might not even cover this area."

"This was the only guide, and I assume it's for here." Beth smirked and crossed her arms, the guide tucked in her armpit.

"Can I see it?" My tone softened.

Beth sighed. "Give it back." She unfolded her arms and thrust the book toward me.

A Pocket Field Guide to Flora and Fauna, as read on the inside cover page, was small, thick, and well-used. Faded coloured pictures of various plants with easy-to-understand descriptions covered the pages. It wasn't just a field guide but a survival book. Flipping through, my eyes took in the information and forwarded it to my brain for storing. After a few more moments of careful perusing, I handed it back to my sister. "Guess it'll help well enough."

"So, do you want a blueberry? They are so good." Beth had picked another handful of the wild berries while I'd read. The delicate fruits sat in her palm.

"And what about that?" The decomposing remains of the bird once again in my focus.

Beth shrugged. "Th-there are two more back th-there." She nodded toward the route we'd travelled. "Crows too, I th-think."

"Two! And you said nothing?"

"Not a big deal." Beth picked another blueberry and stuck it in her mouth. "Are you going to eat any?"

"Fine." I chose one and popped it into my mouth. Sweet goodness spilled across my tongue as the tiny orb burst. I closed my eyes and swallowed. The taste evoked a memory. "Dad picked us wild blueberries when we were camping."

Beth squeezed her eyes shut for a moment. "Nope," she said shaking her head. "Don't remember th-that." She tucked the book back into the pack, and I helped her as she pulled the straps over her shoulders and clipped the buckles up front, securing it in place.

"That was years ago, we were young."

"How do you do it?" Beth licked the berry juice left on her hand.

"Do what?" The stubborn purple stains remained on my fingers despite my efforts to remove them.

"Remember."

"These stains don't come off so easily," I muttered. "Give it time, your memories will return."

"Some memories are coming back, but you're different."

I didn't like being called different. "What do you mean?"

"Just that you can see s-something and remember it. That's not s-something I th-think I can do."

The gift was not the same for Beth. "Trust me; it's not always that great."

"If you can do th-that, recall everything you read—see.

Maybe you sh-should have a good look at that journal, a really good one, before we waste any more time."

Beth kept her focus on the road ahead, wavy hair bouncing with every step. From a distance it was possible to mistake her small frame and shorter stature for that of a child. And though she might appear meek she was anything but. The way she carried herself she exuded confidence and commanded respect. Thunderstorms were the only thing that reduced Beth into less than what she was, and she worked on taming that fear. In a few days she had regained her strength, and it showed in her gait. *A firecracker*, our father had called her. Beth's brain might not remember everything about her life before, but her body and mouth did, in that regard she was the same. I admired her.

Beth was right. I needed to read the journal, learn every detail, and absorb every word written on every page. Tingles started at the top of my head and travelled along my arms at the thought. The hot sun did little to comfort me from the sudden fear that crept over my body. That book held secrets, clues, and answers. There was no more time to waste.

Beth gripped my arm, stopping me in my tracks, and returned me to the present. Wide eyes stared at me. "What the hell was that?"

"What?" My heart raced.

Beth pointed toward the trees, and my eyes searched the forest beside us. "What did you see?" I whispered.

She shook her head and whispered back, "I didn't s-see anything, just heard."

"What?"

A distant bark, followed by another yelp, answered my question. The barks and yelps evolved into howls.

"Walk," I said. "Don't run, just walk... fast." My pulse quickened as did my pace and reignited goosebumps.

"Wolves?"

I nodded. "We probably disturbed a sleeping pack."

"I'm sure they're just letting us know th-they're here."

"I don't want to find out. Do you?" I looked down at my shoelaces bobbing with every quickening step.

"Nope!"

The barks and howls grew closer.

13
EVER-WATCHFUL EYES

"Do you think they're out there?"

We rested in a small clearing between the road and the forest. It took Beth three tries to light the campfire with the wood matches we found in a tin at the house. The old fire starters ignited and fizzled out in the same instant. The odour of sulphur followed by a white curling tendril of smoke extinguished any hope with each try. And as daylight faded, our impatience grew. On the second strike the third wooden stick burst into flame with a hiss. Beth touched the match to a clump of dried grass, adding twigs and then the branches we'd gathered. The dark descended, but we had a fire.

A loud snap erupted from the flames sending a spray of tiny orange sparks into the air. Each fiery particle twinkled and danced for a moment until one by one the tiny embers burned out. The blackened, lifeless remains drifted back to the ground.

Beth tugged at a piece of jerky with her teeth until a chunk ripped from the larger part in her grip. She wrinkled her nose and chewed open mouthed, smacking her tongue. "This tastes like crap!" She drew the back of her hand over her mouth, wiping away the spittle that had formed in the corner of her lips.

I yanked off a strip of dehydrated meat and nodded in agreement as my teeth worked to grind the tough and tasteless dried beef. After several seconds of trying to breakdown the insoluble bits into a mash suitable for swallowing, I gave up. The rough pieces scraped my throat. I had put off eating this food stuff and with good reason; it didn't impress.

"Hope not." I finally answered her question and scanned the area. Obscured by darkness the forest appeared ominous and played on my imagination. Invisible figures moved among the shadows. Unseen, black eyes watched through the trees. The heel of my hand pressed and rubbed my thigh as I fought the urge to stand and run. Adrenaline pumped through my body with my increasing heart rate, and I took a sip of water and swallowed hard. My ears trained on the surroundings and listened for sounds that would alert us of their presence. An owl hooted in a nearby tree, and we yelped.

Beth's eyes widened, and her jaw fell open. She placed her hand on her chest. "Th-that scared the crap out of me."

"Me too." The fluttering in my chest slowed as I blew air through my lips.

"What I asked before, I didn't mean the wolves. What I meant was Mom, Dad, and Caleb. Do you really th-think they're out there?"

Imaginary creatures dissolved into faint apparitions, mere whispers of their former selves. "Yes, I do. And maybe even others." I picked up a small piece of wood, placed it on the fire, and changed the subject. "Aren't you afraid?" The slight disturbance caused a few more sparks to erupt from the flames with sizzling cracks and pops. A cloud of smoke rose bringing with it the musky smell of pine needles and dried leaves. The heat warmed my cheeks.

"Of what?"

"Of what's out there, watching us from the trees?"

The firelight cast an orange glow over Beth's face. "Just the unexpected noises and you know, mice that jump out at you. Are you?"

A mosquito's shrill whine interrupted the soothing crackle of the fire, and I swatted it, squishing the insect against my arm. "Don't these things ever bite you?" My finger flicked the pulverized body into the fire.

"Maybe I'm just not as s-sweet." She smiled. "Don't worry; wolves don't like fire." Beth jutted a thumb over her shoulder toward the trees. "Wish we had a cell phone." She tossed the last morsel of her jerky into the flames.

"Beth! Don't waste food."

"The st-stuff is effing gross. Besides, I'm not hungry anymore."

A small portion remained in my hand, and it tempted me to do the same, but I resolved to eat it instead. "So, you remember cell phones," I said after swallowing the tough meat.

"Yes! And I even recall the time Mom lost hers in plain sight."

"Do you?" My voice came out louder than I'd intended.

Beth drew her legs up to her chest, folded her hands, and rested her chin on top of them. Her black sweatpants still rolled to her knees while my pantlegs were tucked inside mismatched socks. The idea was to deter any more insects from attacking my ankles. "Mom had one of those t-transparent ones and set it on a s-stack of papers."

"She searched for hours." The memory caused a wide smile to spread across my face. The earlier imagined shadows were an imperceptible blip in my head.

Beth unrolled her sweats. "Mom was really s-smart."

"And very absent minded." I tossed another stick into the

campfire. The hungry flames ignited and jumped on the piece of wood, consuming it in an instant.

A peaceful silence settled, and we gazed into the fire. Transfixed by the small blaze and lulled by chirping crickets, my mind focused on the memory Beth had prompted.

"Are you planning on reading th-that?" Beth's low voice interrupted my thoughts.

My eyes narrowed. I did not understand what she meant, and then a weight on my left thigh reminded me. The leather-bound journal rested on my lap; the black cover enticed me to open it. "No." I picked up the diary and put it back inside the backpack. "Anyway, it's too dark now. The morning would be better."

"Whatever." Beth sighed and lay on her blanket with her pack behind her for support. She stretched her arms toward the sky and named the stars and the constellations.

I lay on my bedroll and listened to her quiet voice, trying to pick out the tiny points of light she mentioned, trying to keep my mind off the journal. Her words comforted me, and I smiled. Beth had always excelled at science, biology, chemistry, astronomy, while I could not care less. Her instinctive memory returned.

The stars blurred under my heavy eyelids as the din of crickets lulled me into a hypnotic state. The sound only interrupted by the occasional owl hoot or Beth's soft snore. My lids closed. Though I sensed watchful eyes boring into my body, exhaustion did not allow for imagination to rule. My muscles relaxed with each exhale as sleep took a gentle hold and eased me into unconsciousness.

"Get dressed, April. Your uncle will soon be here," Mom said, poking her head into Dad's office. Waves of brown hair sat on her shoulders, except for one lock held in the absent grasp of Caleb's one-year-old fist. Mom untangled the strand from

between his little fingers and shuffled him onto her other hip. She spun around, her voice soft and loving to Caleb as she walked out of the office and down the hall.

"He's not our uncle, is he Daddy?" I climbed off from his lap and Daddy shut the lid of his laptop. He had been showing me a map of the world. It was a game of ours. He pointed out a country, and I told him the name.

"No, Av, he's not. But he doesn't like being called mister because he says it makes him feel old."

Daddy followed me out of his office and closed the door. "Why can't we call him by his name?"

"Because," Daddy patted me on the top of my head, "he wants you to call him Uncle."

I shook my head as we ambled toward my bedroom. Mommy's voice called out from Beth's room. "Your dress is on the bed, April."

I faced Daddy at the entrance to my room. "I think it's silly."

"No, I hate the blue dress!" Beth's voice shrieked.

Daddy smiled. "Between you and me," he raised his eyebrows, "I think so, too."

My green dress lay on my bed. I scowled, I hated that dress.

Cecil's face suddenly flashed in front of my closed eyes.

"Girls!" Mommy's disembodied voice whispered. "This is your uncle."

A scream ripped through my dream. I sat up, disoriented from the sudden commotion, my heart racing. The moon had disappeared, and all that remained of the fire were small, glowing embers which did nothing to show the action occurring on the other side of the campfire.

"Help... me," came Beth's muffled voice.

14

UNWANTED GUEST

I SCRAMBLED TO MY FEET AS THE SOUND OF SCUFFLING and low groans replaced the chirping crickets. Beth shrieked. The high pitch shrill reverberated around me. She yelled again but deeper and angrier. I stood motionless by the unexpected attack. Frozen to the earth, my eyes followed the dark shapes struggling on the ground. While I could not see Beth's assailant my imagination drew several pictures, from maniacal villains to blood thirsty beasts.

"Help!" Beth gasped. Her voice snapped me out from fear and in to action. A big piece of wood that lay beside me became my focus. The dying glow of the campfire guided my urgent hands. Seconds later they bumped into the rough object, the log solid and heavy in my grasp.

I raised the large piece of wood above my head and hesitated. *Which one is Beth?*

"On. Top. Of. Me," Beth grunted.

I stood over my sister and her attacker and threw the log. A thunk followed as it connected, and my heart skipped. *Did I hit the right target?* Something groaned then gasped.

"Get. Him. Off." Beth's muffled and breathless voice came from underneath the dark form.

Adrenaline continued to drive my actions. Half-expecting to meet the thick fur of a wild beast, my hands recoiled for a second when they touched cool fabric instead. I shoved the attacker over, and he rolled onto his side and coughed.

"Are you okay?" I knelt beside Beth.

"Took you long enough." Beth's snarky response answered my question.

The shadowy lump wheezed, and a flash of blue-white light lit up the dark. I gasped. A young man close to my age, though it was hard to tell, curled into a ball. Matted, blond hair tumbled forward and clung to his dirty face as he moved to his hands and knees. His back rose and fell with each struggled inhale and coughing exhale.

Beth trailed a shaky light beam along his body. He wore grey cut-off shorts with one side shorter than the other and both frayed at the edges. A matching T-shirt riddled with small holes and tears, the ensemble reminded me of hospital clothing.

"Is he dying?" The thought occurred, and I covered my mouth. The action meant to keep either screams or vomit from escaping. I wasn't sure which, but I clamped it there with my other hand.

Beth knelt beside the guy and placed her palm on his back. "Nope, just knocked the wind out of him." She rose and stood by my side.

I was glad I hadn't killed him but a small part of me wished I had. My heart kept its adrenaline-filled pace. Beth's attacker could regain strength at any moment.

Beth stretched out her arm. "That little sh-shit bit me!" The flashlight still in her grip shone over her injury.

"Beth!"

"What? He did—s-see!" She held out her arm.

The light showed a distinct bite mark below the sleeve of her grey t-shirt. The assailant's teeth had dented the soft flesh on the inside of her upper arm. I touched the spot with my fingertips, and she hissed through gritted teeth. Blue and purple bruising dotted the tender area.

"Well at least it didn't break the skin." I pulled my fingers away.

"Lucky for you." Beth jutted her chin toward the young man still in a crawling position, but his breathing had eased.

"What now?" My gaze fixed on the boy, waiting for his next move. The log I'd hit him with lay nearby, and I picked it up, just in case.

"Don't know about you, but I'm going back to s-sleep. He ruined an awesome dream." Beth returned to her blankets.

"Beth?" Her nonchalant demeanor surprised me.

"Look at him, he's harmless."

"What! Harmless! He attacked you!"

"Well, I wouldn't say attacked. Yes, he was on top of me but once I woke up, I realized he was just lying th-there like a big lump. I was doing all the s-struggling 'cause I couldn't get him off me."

I pointed to Beth's arm. "What about the bite?"

"Ya, he only bit me after I s-scratched him."

"But—"

"Look, if you're that worried, we'll tie him up."

"And why would he let us do that?"

"Because he will if he knows what's good for him." Beth shined the light in his direction. Amber, vacant eyes stared into the dark as though we didn't exist. The young man shifted to a seated position; his shoulders and chest moved with easy breaths. If he had any plans of attacking again he didn't show it. He continued his blank stare and gave no sign he'd heard or understood.

Beth reached for her shoes and pulled out the pink shoelace from one and the black from the other. "Will need yours too."

The green and blue laces from my runners tied his hands at the wrists while Beth attended to his ankles. There was no complaint or attempt to flee as he sat and allowed us to secure him. "Be careful those aren't too tight." I motioned with a head bob towards the shoelaces Beth knotted.

Beth sighed and tucked a finger underneath the coloured strings. "See, not too tight, okay?" There was an unmistakable cranky tone as she crawled to her nest of blankets and within seconds, quiet snores merged with the chirping crickets.

I stayed by his side, shined the light toward his face, and inspected his features. Slow blinking eyes fixed straight ahead. A layer of grey mud caked his cheeks and stuck in his stubble covered chin; pine needles and twigs tangled in the knots of blond hair. Thin, cracked lips pressed together under a straight nose. The stretched and torn neck of his shirt made it possible to see his collarbone; a small white scar decorated the left side. He was slender but not starved. Scratches, bruises, and insect bites covered his arms and legs; a fresh scratch on his upper arm oozed blood. A gentle breeze stirred the air. He smelled of dirt, and leaves, and sweat. I sniffed my arm and wrinkled my nose; my scent was no better. The portrait of Caleb came to mind, but the boy beside me was not him. He was too old and anyway Caleb's eyes were blue.

The flashlight beam flickered, but he paid no attention and cared little that I had left him for a moment. "Here, lie on this." I spread out a blanket taken from my bedding. The man sat quiet and unmoving.

Back at my bedroll, I dug into the front pocket of my pack, the heavy knife an instant comfort as I pulled it free. With a slight tug the blade opened, and I ran my thumb along the dull edge and touched the tip. The point would serve its purpose. The flashlight dimmed; I shut it off, and tucked the open pocketknife underneath my blanket by my head, the pearl handle secure in my grip. My mind flashed to the night when I'd gripped the nail file in the same fashion. That time I had waited for Cecil to attack. I dared then, and I did again tonight. Only now my weapon offered more protection.

The adrenaline dissipated with a slow and long exhale. Muscles relaxed and my heart slowed. Despite my fight to stay awake the pull of sleep enticed. *Who is he, and what does he want?* My mind questioned at the last before I drifted away.

15

HE WHO HAS NO NAME

"This doesn't make s-sense."

My eyes fluttered open. Fragments of a dream demanded attention, but I ignored them, and the visions faded. A single star twinkled high in the still-dark sky. The beginnings of bird songs floated through the air. One tune started another until the forest erupted into a din of melodies and bathed me in peace and contentment, my body light, my mind at one with nature. It was the cusp of dawn and soon the rest of the sleeping world would rise.

I rolled over and propped my head on my hand. A small campfire crackled. Beth sat on the other side with a blanket draped over her shoulders, her figure blurred and distorted by the heat rising from the flames. The damp morning air caused me to tremble, and I sat up, warming my hands by the fire. My view of Beth cleared. "What doesn't make sense?" I yawned.

"Nothing—never mind."

I sat up and pulled my blanket around me. "What?"

Beth sighed. She dug at the ground with a small stick then shrugged. "Nothing makes s-sense."

"Oh." Beth was right. There was still so much we didn't understand, including who the stranger was that wandered into our camp in the middle of night. Why he'd pounced on Beth, and even more confusing why he'd acted like we didn't exist afterward. Thinking about everything hurt my head, and my focus drifted to the intensifying cacophony in the trees as the sky lightened. Daybreak defined the forest edge, their forms no longer lost to the shadow. A loud snort startled me and pulled me back to our camp. I looked over at the sleeping boy lying on his back on top of the blanket. A sharp intake of air filled my lungs as I noticed the shoelaces missing from his wrists. "He's loose! When did that happen?"

Beth threw the stick she'd been playing with into the fire. "When I woke up. He didn't look very comfortable."

The young man snored again and curled into a ball.

"And now he looks cold." The campfire was further from where he lay. Beth rose and dropped the blanket that hung from her shoulders onto the sleeping figure. "What month is this?" She sat again with knees drawn to her chest and arms wrapped around them.

"Mid-August?" It was the best guess I had.

Beth cocked her head. "Is it? Can you be certain of the time spent in th-that—house?"

The time that had passed didn't concern me, and I shrugged. "I marked the floor every day, except at first. Guestimating what I missed, two and a half, three months." I picked at a small piece of grass and twirled it in my fingers before tossing it into the flames.

"S-sometimes..." Beth hesitated, "sometimes you scratched the floor twice... in one day." She flashed an apologetic gaze. Her face no longer tinged orange under the morning sky.

"What?"

"Twice in one day." She shrugged.

"But, I..." My eyes closed for a moment. "No, every day—one time."

"You weren't as aware as you th-thought. Neither was I." An ant crawled on her leg and she flicked it toward the fire.

"How do you know? You hardly remember anything," I said. Beth's eyes dimmed, and I regretted my words. "I'm so–"

Beth held up her hand. "Th-that's just it. While your brain is busy remembering memories, mine is busy s-sorting out what we know. And nothing makes sense."

"Maybe," I whispered as what she said sunk in, and I understood.

"We weren't there that long. No more th-than two months. And if this was mid-August, I don't th-think there'd be s-so many blueberries. I'd say mid or the end of July."

The days of our imprisonment at the house rolled through my head. Sometimes one day ran into the next, when we received inconsistent meals, and when Cecil deprived us of the sun and moon. *How could we know?* "Sometimes twice?" I said.

Beth nodded. "And at least three times on one occasion."

"And you said nothing."

"I didn't care." Beth shrugged.

I turned my head; the green backpack came into view. The journal inside begged me to read it in its entirety.

"Remember when Mom and Dad left us with that sitter from hell for a week. All she prepared for us to eat was peanut butter s-sandwiches." Beth stretched her arms above her head and yawned.

"You remember that?"

Beth nodded. "Just came to me."

"And it was only three days, Beth, not a week." Even my memory had deceived me and led me to believe they'd left us in misery for much longer. But our parents had assured it had only been a few days.

Beth smiled.

"Okay, okay, I get your point. But why does it matter? June, July—August?" The small rock I'd been picking at came free. Though rough and cold against my palm its weight comforted. I held it up and turned the stone in the firelight, tiny flecks of white quartz sparkled. My thumb rubbed off a spot of dirt before I enclosed the small pebble in my fist.

Beth shrugged. "It matters if we're going to be..." she tilted her head back and gazed at the sky, "in all of this." She waved her hands around us.

"It will not snow anytime soon, if that's what you're worried about."

"No, but... I wish we had a better idea."

"Does it matter right now?"

Beth opened her mouth to speak, but whatever words she meant to utter next became unimportant as our guest stirred and sat. He stared with blank eyes at the flames. Matted blond locks stuck out in every direction. Clods of dirt and other debris contained the rest of his hair. He pulled the blanket around his shoulders and moved closer to the early morning fire.

Beth grabbed a log, and I grabbed a nearby rock. "You said you weren't worried about him."

"Ya, well I could be wrong," Beth said

My eyes narrowed and inspected the boy's features, now easier to see in the light of day. His face, although caked in dirt, did not look familiar and he resembled none of the faces found on the digital photo frame back at the house.

"Do you recognize him?" Beth spoke in a low voice.

I shook my head.

"What's your name?" Beth asked the young man who

looked older than Beth's sixteen years of age and closer to my nineteen years.

The vacant expression continued, and he stared through us as though we weren't there.

"Your. Name," Beth repeated in a louder voice.

His gaze shifted to the dying flames.

"Could be he doesn't speak English."

"Votre nom? Tu nombre? Ti chiami? Uw naam? Dein name? Ditt namn?" Beth said in several tongues. At a young age, she had a penchant for languages and learning them came easy. Second nature, Dad had said. My sister continued to expose her skills and personality on a subconscious level. She shrugged. "And you say I'm stubborn."

"Well that was impressive! And he's not stubborn. He doesn't talk." A disembodied voice spoke from the trees.

Beth leapt to her feet, jumped over the smouldering logs, and joined me at my side. "Who the hell are you?" She hissed.

Once again I sat motionless, unable to move. My eyes darted from the young man's face as he kept his gaze focused on the embers, and then to our new visitor. He smiled.

16

MARCUS

"Easy, there's no threat here." His good looks were hard to ignore as deep brown eyes reflected the sincerity in his voice, and he sat beside the young man. He reached out and patted him on the shoulder and smiled.

Whatever paralyzed me released, and I jumped to my feet and stood closer to my sister with the rock still in my grip. "Who are you?"

"Hey, I'm Marcus. This here is Shaun." Marcus' sleeveless shirt showed off muscular arms and shoulders.

"Why doesn't Shaun talk?" Beth interrogated.

"Not sure if he ever spoke, but maybe at one time." Marcus pointed to his head. "Erased."

The word erased caused a knot to form in my stomach. "What do you mean?"

"Did you come from C.E.C.I.L.?" Marcus rubbed the heel of his hand over the stubble that covered his chin.

My heart skipped at the mention of the compound.

"Why?" Beth wasn't any less suspicious, and her knuckles

whitened as she tightened her grasp on the log still in her hands.

"Relax, girl, just wondering."

"Don't call me, girl."

"What should I call you?"

"None–"

"Beth and April." I interrupted. "And to answer the first question—we are." I needed to know if they had been imprisoned like us or worked there and telling them who we were might help me find out.

"Av!" Beth disapproved.

"Okay, us too, roomies even. Not too sure how we escaped the fire but we've wandered around for weeks, or whatever it's been. Everything was all hazy, right?" Marcus looked at Shaun and scratched his head. Curly black hair stuck out, but unlike Shaun's, it was free of any visible bits of mother earth. "Anyway, after some time, memories returned, not all but most. Unfortunately, ole Shaun here... nothing." He patted the boy on the back.

"How do you know his name th-then?" Beth said.

"Don't, really. There was a guy who looked like him back home named Shaun. Anyway, I had to call him something, right? Couldn't keep saying 'hey, you', that got old quick."

"Why do you say he's erased?" The term bothered me.

"Just something I came up with. Figured the shot I remembered getting had something to do with it. Guess I think it took away whatever he remembered, like it erased his mind."

Jasper had told me once that reducing the memory-blocker drug too fast could cause someone to lose their entire memory. I glanced at Shaun. His blank stare focused on the fire; the orange glow bounced from his pupils. It saddened me the only light ever to shine from his eyes again would be a reflection.

There was a flutter in my stomach. "Are there others?" A conversation from the past came to mind.

"Where does he g-go?" Beth questioned.

My gaze shifted from my sister and fell back on Jasper. I was curious about that too and waited for his answer.

Jasper inhaled, his lungs rattled, and his throat whined as the air passed through. "To find others. To look for food—secrets." He shrugged.

My eyes widened. "Others?"

"Those who escaped that night." Jasper reached for the bottle of water with one shaky hand while the other tried to turn the lid. After a second, I reached over and unscrewed it for him. His mouth twitched as though trying to smile. "Thank you," he whispered.

Marcus stretched out his legs and leaned back on his hands. Black running shoes adorned his feet. The same kind Beth and I had worn at the compound. One jagged hem of his navy pants ended at his knee and the other halfway up his thigh. Loose threads hung from the frayed edges. Like Shaun's outfit, Marcus' shirt and pants matched.

"We've seen no one else, up 'til now." Marcus flashed a smile.

"You sure?" Beth said.

"Beth." I shook my head.

She changed the subject. "What happened to your knee?"

Below the edge of his torn pant leg, dried blood stained his brown skin. Marcus pulled the tattered material up higher. "It's just a scrape. Nothing too bad. You get lots of 'em running around the woods. You two look okay though." He jutted his chin in our direction.

We may not have any outward appearances of injury, but

we were far from unscathed. Our scars ran deeper than what was visible. I looked away from him.

Beth flicked a small bug off of her thigh. "We haven't done much running around."

"Where are you going?" I placed the focus back on Marcus.

Marcus sat forward and folded his legs. He poked at the smouldering piece of wood with a stick he'd picked up from beside him and trailed it across the cracked charred surface. The tip of the branch sank into a small fissure and exposed an orange glow.

Marcus shook his head. "I have no idea, nowhere I guess."

"You could come with us." I suggested as I would rather have them with us instead of lurking in the trees where we couldn't see them.

"Av!" Beth whispered a warning, but I ignored it.

"Where are you're heading?" Marcus dropped the stick on the glowing embers and within moments it burst into flames.

"Nowhere, we're just looking."

"For what?"

"Our parents." The reignited fire held my attention. That I had no clue where to start in this endeavour, I kept to myself.

"Hate to bring you down, but they might not even be alive." Marcus picked up a tiny twig and stuck the end in his mouth.

"What do you know?" Beth hissed and glared.

Shaun looked away from the fire for the first time since Marcus arrived and stared up at Beth, no change appeared in his vacant eyes.

Marcus glared back. "All I understand is some virus was wiping out the planet."

I stared at Marcus. "How do you know it was wiping out the planet?" I used his words. If he was a resident, prisoner, who had received the hypno-drug, he would not have known. It was Jasper who had informed us of the virus and whether we had that knowledge before receiving the drugs was unknown. That information no longer remained or was temporarily unavailable. My grip tightened on the rock once again.

He raised an eyebrow then narrowed his gaze. "When did you arrive?"

"I asked first."

Marcus sighed. "It was about a year ago when I showed up at the place. Things were a mess. When I found the compound, it was sealed up tight."

"Just you? Where's your family?" Beth shifted her weight and leaned closer to me.

"Dead. Virus killed them—everyone." Marcus threw the gnawed stick from between his teeth into the fire.

"So how did you get inside the compound?"

"When my family died, I left. Drove for a bit, but there was panic everywhere, and they turned cars back from wherever they came from. So, I ditched the car and headed out on foot. My plan was to head north. I'd've gone further too, only..."

He'd piqued my curiosity. "Only what?"

Marcus leaned forward. "Only, here I was in the middle of nowhere, and there's this wall. I climbed it, walked through the woods, and found C.E.C.I.L. They wouldn't let me in, at first." He laughed. "I told them I'd been exposed and never got sick. When they heard the story, the doors opened. They quarantined me for a while. I guess they thought my blood was the antidote or something."

I turned away from the staring match between Shaun, Beth, and Marcus and had my own with my backpack—one sided. Whatever doubt or fear I had evaporated, and I had to read the journal.

"So, what makes you think your folks are still alive?" Marcus' voice broke my concentration.

"Because, they were at C.E.C.I.L." A light breeze swept over me causing the skin on my arms to prickle.

Marcus squished a mosquito that had been feeding on his arm. "What if they didn't get out?"

"They did." I watched as he flicked the body toward the fire, and half-smiled, happy that there was someone else on which they liked to dine.

Marcus nodded. "So, your parents are out there looking for you too?"

"Yes." My heart skipped at the thought; at least I hoped they were looking

"Unless..." Marcus poked at his teeth with another twig.

"Unless what?" Beth said.

"Unless they think you're dead."

17

INK

Black ink words levitated as bright sunlight reflected off the white pages of the journal. The sun-warmed sheets attracted winged insects, and they landed on the floating script pushing it back into place. Segmented bodies shimmered in the sunbeams; delicate wings fluttered and carried the tiny flies off with the breeze. The text hovered once more as the bugs lifted. I squeezed my eyelids shut over burning and blurry eyes and shook the illusion away.

Distant melodies drifted through the air and mixed with the occasional buzz and the murmur of voices. But I paid no attention to any distraction. My focus was on the writings as each paragraph entered my pupils and imprinted in my memory. The diary held secrets, truths, and mysteries, and my stomach rolled with every turn of the page.

Shaun slept in the shade, oblivious of the surroundings, while Beth and Marcus studied the nature book, absorbed in the natural world around them.

Were all the residents exceptional? I swept up damp hair with one hand and lifted the locks off my shoulders. A warm breeze blew over the hot, clammy skin at the back of my neck. The current of air cooled me as I gathered my hair into a ponytail, twisted it into a bun, and secured it with two small sticks. Damp tendrils framed my face.

I closed my tired eyes. A bead of sweat trickled down my nape and reminded me of the entry I'd just read; I needed to know if the words spoke the truth. Another gust rustled the leaves and fluttered the journal's pages as it rested on my lap. Tiny bumps erupted on my arms. I drew in a deep breath and forced it back out through pursed lips.

"Don't think your sister likes me much."

My eyes blinked open to Marcus standing beside me. Without hesitation, I closed the journal; the pages slapped together. "What makes you think *I* like you?" I half-smiled at Marcus. While I'd found him attractive from the moment I saw him, under the circumstances I could not allow those feelings to surface.

Marcus shrugged. "Seems like you do."

"Don't worry about Beth; she takes a while to like anyone."

"So, what's Av?"

"What?"

"Beth, she calls you, Av, sometimes."

"*Family* nickname, short for Avril, April in French," I said, emphasising the word family.

Marcus put up his hands. "Got it. Listen, even though we just met, you can trust me. Both of us." He jerked his head toward Shaun who lay sleeping in the shade.

The look in his eyes read as sincere but only time would prove if his words were true. I gave him a polite smile. "Okay."

"April, you should get out of the sun; you're turning pink." Marcus held out his arm and compared it to mine, the deep brown contrasted with my rosy skin.

I tucked the journal inside the backpack and rose to my

feet. Dirt and grass stuck to my legs, and I brushed the bits off as I stepped over the long-dead fire and walked with Marcus toward the trees. We sat near Shaun, but the shade wasn't much cooler.

Shaun snorted and rolled closer to the trees. His dirty, grey shirt clung to his back. Wisps of blond hair matted at his neck and stuck out in every direction.

I stared at Shaun for a moment and wondered what he thought about the situation or anything at all. Jasper's writings once again replayed in my head. *He has even marked his chosen ones* floated in front of my eyes. There was only one way to know for sure, and I needed to find out before I told Beth. I took a deep breath and allowed it to rush out from between my lips.

"What's the matter?" Marcus said.

"Nothing. What makes you say that?"

"Well," he picked a blade of grass and tucked the skinny leaf between his teeth, "there's this thing."

"What thing?"

"Well, like I said, we haven't known each other long."

"No, a few hours."

"Not trying to pry or anything. Anyway, you sorta blow air out through your lips sometimes, figured something was bothering you, maybe."

"When did I do that?"

"Just a few seconds ago and before, reading that book. You did that a lot when you were reading."

"Were you spying on me?" I folded my arms, questioning my decision to trust Marcus and the favour I planned to ask of him.

Marcus shook his head. "No, not spying, observing. Anyway, didn't mean to pry."

"No, it's okay." I rubbed my forehead. "Listen, I need you to do something, but it's weird... sort of."

Marcus raised an eyebrow. "Okayyy," he drew out the word.

"Okay." I took a deep breath and turned my back to Marcus. "Is there anything on my neck?" I bent my head forward.

"Like a bug or something?"

"Yes, but a tattoo of a bug, a butterfly to be more specific." My pulse raced as I waited for Marcus to look.

Marcus' fingers swept away stray hairs. His gentle touch made my skin tingle, and yet another part of me made me want to tell him to forget it. The tip of one digit pressed against my skin. "There's a tattoo, a butterfly."

The news made me gasp despite my intuition.

"Hey, you okay?" Marcus' strong hands rested on my shoulders, and I flinched.

I pulled away and faced Marcus again. "Can I see your neck?"

"Sure." He agreed, but I felt he was humouring me as he scooted around and moved away his dark curls.

"Where is mine, exactly?" I rose on my knees and searched Marcus' neck.

"You don't know?"

"No." My tone fell somewhere between normal and a whisper.

"It's about here." Marcus touched the back of his neck right at the hairline.

"Is there any colour?"

"Nope, just a small, black butterfly."

I combed through his hair, parting sections and untangling curls as I inspected the skin underneath. With every second my searching grew more frantic.

"Ow! Was I that rough?"

"No, sorry." I sat back on my knees. "Nothing," I whispered.

From his treetop perch the long call of a cicada buzzed and vibrated through the air. I picked at the ground, plucking tiny blades of grass and other small plants. Beth lay on her stomach under the shade of a stand of maples, consumed by the contents of her field guide.

"What made you think I had a tattoo like you?" Marcus' voice startled me.

"Something I read." Jasper's writing floated before my eyes as I stared at my backpack.

"In that book?"

I nodded.

"What does it mean?"

"That we're exceptional," I said.

"In what way?"

I stretched my legs out in front of me. "You said you arrived at C.E.C.I.L. about a year ago?"

"Uh-huh!"

"I don't think you can be exceptional—anomalous." I shrugged.

"Pfft! Thanks! They used my blood for the vaccine didn't they?" Marcus slapped a mosquito feeding on his calf.

"Just going by what you told us. Anyway, I don't mean you aren't exceptional in your own right." I crawled toward a still-sleeping Shaun.

"What are you doing?" Marcus whispered as he crept along beside me.

Shaun's blond hair stuck to his neck, but I swept it away and probed his hairline with my fingers. The black butterfly came into view. "Like this one?"

Marcus nodded. Shaun startled, and we moved back, giving

him room to sit. He scratched his head and yawned; vacant eyes stared in Beth's direction. At one time, Shaun was exceptional too. Now his brain registered nothing. He only existed.

"Beth, come here." I waved for my sister to join the three of us. She gave a brief consideration but resumed her engagement with the book again. "Beth!" I called louder.

She sighed; the sound was heavy with annoyance. "What?"

"Just come here, please."

Beth closed her book and shoved it into her nearby pack. She walked over and glared. With folded arms she tapped her foot on the ground. "What?"

"Sit." I pointed at a patch of grass beside me.

Beth frowned but did as I asked. I crawled around behind her and brushed her damp hair from her neck.

"What the hell are you doing?" She spun; her dark waves fell away from my hand and back onto her shoulders.

"Looking for a butterfly."

Beth's eyes narrowed. "What the–"

"Beth, please let me look."

"Fine." She turned and pushed her hair away from her neck.

After a few seconds of prodding, I found the tattoo. "She has one too." There was not much detail to the small inking on her skin, a simple but obvious design.

Marcus looked. "I'm feeling a little left out now, you know."

"Would someone t-tell me what the hell you are talking about?"

"This here." With my back turned and Marcus' help, he pointed out the tattoo on my neck to Beth.

"Same as this," he said.

"Shaun, too!" I said turning to face my sister.

"What does it mean?" Beth placed a hand on her neck.

"Apparently, we're chosen."

Marcus raised his eyebrows. "I thought it meant you were exceptional."

"Exceptional, special, different—chosen."

"In what way from everyone else?" Marcus spoke.

"According to the journal, intelligence and/or special gifts, talents." I reached for the backpack and pulled out the journal, showing Beth the entry about the tattoo.

"Your memory," Beth said, "and your creativity."

"Could be. And yours?" As far as I remembered Beth showed no extraordinary talents, other than her penchant for science.

"I'm working on s-something." She smiled.

My eyes widened. "What?"

Beth waved her hand, dismissing my question. "And his?" Beth pointed toward the vacant Shaun. "I guess we'll never know."

A distant rumbling echoed through the trees. Beth's head snapped back, and she stared up at the cloudless blue sky. Though she coped, she hadn't gotten over her fear of thunder storms.

"We better go." Marcus' lips tightened into a line and his jaw tensed. The sinewy tendons in his neck twitched.

"Why? What is that?" I rose and stood beside Marcus.

Marcus pulled Shaun up and grabbed the blanket that lay on the ground. "A truck. Come on, grab your stuff."

Beth hurried over to her pack and bedroll and gathered them into her arms.

"Into the trees," Marcus said, dark eyes wide with concern.

"Who is it?" My pulse raced.

"There's no time to explain." Marcus seized my hand and pulled me toward the forest. "Help Shaun!" he yelled to Beth.

Beth grasped Shaun's arm with her free hand and disappeared into the woods.

"I have to get my backpack!" I called and tugged my hand.

"There's no time!" Marcus warned.

I pulled from his grasp and ran the few steps for my pack and bedroll. My heart thumped in my ears as I scanned the road. A cloud of dust billowed toward us in the distance; the engine's roar grew louder.

Marcus grabbed me by the arm once again and tried to lead me to safety. My feet stumbled over the remains from the fire. The pull of gravity was strong as my body lurched forward. Beth peered at me from the bush. Marcus' fingers slipped away, and I landed with a thump.

18

TRUTH

Tiny blue, green, and white lights twinkled behind closed eyelids. Each deliberate inhale and exhale slowed the fluttering in my chest and the thrumming in my ears. The thump so loud it drowned out the whispered voices.

"You okay?"

The voice pulled me from within, a warm hand rested on my forearm, and I shook it free. Rivulets of blood ran from a scrape on my right knee. Pieces of skin and dirt protruded like little islands. I plucked a small stone from the abrasion.

"Are you all right?" Beth dropped the black pack and rifled through its items.

A shaky breath blew from between my lips as my heart slowed. I nodded at my sister then turned my attention toward Marcus. Anger burned my cheeks. Jaw tensed and teeth gritted. He had denied others existed. My eyes narrowed as we held each other's gaze.

"Ouch!" I cried as Beth dabbed at my injury with an alcohol swab. She wielded a small pair of forceps.

"There's one more. Th-this might hurt." The pincers moved towards my knee, but I caught the hand holding the tool.

"Careful."

She smiled and patted my arm. "Don't worry." Her eyebrows knitted in concentration, and she went back to work.

A sharp suck of air hissed through my teeth as she plucked out the final grain. With diligent hands she cleaned and bandaged the wound.

"There, all better." Beth tucked the first aid supplies back inside the pack then glared a warning at Marcus. After a moment she left and sat beside Shaun who leaned against a tree and stared off into the forest. The tune she hummed carried to my ears on a breeze, the only song she remembered—Cecil's ballad.

"Who was that?" The minor procedure had not made me forget my anger.

Marcus shook his head. "I don't know. Someone from C.E.C.I.L."

"From C.E.C.I.L.? How do you know this? Are there others? What does he want?" One after another questions rolled out of my mouth while more queued up in my head. *Mom and Dad?*

Marcus shrugged. "Us."

"Why?" A mosquito gnawed on the back of my neck, and I slapped the annoying bug.

He shook his head. "We've been hiding from that guy for days, weeks." He kept his voice low.

"WEEKS!" The word came out louder than intended.

"I didn't want to say anything. Didn't want you to worry."

"Maybe he wants to help?" Not everyone from the compound was malevolent. I thought of my parents and Jasper.

"Well, he doesn't."

"He might have information about my parents." As I spoke

it occurred that hiding in the woods could ruin any chance at finding them. I jumped to my feet, ignoring the sting in my knee from the sudden movement. The underbrush brushed against my calves, and my hands pushed away low branches. Tree roots tripped me, but I maintained my balance.

"Where are you going?" Beth called, but I ignored her too.

"STOP!" Marcus' loud voice caused me to hesitate for a moment but then I continued until his hand grabbed my elbow.

"Let. Go!" I tried to shake my arm free.

"Stop!" Marcus said again. He clutched both of my arms and forced me to face him. "That... maniac has no intention of helping. There were more of us."

"What!" I gave up the struggle.

"There were others." Marcus released his grip and stared at the ground.

"What's going on?" Beth had caught up; she folded her arms and waited for an answer.

"Where's Shaun?" Marcus focused his gaze over Beth's head.

"At the tree, s-still s-staring off into s-space. Now tell me what the hell is going on?"

I pointed at Marcus. "Ask him!"

Beth glared. "Well!"

"There were others... like us. Seven more."

No words tumbled from my open mouth. *Beth was right not to trust Marcus.* I pushed the thought away and dropped the backpack. With trembling hands, I unzipped the bag, opened an inside pocket, and pulled out a piece of paper. "Was this boy part of the group?" The folded paper dangled from my fingers.

Marcus took the wrinkled sheet and unfolded it. Eyes narrowed, and lips pressed as he studied the portrait. My fists clenched, and I swallowed hard. The tense moment lacked a ticking clock.

"No." He refolded and held out the drawing.

"You're sure?" My breath hitched as I tried to draw in air. The feeling reminded me of the time I dangled from a tree branch, my feet not too far from the ground. My fingers slipped, and I fell, landing on my back. The air had rushed from my open mouth, and on hands and knees, I gasped, waiting for my lungs to expand.

Marcus nodded. "Who is he?"

I was mute.

"Never mind. Where did the others go?" Beth said.

Marcus sighed. "Most of us had come out of our daze when he showed up. Just walked into our camp. Said he was looking for someone and wanted to help. I didn't trust him."

"How can you be certain he was at C.E.C.I.L.?" My voice returned.

"His clothes, a badge around his neck, though I couldn't see his name," Marcus said.

"What happened?" Beth said; neither tone nor gaze was any softer.

"He asked for our names. Some remembered. Some didn't and told him that. Then he asked Shaun." Marcus glanced back toward the tree and the ever-silent Shaun. "When he didn't answer, that asshole took a hold of him and put a knife to his throat."

I gasped. "Oh, no!"

"One girl, Grace, she..." Marcus stopped and blinked. "She rushed him, pushed Shaun out of the way, and he slit her throat.

"Shit!" Beth let her arms drop to her side.

"I grabbed Shaun and ran. We split up from the rest, and I haven't seen them since. When Shaun stumbled on you last night..." Marcus looked at Beth.

"You s-saw th-that?"

Marcus nodded. "I thought you were part of the group. Shaun must have thought so too. He might be erased, but sometimes he reacts to things. That's why I think he jumped on you."

"He wouldn't get off of me! I scratched his arm and then he bit me!" Beth yanked the sleeve up and showed Marcus the mark.

Before Marcus had time to react to Beth I interrupted. "Then why did you stay in the trees? Why not come out? How did you know we wouldn't hurt him? I threw a log at him!" Several other questions popped in my head.

"I was about to, but something snapped in the bushes behind me. I took the chance Shaun'd be okay and lead whatever made the noise in another direction. By the time I snuck back, you were curled up by the fire, and then I fell asleep. You threw a log at him? Guess I missed that."

"Why didn't you tell us the truth earlier?" I folded my arms.

Marcus scratched the top of his head. "Like I said, I didn't want you to worry."

"Hmph!" Beth snorted. She spun, and I followed her with my eyes as she went to Shaun.

"So, there is someone inside that head," I said, keeping my eyes on Beth as she stood by the tree where Shaun sat. I couldn't see his face but could imagine his blank stare.

"There's no hope for him."

"There's always hope." I walked away to join Beth and Shaun, leaving Marcus behind, the memory of when I'd given up on ever being free fresh in my mind.

We followed Marcus through the woods; the dirt road was no longer a safe choice, at least until we had a better strategy. And while we had freedom of movement, every step was a grim sign that once again something trapped us. The trees reminded me of prison bars, tall and strong. Until we had a way out, we would stay hidden among nature's bars.

My feet stumbled over roots, rocks, and downed branches. Thorny underbrush caught in the soft material of my rolled sweatpants and scratched the exposed areas of my shins and calves. The smell of sweat and blood oozing from my skin drew biting insects. I grunted and groaned my way over the rough terrain, up and down hill, and over and under fallen trees.

"Did you hear them yesterday morning, the wolves?" I called to Marcus, remembering he'd said he led something away from the camp.

"No, but I have before. Seen them too."

The information worried me. "When?"

Marcus stepped over a large branch and the rest of us followed. "Last week maybe, I don't remember. Why?"

"They freaked her out," Beth said. I glared at my sister. "Us, I mean."

"Don't worry, there's only four."

"Four? Sounded like a lot more than that." The invisible silk thread of a cobweb strung between two trees caught my chin. "Ugh!" I groaned under my breath.

"Nope, only four."

For a while the only sound came from stomping and tripping feet as we wandered through the trees and underbrush.

"Where... are... we... going?" I huffed breathless.

Marcus stopped and waited for me; Beth and Shaun trailed behind us. He smiled, his brown eyes brightened. "It's not much farther, the walking will be easier." He turned and kept hiking though his pace had slowed.

We emerged from the tangled mess of thicket, fallen timbers, and wayward rocks onto a trail that cut through the forest. Apart from a faded blue trail marker nailed to a tree the path reminded me of the simulation room.

"This way," Marcus said after hesitating at a fork in the pathway.

The muscles in my legs relaxed as the passage was less encumbered by obstacles. I adjusted my pack, its weight lighter now I wasn't stumbling, ducking, or climbing.

"Where are we?"

"What do you mean?" Marcus answered my question with another.

"You said you headed north after your family died and then you found C.E.C.I.L. Don't you know where we are?"

"I fled north." Marcus nodded. "But I was on the road for weeks. Drove a little, walked most, but hitched some too with whoever wasn't afraid to have me, and we travelled a lot at night. I told a few rides I headed as far north as they were heading. Sometimes the drives were long. Sometimes we travelled west, sometimes east, but always further north than from where I started. By the time I arrived at C.E.C.I.L., I lost all track of where I was. Anyway, why does it matter?"

Marcus' explanation rolled in my brain. *How is it possible to not know where you'd travelled? Is he holding back something? It wouldn't be the first time,* I argued with myself. *How is this any different?*

"Anyway, who cares where we are when we've got this?" Marcus waved his arms out in front of him and stepped to the side.

The earthen ground beneath my feet changed to rock. The flat rock we stood on stretched ahead of us and disappeared into shimmering blue water.

19

FIRST WORDS

THE CHEST DEEP WATER REFRESHED MY BODY. HANDS AND fingers dipped and splashed; feet and toes dug into the gravel. White water lilies with brilliant yellow centres floated in the shallow depths further down the shore but their fragrance carried to me on warm breezes. Air filled my lungs, and I ducked under the stillness. The cool liquid rushed over me, and my skin tingled. I opened my eyes and swam closer to shore above the rocks and sand. Fish the size of my hand scattered in every direction. Sunbeams pierced the surface, refracted, and highlighted whatever lay in its path. The remains of a freshwater mussel shell shimmered.

In the shallow water I rolled onto my back and grabbed a large rock. My legs drifted, weightless. The blue sky distorted and blurred, in the centre the sun blazed, but I felt no heat. I allowed a hand to float upward and stretched my fingers as though to grab hold of something out of reach.

Bubbles gurgled and rose. I released the rock and floated up with the air-filled orbs. My face broke through the surface. Warmth touched my skin, and I closed my eyes against the bright sun. The light turned the underside of my lids a brilliant red. Water clogged my ears and muffled sounds; my heart beat steady and rhythmic in my head.

A shadow fell across the brilliance, and I opened my eyes. Through wet eyelashes, Beth's face smiled above my naked body.

"Lunch," she said and held out a purple blanket.

I took the offering as I stood and wrapped it around myself. The soft microfiber caressed my skin and absorbed the remaining water. "Let me guess." The water sloshed at our knees then splashed our ankles as we waded toward the shore. "Fish!"

Beth laughed. "There's no s-surprising you." We'd eaten fish every day since arriving at the lake, sometimes twice.

Weeks before, Marcus, Shaun, and their group had camped on the other side of the small lake surrounded by trees and rocky outcroppings. They'd lived on snails and frogs and the odd fish, which had been difficult to catch but not impossible. They drank from a stream that emptied into the lake and it was from there where we filled our bottles and canteen. Fishing was easier for Marcus now. Not only had his skill improved, but we had provided line and hooks from the small tackle box we'd found at the house.

For three days, we ate, rested, and grew stronger. When we weren't hunting or exploring, Beth busied herself with the nature book, studying everything and learning which plants we could eat and the skills for outdoor survival. I buried myself in Jasper's journal, reading every entry that detailed how we came to be in our current predicament. The secrets and information etched into my head, and I divulged nothing because there was more to read—and because nobody asked.

Stiff clothes hung from a branch but they were clean and dry. Marcus had used the pocket knife to cut the legs off one pair of sweatpants. He'd wanted to do the same to the other pair, but I didn't allow it.

The blue t-shirt crunched in my hands as I softened the stiffened material before pulling it over my head. And I repeated the process with the cut-off shorts. The purple blanket took their place and spread out over the bush to dry in the sun.

"Are you ever going to wear the other shirt?" Beth said as I tightened the drawstring of the grey shorts. Beth smoothed her hands over the spare, pink tee she donned and smiled.

"Don't need to, not now anyway." The second tee in my pack was orange, and I put off wearing it as long as possible. Had there been another that fit, I would never have taken it. The colour reminded me of the pajamas I'd worn the night they had taken us back to C.E.C.I.L. to live on a permanent basis. The same pajamas we'd found in the wardrobe at the house.

We walked barefooted back to camp. Shaun rested by the campfire as Marcus turned the sticks that held our lunch. The smell made my stomach rumble.

"One each, today!" Marcus flashed a proud smile.

"Impressive!" I said and sat beside Marcus. Beth took a spot by Shaun.

Marcus removed two skewers from the fire, and I passed them to Beth. Then he took out the remaining two and gave me one. I blew on the steaming fish, pulled off a small bite, and popped it in my mouth. Beth did the same but instead of eating it she handed the piece to Shaun. With an automatic response, he placed it in his mouth, chewed, swallowed, and waited for the next offering. The back and forth feeding continued; first a chunk for Shaun and then Beth took one for herself. Since wandering into our camp four days ago, Beth assumed most of the responsibility for his care, except bathroom duties; Marcus took him on those outings.

"Shaun can feed himself," Marcus said, picking at his own fish. This debate was one they had yet to resolve.

"He'll burn himself," Beth countered.

"Only once."

"Fine!" Beth glared at Marcus, and she held the skewer out to Shaun.

"This doesn't seem like a good idea." My gaze shifted between Marcus and Beth. That she would give in to him never crossed my mind. It was a rare thing to sway my sister and now that Marcus had, it concerned me.

"None of us hand fed him before." Marcus shrugged.

"You didn't have cooked fish before." Somehow I had taken over Beth's argument.

"We did—just not often. And I have to tell you, this tastes so much better. Less slimy and gooey, you know? Oh, and less chance of it coming back up." He popped a piece in his mouth and licked his fingers.

I held up my hand. "Please, no more detail."

He chuckled. "You sure you don't want to hear about the snails?"

"Take it!" Beth's voice interrupted my discussion with Marcus.

The seconds passed as Shaun stared at the stick held out to him. Beth widened her gaze; she rolled the wood skewer between her fingers, the pieces of fish twirled in silent temptation. Shaun's hand rose from his lap. His fingers wrapped around the skewer and pulled it from Beth's grasp.

"Be careful," she warned, "it's hot."

Shaun glanced at Beth then turned his attention to the meat. He stared at the food for a moment then brought it toward his mouth and took a large bite from the side. I sucked in my breath, realizing as I did that my fish had cooled. His would be no different. A quiet calm settled over us as we consumed our meal.

With the last bite in my mouth, I tossed the stick into the fire. I closed my eyes and revelled in the flavour, remembering tartar sauce and lemon. And fries, I licked my lips at the thought.

A sudden groan followed by three quick 'Ows', and my memory of fish and chips disintegrated. A moment of stunned silence fell on us as I scanned over each surprised face.

Shaun gripped the thumb of one hand with his other. A small trickle of blood oozed between his fingers.

"What's happened?" I said, bewildered by their expressions.

Marcus shook his head. "Not sure."

Beth grabbed her pack from behind her and rummaged through it. "He was eating and then he stabs his th-thumb with the s-stick." She pulled out the first aid kit and opened the box. "Let me look." Beth pried away Shaun's hand from his injured thumb. "Oh, it's not s-so bad." She washed away the blood with water from her bottle, then tore open one of the alcohol swab packets. "This might sting." She dabbed at Shaun's wound, but he didn't flinch. Beth applied a bandage. "There, all better." She smiled and patted Shaun on the back. Her eyes softened as she looked at him.

I shook my head. "I knew something bad would happen."

"Bad?" Marcus' voice startled me.

"Yes, bad. Shaun hurt himself or were you not paying attention?"

"Neither of you were paying attention." Marcus tossed his skewer into the fire.

"What do you mean by th-that?" Beth shifted her focus away from her patient, and her soft eyes turned to a harsh glare.

"Don't you see what really happened?" Marcus said; his head swiveled between Beth and me.

"He. Got. Hurt." My words were slow and deliberate.

"Jabbed his thumb with a stick." Beth filled in the detail.

Marcus shook his head. "No."

My eyes narrowed as they searched his face for understanding.

Marcus sighed. "Shaun spoke."

20

SELECTIVE HEARING

The cicadas crescendo pierced the hot afternoon. Birds sang, warbled, and chirped; each note carried on warm air currents. A light breeze disturbed the trees and leaves shushed. A butterfly fluttered its colourful wings; tiny feet clung to a nearby flower as it drank its fill of nectar before drifting away. Where there was noise there was also tranquil silence, from screeching to melodious, from a quiet hush to the imperceptible. It was a matter of concentration, to separate the din that flooded our ears, focusing on what we wanted and ignoring everything else. We chose what and what not to hear. While Beth and I had heard groans of pain, Marcus had discerned words. One word repeated in succession—ow.

"Is it really a word?" Beth crossed her arms.

"Can you spell it?" Marcus questioned back.

"O-W."

"Yup, it's a word." He smirked.

Beth stuck out her tongue. "Groan sounds can be spelled too."

Marcus raised an eyebrow and mirrored Beth's stance.

"A-r-g-h, or u-r-g-h, and even u-n-h-h." She scowled back.

"Come on, they're just noises."

"So is ow!" Her voice rose.

"Ow is a legal Scrabble word." Marcus flashed a smile in my direction as though he'd uttered checkmate.

"He's got you there," I said to Beth, tired of the bickering, and then to Marcus. "Shaun's never said it before?"

He shook his head. "Never, only grunted or groaned, but mostly, he's silent."

My attention returned to Beth. "Maybe he's becoming aware?" The tiny muscles in her face relaxed as her tense disposition melted.

"Come on, Sh-Shaun, let's get water." Beth stood and helped Shaun to his feet.

They walked through the brush toward the stream. When they were out of sight, I turned to Marcus. "Beth will never like you if you keep that up."

Marcus shrugged. "She's fun to bug."

I shook my head and laughed.

The worn, black leather cover was smooth as I brushed my fingertips over the delicate material. The sensation evoked the distant whisper of my childhood voice. *"Daddy! What do you write in here?"* *A small hand with bright coloured fingernails rested on a book—my hand.* I let the image in my head unfold and tell its story.

My feet dangled from the office chair, legs too short to touch the floor. Daddy stepped further into the room, lifted me up and sat me on his lap. He picked up the journal from his desk and thumbed through the entries. The ink filled pages fluttered my hair as they flipped by. "I write a little of everything, Av." He pulled open the desk drawer and placed the journal inside.

"Like what?" The secrets his journal held captured my imagination.

"Well…" Daddy closed the drawer and locked it with a small key he took from his pocket. "I write about my day, my thoughts, my feelings, that sort of stuff."

I stuck a piece of my hair in my mouth as I contemplated what Daddy said. "Do you write about Mommy?"

He shifted me over to his other leg. "Yes."

"And me, and Beth, and Caleb?"

"Yes." Daddy chuckled.

"Good or bad?"

Daddy tipped me back, and I giggled. "Only the good stuff." He winked.

"Daddy? Could I have a book like that?" My small finger pointed to the locked drawer.

Daddy stood me on the floor. He leaned over and pulled open an unlocked drawer. "It's all yours," he said, handing me a black journal. White butterflies decorated the glossy cover.

My finger traced over the design. "For me?"

Daddy nodded. "For you."

"Thank you, daddy!" I stood on tiptoe, kissed his cheek then skipped out of his office.

The black covered book sitting on my lap was plain with no fancy design other than a natural grain pattern. It was a large journal. Jasper's neat handwriting saturated the pages with many short entries. The notes were blunt though sometimes I found it cryptic, like he feared an invasion of privacy. The writings spanned five years and almost filled the diary. After several hours, over four days, my brain had absorbed most.

I picked up the journal and stood it on its end, the edge darkened by dirt and age. Next to the spine and tucked between the pages was the faded black ribbon that marked where I'd last read. The marker's position was near the back, and I suspected to finish reading long before nightfall. A part of me dreaded reading what remained. Before I could begin the last entry came to mind.

Thursday, May 17, 2029
I was not allowed to see April and Beth this morning and may never again. I fear that the dose they received today will set them back, particularly Beth. And in time, even April will have slipped too far if I am never to care for them again.
I closed my eyes hoping to stop the memory, but it only made it clearer.
Outlook for the future has improved somewhat. Cecil visited me this evening and told me he has rethought his decision to remove me from their care. He believes that making them aware would be of more benefit to him though I am not sure how. I must get them out of here as soon as possible.

With a deep breath and a slow exhale my fingers opened the journal. I moved the ribbon, and my eyes fell on the date of the next entry, May 18. A giggle pulled my thoughts away before I could start. It was a welcome interruption, but it added to my procrastination. Quiet voices held my attention.

Beth sat with her nature book in her lap between Marcus and Shaun. She and Marcus were in deep discussion, but their words were not harsh. Shaun sat quietly, lost in his thoughts—if he had any. Oblivious to my gaze, I watched them for a while until the weight of the journal pulled my focus back toward its pages like a magnet.

I sat in the shade and read the final entries, resisting any urges exclaiming shock, surprise, anger, and even confusion.

Friday. May 18, 2029
I took a great risk this morning and gave neither girl any of the

hypno-drug, instead a placebo, for the camera's sake. Yesterday's full dose set them back, and I need them to be as lucid as possible. I managed a quick meeting with the Ls. We are ready for tonight. They gave me two necklaces, one I'd seen before on the night they'd returned to the compound, the other an identical match.

My mind absorbed every word as my skin prickled and goosebumps settled in for what seemed a permanent state. Once or twice my jaw fell open in disbelief, and I caught my lips uttering silent words. Mosquitoes fed on my arms and legs; so engrossed by the text my feeble swats did little to deter them. As I delved deeper the sounds of singing birds, buzzing insects, rustling leaves, and the low murmurings between Beth and Marcus faded as though I sat in a vacuum.

My attention solely focused on the writings.

Cecil. He was in the simulation room where I set the fire. Where I knew he would be. I locked the door as I left. I had never seen fear in his eyes before.

My hand flew to my mouth holding back the shock that quickened my heart and brought the sound of my breath to my ears. *Jasper thought Cecil had died in the fire!* The revelation spurred my fingers to flip the page.

The loops and strokes in his writing revealed emotion and anxiety. The nervous energy transferred into my bones; my hands trembled. Jasper's hurried scrawls no longer showed concern for spelling or grammar. My eyes narrowed as I worked to comprehend the sometimes confused and jumbled words, Jasper's illness evident in his writing.

Jul 1, 29
Only no date 'cause he said country bday. So tired. Sik. 6 weeks alive is record. Wish dead. No contact Ls. No help. Girls alive?

Last saw they said let go. But so fraid he catch them. Should have let go. Now we all die. Hope him too, somehow.

As the last accounts Jasper wrote buried themselves deep in my brain, unannounced tears leaked from my eyes. A rogue drop fell and landed after the final word as though to punctuate it.

Jasper had logged everything; his arrival; my family's arrival both voluntary and involuntary; meeting my parents; meeting me. He described the hours and days spent searching for an adequate vaccine against a virus nicknamed The Butterfly Flu. This virus morphed into a stronger version of itself whenever they got close. He journaled about his admiration for Cecil and later he wrote of his disdain. He'd known nothing in the beginning and by the end—he'd known too much. His words showed how he'd gone from loyal to disloyal, from ally to foe, from confidant to spy, from a guardian to an arsonist, from healthy to sick. I closed the journal and rubbed my hands over the black leather, the need to open it again no longer a concern. Every word etched into my memory forever.

Surroundings came into focus and sounds sharpened as though someone turned up the volume. A quick slap ended the life of a mosquito feeding on my arm. Red blood squished out onto my tanned skin. I flicked the tiny body away and scratched at the several welts that covered my body. Distant laughter floated to my ears and for the first time I saw that I was alone. I reached for my pack and placed the journal inside, burying it underneath the other contents. Standing, I stretched my arms over my head, audible snaps and pops rippled up my spine. The burden of having to read the journal lifted and my steps lightened as I walked toward the lake. I had information to share. The corners of my mouth tugged into a melancholic smile as I thought of the final entries.

The flat rock disappeared under the cool water. Beth and Marcus waded in the shallows with Shaun, thigh deep. Their voices echoed off the surrounding cliffs in the late afternoon sun.

"Who wants to listen to a story?" I called.

21

THE TRUTH IN THE STARS

THE MOONLESS NIGHT GAVE WAY TO PLANETS AND DISTANT
stars scattered across the dark sky like dust on a black surface.
Tiny specs of light shimmered and dotted the Milky Way. The
vastness of the galaxy overhead overwhelmed me, and in that
moment, I knew my father saw the same speckled canvas. My
flesh prickled with the thought, and I filled my lungs with the
dewy night air. The hickory scent from the fire eased the lump
that formed in my throat. I closed my eyes and savoured the
fading smell.

Like the millions of stars that bewildered eyes and mind
with their sheer distance, millions of crickets did the same to
my ears. Their chirps became one long and unending hum.
The din rattled my eardrums, and for a moment I wondered if
the sound was really from the insects or a sudden and random
case of tinnitus. I squirmed as every minor bump and nodule of
the ground underneath pressed into me like a hundred marbles.
My eyelids blinked open to the sparkling heavens. The texts in
the journal embossed the undersides, and I could not keep

them closed for any length of time before they haunted me. Sleep was unattainable.

A hard object dug into my hip as I rolled onto my side causing me to suck in a sharp breath and wince. I shifted and settled closer to the campfire. Orange embers glowed beneath the dying flames; the heat unnoticeable in the still air. Tendrils of smoke tickled my nose and reminded me of barbecues and bonfires from long ago. I focused beyond the remains, looking past the lumps of sleeping bodies and into the dark. A wall of inky blackness surrounded us, unable to creep closer, held back by the remaining fiery glow. Fireflies blinked in the shadows, their tiny beacons the only offer of comfort in the dark. And if I weren't lying on my side, I would have believed I looked at the night sky.

My mind wandered as I stared at the flickering lights. Thoughts of earlier conversations rambled in my head, what I had said, wished I hadn't. I analyzed, argued, and finally accepted that no amount of ruminating would change things. I had divulged Jasper's journal in its entirety to Beth, Marcus, and Shaun, though I doubted Shaun understood. All throughout our fish dinner until well after dark, I retold the entries, the words I remembered verbatim, my audience rapt in every word. Beth was relieved to hear, though our parents worked for Cecil, they had been unaware of his devious plan, his manmade virus, and the warped idea to alter humanity.

I closed my eyes again; only to see Jasper's handwriting. Poor Jasper, Cecil duped him into believing he had nothing but good intentions, how awful it must have been when he discovered otherwise. Even worse to have had Cecil mistrust him and remove him from his work in the lab to become my nursemaid. At least he'd had our parents to confide in, that must have meant something.

And what about Marcus? I looked toward his sleeping figure. *What had it been like for him?* The future had looked bleak, Cecil's virus out of control. Then Marcus arrived, a survivor, literally knocking at the door. *Had it not been for Marcus, would they have discovered a vaccine?*

My eyes wandered over to Shaun's sleeping body, still in the same position he'd fallen asleep in hours earlier. Beth snorted, and I redirected my attention. She slept as sound as ever. *Did she even dream of the things I told her? Did they even haunt her?*

Beth's earlier question came to mind, her voice so clear inside my head that for a moment I wondered if it was real. Beth snorted again and confirmed that she slept. *So, where's mom and Dad now?* Beth's voice echoed in my head. The image of her face flashed in front of me. Her blue eyes turned amber by the orange glow of firelight.

Jasper's entry was as clear in my memory as though I held the journal in my hands and read his words. He wrote how we would leave the house when we could. When he knew no one had followed and the threat to our safety was minimal, then we would meet up with the Lindens in a nearby town. I stared back at the dying fire. A small flame ignited the tip of a stick I'd stuck in earlier. I pulled it free. The flame snuffed out and smoke curled from the glowing end. A thin wisp rose toward the starlit sky. "Are you still there?" A star twinkled as though answering my question. I gazed, unblinking, and for a moment became lost in the tiny points of twinkling lights.

And now? Beth whispered. Once again, the clarity of her voice inside my head made me look in her direction and make sure she still slept.

Now, we find that town. My answer resounded. Eyelids grew heavy and shut out the orange glow. The hard, lumpy ground softened underneath my weight as my mind shifted between consciousness and sleep. The piercing chirp from crickets faded as though someone turned down the volume. Whiffs of dirt and ash from the ground near my face replaced the aroma of hickory smoke. *Now we have a place to start,* my thoughts whispered before finally becoming silent.

22

WITH THESE HANDS

*T*HE WHITE DOOR SLID OPEN; AN ECHOED WHOOSH ENGULFED *the room. Disjointed memories interrupted quiet thoughts, and I squeezed my eyelids shut and shook my head. Reality and dreams blended, and I could not tell the difference between them anymore. I blamed the injections, and every day I slipped further away from reality and deeper into a perpetual dream*

Soft blankets wrapped around me, protecting like a cocoon. I snuggled into their comfort, and my body sunk into the mattress. My eyes fluttered open to the white room, and from the safety of my bed I gazed at the open door.

A figure stepped across the threshold. A baggy white suit covered the visitor from head to toe and hid the shape and form of the body it covered. I rose from my bed. My feet slapped on the tile as I crossed the room to the table by the entrance, every movement automated. What is happening? I sat down and waited for my guest to approach.

The door closed with another distinct airy sound. The chair across from me slid out from the table. Metal feet scratched across the floor; the high-pitched squeal caused my skin to tingle.

As the white blob took a seat, its suit made a quiet swooshing sound.

I drummed my fingers on the surface of the table and focused on my bare fingernails. My concentration shifted to the reverberating taps and reminded me of a galloping horse. Seconds later, my attention drifted again, and I stared at my nails. When did I last wear polish?

"April!" A woman's voice whispered from underneath a pale mask. Icy-blue eyes stared from behind large goggles with black frames.

The faint aroma of delicate rose petals evoked another rush of thoughts and memories. "Mom?" I blinked my tear laden eyes.

The visitor reached across the table and stilled my tapping fingers with blue rubber gloves. "Yes, Av, it's me."

"Mom, can we go home?" My voice shook.

"Not yet, honey, but soon." The skin creased at the corner of her eyes, and I pictured a smile behind the mask.

"Where's Dad?"

"With Caleb."

"Caleb's here?"

Mom nodded.

"And Beth?"

She nodded again.

The night I woke in the van to find both my sister and brother bound and sleeping came to mind. How long ago was that? I narrowed my gaze as the strange sensation we'd had this same conversation before flitted in my thoughts and then vanished.

"Is Dad coming next?" I glimpsed the camera; the red eye kept a close watch.

"He'll be here soon, after I leave." Mom squeezed my hands.

"What's happening?" A hot tear spilled and trailed down my cheek.

"Oh, honey, I'm so sorry." The goggles fogged at the edges; her chin quivered.

Again, a whoosh echoed in the room. *"I have to go."* Mom stood up and hugged me in the chair. *"I love you,"* she whispered.

My head bobbed, and she stepped over the threshold. The door slid shut. Fingers tapped on the table; the rhythmic drumming reminded me of rain pelting a metal roof like the one on the old camper. The soothing tempo lulled me into a relaxed state. Tension drifted away as a fog descended in my head.

Large, green rubber gloves stilled the tapping. Cloaked in white, the owner of the hands stared at me with unrecognizable eyes through black rimmed goggles. Thin lines stretched out from the corners. *"Hi, Av."* A voice escaped from under the mask.

The confusion lifted. *"Dad?"*

"Yes, honey."

"Dad, can we go home?" There was an ache in my throat, and I swallowed hard.

"Soon, Av, soon." He patted my stilled hands.

"Where's Mom?"

"Gone to see Beth." His voice cracked.

"Beth's here?" I asked a vaguely familiar question.

Dad patted my hand again. *"Yes,"* he whispered.

"And Caleb?"

Dad nodded.

The bed across the room caught my attention. Soft blankets and the supportive mattress made me want to crawl into its comfort and sleep. *"Is Mom visiting next?"*

Dad blinked; the corners of his lips turned down. *"Mom will visit again soon."* He squeezed my hand. *"Time for me to go now, honey."* He stood, and I followed. Strong arms wrapped around me and held me close. His white suit engulfed my body, *and I was sure that whoever watched on the other side of the camera thought I'd disappeared.*

Dad broke from our embrace. "I love you, Av." His voice softened. He kissed my forehead through his mask then rushed out the sliding door.

My slow and light steps carried me, and I could not sense the floor underneath my feet, as though I floated toward my inviting bed. A ripple of snaps and pops ran up my spine as I stretched my arms above my head. The faint aroma of roses tickled my nose. It must be the sheets, I thought as I climbed into my nest of blankets. Tired muscles relaxed, and the fog eased into place—erasing thoughts, dreams, and memories.

A solitary star shone bright and high in the purple-blue sky. Thin lines of light edged the tops of the trees as dawn crept in and changed night into day. Warm, damp air fell heavy on my face. It was the start of another humid morning.

"Okay, I have questions." Beth's voice drifted from across the fire pit.

I rolled over onto my side and propped my head in my hand. My right hip ached as it pressed against the solid ground. For a moment it reminded me of the hard wood floor of the attic room, and I sat up to erase the memory. The quick movement fanned the air over the burned remains. A whiff of smoke and ash stung my nose, and I recalled C.E.C.I.L. and its fire damaged rooms.

"About what?" A huge yawn stretched my mouth wide open, the taste of last night's dinner still on my tongue.

Beth scratched a bug bitten ankle. "Did they really visit us?"

Visions of my dream played in my head. "Yes, I remember it, though it's a little fuzzy."

"Do you think they're s-still there?"

I shrugged. "Who knows, but we're leaving this camp today. We've been here long enough."

"Jasper only wrote a nearby town. Th-there was no name, no direction. How can we ever find it? Which way do we go?"

Beth was right. Jasper never mentioned the name of the town or directions to it, only that it wasn't too far from the compound. "If we get back to the road, we can follow it out, and we start with the first place we come to."

Marcus stirred. He sat up and stretched muscular arms toward the sky and yawned. He smacked his lips and rubbed the sleep from his eyes. "What's goin' on?"

"April wants to leave," Beth said as she drew her knees up to her chest and hugged them.

Marcus nodded. "Good idea. Shouldn't stay here any longer. These trails go forever, they gotta lead somewhere."

"No, we're following the road," I said.

Marcus' eyes widened. "Seriously? He's still out there, you know."

"We've been sitting here for four days, and we're not that far from the road. If he wanted us, he'd have found us by now." I tilted my head back to a much lighter sky. The solitary star was no longer visible. My arms prickled, and I looked behind me, narrowing my gaze as I surveyed the dense bush. The forest lived. Birds chirped and sang, small animals chattered. If anyone desired, they could sneak up on us with no problem. Paranoia made my body tremble. *Will this feeling ever go away?*

Shaun uncurled and sat up, his eyes always vacant.

"That's a bad idea." Marcus rose, walked over to Shaun and hauled him to his feet.

"Who said you had to come?" I twisted my hair into a bun and poked a stick through the gathered locks, securing it in place. The back of my neck cooled in the warm air.

"Well you should take another day. Think about it." Marcus headed for the bush and disappeared with Shaun by his side.

My jaw tightened, fists clenched. "Enough time has been wasted already. Beth and I are leaving after breakfast," I yelled at the trees.

"Now wait!"

I glared at Beth.

"Maybe we need to th-think about it."

"What the hell!" I yelled again, not caring about the volume.

Unfazed by my outburst, Beth continued. "If he's s-searching for us, the road is not s-safe."

"He's not looking for us! We've been here for four days." A heat rose from my neck and set my cheeks on fire. *Why didn't they understand?* My eyes burned, and my throat ached as frustration mounted.

"But we can't be sure." Beth shook her head. "I want to find Mom and Dad, too. We have to be sure. And what about Caleb?"

I unfolded my legs and stretched them in front of me. My bare toes touched the rocks that surrounded our campfire. Heat from the night's fire radiated from the stones and despite the humid air, the warmth soothed. My eyes drifted from my feet to my injured knee. The scrape from days ago was almost healed. Bathing had softened most of the scabs and washed them away leaving behind pink, new skin. Only one scab remained. I wanted to pick it but resisted as it covered a much deeper wound and would bleed. My attention reverted once again to the forest, and I waved around my hands. "Where?" I said. "Where do we even search for Caleb? He could be anywhere. He could be with Mom and Dad. He could be dead." The last thought reduced my voice to a whisper as doubt replaced hope.

"Are you giving up?" Beth raised her eyebrows. Mom's face flashed in front of me.

"No, but we have to let them know we're alive. We have to find them before they stop looking." The words caused my heart to skip. *Maybe they had given up and left.*

"Mom would never give up. Not until sh-she knew for sure." Beth spoke what I thought.

Rough calluses covered my palms. Blue veins weaved an intricate pattern underneath the skin. They were hands that belonged to someone much older. They were hands that had pulled floorboards loose to escape confinement, hands that had gathered wood and built campfires; that had dug in the dirt, picked berries, and gutted fish. They were the hands of someone who wouldn't hesitate to protect their owner or anyone else. I flexed and extended my fingers, bones and tendons moved beneath my flesh. The old nail file, used for its true purpose, had filed each fingernail even with the tips.

"We have to follow the road," I said with a steady and calmer tone, and my hands dropped to my lap. Goosebumps erupted on my arms as I studied our surroundings. *Where are Marcus and Shaun?*

"It's not s-safe!" Beth kept up with her side of the argument.

"She's right. It's not."

The unfamiliar voice drove me into action. I grabbed for my pack and dug into the open front compartment. The heavy pocketknife tumbled into my palm as though my hand were magnetic. In one swift motion the blade opened, and I jumped to my feet. Practicing and planning for such an event made my efforts quick and smooth. The weight of the knife in my grip comforted as I turned to face the stranger that had entered our camp. I glanced at my white knuckles as fingers clutched their weapon. They are the hands of someone prepared to fight.

23

SUBLIMINAL MESSAGE

It was hard to tell if our visitor's shirt was grey or light blue under the dirt. The cut-offs she wore appeared to match though they too were filthy. The tattered edges of a sleeveless top exposed slender arms. And the torn and frayed hem of each pant-leg sat mid-thigh. Long, scraped and bug bitten legs ended in a pair of well-worn, black shoes.

My eyes travelled over her flattened chest and landed back on her dirt smudged cheeks. The odd, stringy lock of brown hair touched the top of her shoulders, but most was shorter than chin-length.

"What do you want?" I called to the stranger standing at the edge of the forest. Sweat trickled from my temples despite my hair being swept off my neck, and my heart thrummed. The knife grew heavy, and my fingers ached. I adjusted my grip. *Where is Marcus?* My inner voice questioned for the second time.

The uninvited guest took a step forward. The pearl handle pressed deeper into my palm as my fingers reclaimed their hold and knuckles turned white. "No closer," I warned with as much confidence as I could fake.

Her eyes darted between the knife and my gaze; empty hands rose in the air. "He's still out there, still looking. You should listen to her." A dirty finger extended and pointed to Beth standing beside me.

"Where is he? Have you seen him?" I stared beyond the strange girl and into the trees behind her.

She shrugged, brought a hand to her mouth and chewed on her thumbnail, spitting the piece she'd bitten off onto the ground. "Are you from there?" she said.

"Yes. You?" I loosened my grip on the knife.

She laughed and plucked at the dirty shirt. "Looks like you're outta uniform. Where d'you get that?"

My hand tugged at my blue tee and smoothed over the grey cut-off sweats. "Found them back there." I thrust my thumb over my shoulder though I had no idea where the house was in relation to our current location.

"Yeah, found mine too, the dress wasn't cutting it out here. Pulled this off some dead kid." She smirked.

I envisioned Caleb's portrait. "What did he look like?" Though my voice sounded calm, I held my breath as I waited for her answer.

"That's kinda morbid."

I shrugged with indifference but under the facade anxiety mounted. "No more morbid than you stripping a dead kid."

"Touché." She cocked her head; narrow eyebrows rose. "Didn't care to take that good a peek, but I remember brown hair."

My stomach sank as doubt ate away more of my hope.

"What's your name?" Beth said. Arms folded, she glared at our visitor with piercing, cut-through-glass eyes.

"Caia. Yours?"

"Beth, April." My sister pointed.

I gaped at her, surprised she'd given that information considering she hadn't wanted me to tell Marcus the same.

"What? She's not going to call me 'hey you'" She said, her voice sounding somewhat annoyed.

"Just the two of you?" Caia jutted her chin toward us.

"What happened to your hair?" I said, avoiding her question. With Marcus and Shaun missing I didn't want to divulge too much. Like my initial feelings about Marcus, I couldn't be sure she wasn't working with the man looking for us.

Caia tugged on one of the longer, dark locks that brushed her bare, left shoulder. "Cut it," she said without emotion.

"With what... a rock?" Beth used the same snarky tone she had with Marcus. True to her pre-C.E.C.I.L. self she took her time warming up to strangers especially ones she hadn't engaged first. She was just now speaking with more civility to Marcus.

I turned and looked toward the bush. Marcus and Shaun's disappearance worried me.

"What's over there?" Caia said, taking several steps closer in our direction, near enough to see the colour of her eyes. Green, but not bright, as though a smoky haze clouded over them, like looking at green trees through a fog.

Caia forced a smile, showing off the gap between her front teeth, the space the same thickness as Jasper's I.D. card. She held up her hands and sat on the ground.

Beth and I shared glances then I focused my attention back on Caia. Her arms and legs were thin, but she didn't look as though she starved. She'd chewed her fingernails past the tips of her fingers and one or two of them stained with dried blood.

I sighed and sat across from Caia. Beth remained on her

feet with her arms folded. Her foot tapped beside me, and I reached out and stilled it with my hand. "Sit down, Beth."

Beth grunted, swore under her breath, and joined me.

"So, you have seen him?" The knife rested on my thigh. Heat from the handle, made warm by my hand, penetrated my sweatpants.

Caia nodded. "Two days ago."

"Were you on th-the road?" Beth said.

Caia shook her head. "Never go there. No. In the woods; well I was hiding in the trees, he was on the trails."

"Where?" My head swiveled, eyes narrowed as I scanned the bush surrounding us.

"Don't worry, not around here. Anyway, he went one way, I headed the other."

"If he's on a trail..." the earlier argument and my insistence came to mind, "we can follow the road out of here before he comes back."

"No!" Caia and Beth said in unison.

The agreement made me regard them with utter disbelief. "What is wrong with you?" I said to Beth. "Don't you want out of here?"

Neither one answered. Beth kept her focus on the ground, fingers played with the dirt. Caia picked at her elbow.

After several seconds of silence, Caia spoke. "We can't leave the trail." She licked her thumb and washed away the blood oozing out from under a disturbed scab.

"Always stay on the trail," Beth recited in monotone.

A sign with a red number, counting laps, flashed in front of my eyes. I closed them and willed for a lucid vision of the forest room. The image played like a movie on a screen. Birds chirped and insects buzzed as my feet carried me along the path past plastic trees and imitation shrubs and flowers. In my mind, I relived the moment. Mixed among animal conversations there was something else, some other noise apart from the hush of wind. I concentrated on the memory, blocking out my surroundings. Hidden within the calls of nature a voice whispered. The message was straightforward, concise, and subliminal. "Always stay on the trail," it said. "Never leave the trail."

The sudden snapping of branches pulled me from the recollection, and I spun to see Marcus. He leaned forward and rested his hands on his knees, shoulders heaved as he gasped.

"What's going on? Where's Shaun?" Beth jumped to her feet.

Unable to speak, Marcus jutted his thumb over his shoulder. I cast my gaze in the direction and held my breath, waiting for Shaun to emerge.

"What happened?" Beth hurried to Marcus' side. Caia and I followed.

Marcus straightened, a bead of sweat rolled down the bridge of his nose. He wiped it away with a dirt covered hand and left behind a smudge. His eyes widened as his gaze swept over us, hesitated on Caia, and returned to my face.

"Shaun's hiding. He's back there. We have to find him before he does." Marcus took a deep breath and exhaled.

"Who?" I said, but my question was redundant.

"Him!"

"Truck Man?" Caia said to Marcus.

A loud bang echoed through the forest, and a flock of birds took to the sky, scared up from the noise.

"What was that? Beth's face paled.

"That old truck backfiring, heard it before," Caia answered.

"We better get Shaun," Marcus said.

"Unless he already has." Caia stared into the woods where Marcus had emerged.

Without further hesitation, we headed into the trees.

24

HATCHING A PLAN

BRANCHES SNAPPED UNDER RACING FEET, EACH CRACK sounded as loud to my ears as the truck's backfire. Sweat ran down the hollow of my lower back, dampening the waistband of my cut-offs. I tripped over a root and grabbed a nearby tree to keep me upright. The rough bark scraped across my palm.

Marcus held up his hand, and we came to a halt. "Over there, in that outcrop of rocks," he whispered as he pointed through the trees. A huge rock formation rose from the ground. Large cracks, overhangs, and small caves made it the perfect hiding spot.

"Why is Shaun there?" I said, brushing a lock of damp hair from my eyes.

"I saw Truck Man lurking around and wanted to get back to camp to warn you. Shaun would only hold me up; it was safer to hide him."

"Did he see you?"

"Nah, he walked off in the opposite direction, like something caught his attention. He seemed in a hurry."

My eyes narrowed. "Caia, I thought you said he was nowhere near here."

She shrugged. "Guess I was wrong."

"Let's get him." Beth took a step forward.

Marcus reached out and grabbed her arm. "Wait!"

Beth tried to shake off his grip. "Let go!" She hissed through clenched teeth.

"Look!" He said in a loud whisper and pointed over her shoulder.

A large figure moved through the woods. We ducked and crouched low behind a fallen tree, Marcus and I in the middle with Beth to my right and Caia on the other side of Marcus.

My pulse hammered. "Is that him?"

Marcus nodded. "Ya, but I was sure he left."

From our concealed vantage point we watched him tromp between the trees and push low hanging branches out of the way. The thick vegetation and distance made it difficult to get a good view of his face, but I could see he wore dark clothing. I held my breath and hoped Shaun knew enough to keep quiet. Truck Man, or as I now referred to him, at least to myself, The Collector, approached the large rocks. The new designation I chose stemmed from what he did or tried to do according to Marcus' earlier account, his attempt to capture them, us, for whatever purpose.

The Collector stopped with his back toward us.

"Keep quiet, Shaun." Marcus whispered my thoughts.

"Will he?" I voiced my worry.

"He has to." Beth murmured.

I leaned closer to the tree. A piece of bark tore away from under my hand, and I slipped forward. My hand then knocked a small dead branch poking out from the trunk, and it broke off with a snap.

The Collector turned.

We ducked lower and waited several minutes. Sweat rolled down my neck. The sharp bite of a mosquito made me flinch as more of the annoying insects whined around my ears.

I grabbed Marcus' arm, his muscles flexed beneath my hand. "What are you doing?" I whispered as he was about to peek over the dead tree.

"Checking to see if he's still there. We can't stay here forever, I'm being eaten alive," He whispered back.

"And if he sees you?"

"Better me than you. We've already met before." Marcus peered over the tree.

"What's happening?" Beth said.

"Look for yourself." Marcus replied.

The three of us joined Marcus and peeked over the log.

My eyes scanned the trees. "Where is he?"

Marcus shrugged.

Caia pointed. "There!"

The Collector had moved further away from the rocks and emerged from behind a small cluster of trees. He stopped and headed back again toward the outcropping.

"What's he doing?" Caia said.

We watched for a few more seconds as he ambled, stopped, and bent forward. He stayed in that position for a moment and then continued on his way again.

"Maye he's looking for something," Marcus answered Caia.

"What?" I said.

Marcus shook his head. "No idea."

The Collector neared the rocks again. I held my breath. His pace quickened, and branches snapped in the distance. He stopped and bent down for the second time, and when he straightened, he walked away.

There was an audible collective sigh as we sat on the fallen tree and waited.

"Let's go!" Beth spoke after several seconds had passed.

I placed my hand on her thigh. "Just wait another minute."

"No." She stood.

We walked in single file, lifting our feet over roots and pushing back branches until we reached Shaun's hiding place. The smell of sweat and dirt lingered in the warm air and attracted more mosquitoes.

"Where is he?" Beth said, slapping at an insect feeding on her arm.

"Behind this." Marcus grabbed hold of a moss-covered tree trunk that leaned against a large boulder. Caia side-stepped around us and moved to the front by Marcus. Their eyes locked for a second and had I not been watching it would have gone unnoticed.

Together, Beth and I picked up the other end of the fallen tree. My fingers sunk into the damp moss and disrupted a small beetle. The iridescent bug skittled over the back of my hand, hairy feet tickled as it ran. On Marcus' cue we lifted. The relative lightweight of the limb surprised me. Pieces of rotted wood and the corpse of a chipmunk fell from the bottom as we carried it away.

"Ah, gross!" I blurted.

Caia turned her head and spotted the reason for my disgust. "Just a dead chipmunk."

"I know that, I just didn't expect to see it."

"Well you should. There's lots'a dead stuff out here, you can't be squeamish."

The dead birds, the tuft of fur clinging to a small shrub, and the remains of some animal's body buried under a clump of leaves came to mind.

Beth pulled a twig from her hair. "Ha, trust me. April is not s-squeamish."

Cecil, Jasper, the burned bodies, I had seen plenty of death.

"Yeah, of course," Caia said in an amenable tone, but her raised eyebrow suggested otherwise.

"Come on, Shaun." Marcus crouched beside a wide crevice exposed by the removal of the tree and held out his hand. After several seconds of coaxing, Shaun's fingers reached out, and he emerged from his hiding spot.

"Shaun!" Beth moved to his side, stepping in front of Caia to help him from the small cave.

Caia held up her hands and backed away.

"Let's get our stuff and go," Marcus said as he walked by me with Shaun and Beth close in step.

"To where?" I said as Caia and I stepped in after the others.

"The trails." Marcus' voice drifted behind him.

"We have to stick to the trails," Caia affirmed.

"Agreed, I th-think it's best," Beth said.

"Stop!"

In an instant everyone stopped. All but Shaun focused their gaze on me. "He is out here, right now. Don't you think we'd be better off on the road?" I knew what their brainwashed-answer to the question would be, but I had to ask. As for understanding why the subliminal message at C.E.C.I.L. hadn't worked on me that was something I couldn't answer.

"No." Their voices came in unison, an automatic response with little emotion. They turned back, and we continued in haste to our things.

Before emerging from the trees, we observed our camp, making sure it remained the way we had left it. Satisfied that nothing appeared disturbed, we stepped into the clearing.

"It's good to see you, Caia," Marcus said, picking up the rocks from around our fire pit.

"You know each other," I said out loud, confirming what I'd suspected.

Beth gaped. "Do you?" she said.

"She was in my group before." Marcus lifted another rock and added it to the two he cradled in his arms. His biceps flexed under the load.

"We got separated," Caia finished.

"Have you been alone all this time? What have you been doing?"

Marcus' question softened the tough-girl act and Caia nodded; her eyes brimmed with tears. Marcus smiled, leaned forward, and kissed her tenderly on the cheek. For a split second I wished it was my cheek he'd kissed. I pushed the thought away, now was not the time.

She wiped her eyes and shrugged "Just wandering. Hiding. Looking for the others. For you. What about you? Where have you been?"

"Same. Sticking to the trails and trying to keep Shaun safe. Ran into Beth and April a few days ago." Marcus took a deep breath. "Anyway, we better get outta here, clean up this camp. We should throw all these campfire rocks in the water. Make it look like no one's been here."

Caia picked up the remaining stones, and they headed toward the lake. I watched them leave, an unexplainable heaviness in my stomach.

"We're going to get water." Beth held an empty bottle in each hand. Shaun stood beside her with the canteen we'd found at the house slung over his shoulder.

"Be careful," I called out as they made their way to the stream.

Birds sang peaceful songs; no squawks or squeals of alarm came from them or any other small creatures that roamed the woods. My ears tuned in to my surroundings as I rolled my bedroll, strapped it to my pack, and did the same with Beth's. While we had no choice but to leave, I wasn't looking forward to wandering. The few days spent resting and rebuilding strength had been nice.

The route that had led us to the camp was barely visible. Not far beyond was the road. I was certain it lead back to whatever civilization existed, back to our parents, back to home. But they outnumbered me. The others had no intention of following me, not even my sister. Although the person they feared on the road 'Truck Man' was now roaming the forest, their drive to stay on the trails was strong. I couldn't leave Beth. Somehow I had to persuade them the road was a better choice. Somehow I had to deprogram them. And while we hiked on what I guessed were many paths that looped and intersected there was the potential for a positive outcome—the chance of finding Caleb. Like hanging from a cliff with one finger a small part of me clung to the hope that he lived and roamed the trail system. It was all I had, and I held on despite the odds and the bigger part of me that believed he was dead.

I picked up charred logs from the campfire and carried them into the woods where I scattered them among the forest shrubbery. The knife jostled in my pocket. With everything that had happened since Caia's arrival, I had forgotten I'd placed it there. A sapling became the object of my attention, and I flipped open the saw blade. Twigs and leaves shook as the teeth gnawed through the thin covering. I pressed with one hand above the cut, splintering the green wood. *Sorry tree*, I thought as I bent back the thumb-diameter trunk and pulled. Strips of bark pealed as the last bit that held it together tore away.

The sapling swept the remaining traces of our existence in the clearing—nature's broom. With each sweep my thoughts returned to the road and my problem. But as a solution formed, the sound of quiet laughter and murmuring distracted me, and

Marcus piggy-backed Caia into the camp. Water droplets in their hair caught the afternoon sun and glinted. Marcus set her on her feet; his hand disappeared behind her. Caia squealed and swatted it aside.

"Hey!" Caia flashed her gap-toothed grin.

"Should have swam with your clothes on, it would have done them good." I looked away and continued sweeping, unexpected jealous tears burned my eyes. An awkward silence settled over us, and my attention tuned into the swooshing of branches and leaves on the ground.

"Where's..." Marcus started when the whisper of a familiar tune drifted out from the forest and interrupted.

Beth strode into camp with Shaun behind her. Full water bottles sloshed in her hands with her strides as she hummed, and Caia joined in. It surprised me for a moment she would know the tune, but then again, she had been at the compound, and it had been Cecil's song. I glanced at Shaun and wondered if the tune played inside his head. Their hums turned into words as Beth and Caia sang 'Come to Me, My Children'. I had thought Beth's voice pleasant, but Caia's was so much more. For a moment, she transformed the melody I hated into a beautiful ballad, and I enjoyed the harmony.

The weight of the knife against my thigh brought me back again and reminded me of the crazy idea forming in my head. An idea that meant crossing the line. *But sometimes that's what it takes to survive.* My hand reached into the soft, grey pocket and wrapped around the pearl handle. *The Collector needs to find us.* I gripped the pocketknife tighter. *And when he is no longer a problem, maybe then I can lead everyone out to the road.*

25

HIDDEN TALENT

Marcus took the lead with Beth's pack slung over his shoulders. Caia walked alongside; their hands brushed against each other's. Marcus tilted his head and whispered something to Caia, and she tossed her head back and giggled.

The display of affection between them annoyed me. "Beth!" My sister and Shaun were a few steps behind, and I waited for them to catch up.

"What?" Beth touched Shaun's arm, and he stopped.

"Why don't you two walk ahead?" I shifted the backpack.

Beth narrowed her gaze. "Why?"

Marcus and Caia halted further along the trail but were still within listening distance. He reached out and plucked a chunk of long hair that had pasted to her cheek, tucking the strand behind her ear. "Just do it, okay." I gave no explanation.

Beth sighed and grabbed Shaun's hand. "Come on, Shaun."

"Thanks!"

Beth lifted a hand above her head and waved in response.

The four of them walked away as my feet stuck to the ground and held me in place. I looked over my shoulder. The trail disappeared into the trees. Somewhere beyond those woods was the way home. The pull of the road and my wish to get help spun me around, and I stepped forward.

What happened to bringing him to us? "That will never work; it was a stupid idea." I murmured to myself then hooked my thumbs under the pack's straps and adjusted the belt once again. *We need help and heading out on my own is the only way to get it.* I pulled my shoulders back and raised my chin in stubborn determination, I moved ahead; my mind focused on the situation and not on leaving Beth.

"Are you coming?" Marcus called out, and I stopped. *Run,* my head yelled. *Stay,* my heart argued. The battle lasted mere seconds. *Get rid of The Collector first and then get help.* The rejected plan niggled at the back of my mind. Sighing, I lumbered toward my companions. The call of the road diminished to a whisper. I rejoined my group, and we continued hiking.

The black clouds that blew in on humid air made the edge of dusk darker. Thunder rumbled in the distance, the faint scent of sulphur bothered my nose as lightening flashed and introduced the coming storm. The heavy atmosphere promised rain but the only moisture on my skin was my sweat as beads trickled down my back and between my breasts. My t-shirt clung.

The small campfire, lit with one of a few remaining matches, illuminated the looming dark and waited to cook whatever Marcus and Caia hunted. I peeled the blue tee from my hot flesh and flapped the hem, sending puffs of warm air across my belly. The fanning of the shirt caused sweet smoke to curl and rise upward to meet with the gloomy sky.

Beth's whispered words drew my attention. Shaun's head

rested on her shoulder as she read from the nature book. Shaun stared, and I wondered if he understood what she said as she pointed to the pictures and flipped the pages with one hand. The other twisted a lock of hair around her index finger.

Laughter interrupted my thoughts, and my jaw tightened. In the same instant, I scolded myself. I tugged at my damp top and forced a smile.

"Dinner!" Caia announced and set down several frogs' legs on a rock by the fire. The sight made me wrinkle my nose.

"Here." Marcus ran the knife over the leg of his cut-offs and wiped it clean; the blade glinted in the firelight as he folded it back inside the handle. "Used it to clean up a little too. That beard was driving me nuts." He ran a hand over his face. The longer hairs trimmed closer and, in some places, shaved down to the skin and replaced with specs of dried blood. The closer shave made him even more attractive.

I held out my hand, and he returned my knife. Scenes from the day we found it flashed in my head.

I took the box and turned it in my hands. I looked over toward the cabinet and the rough carvings inside.

"It's his, isn't it?" she said, pointing to the ID on the box and the one scratched inside the large wardrobe.

I nodded.

I placed the box down on the floor in front of me, and we stared at it. Finally, Bethany reached over and pulled off the lid.

My focus returned to the present for a moment. The width of the pocketknife was not much larger than my thumb, its length stretched from the heel of my palm to the tip of my middle finger. And then the memory forced me back to relive the moment.

Bethany reached inside and pulled out a small, brown teddy bear. I gasped, not expecting the stuffed toy.

"Oh, he's cute!" Bethany gave the little bear a cuddle, before

laying it down beside her. Her hand dipped into the box again and pulled out a heavy metal object. "W-what about this?" she smiled as she held it out to me.

I took the object and turned it over. My head swivelled back in the direction of the cabinet. "This is what he used, I'm sure of it."

I remembered inspecting the pocketknife, pulling out its implements and snapping them back.

A smile crept across my face as my hands pushed the pieces back into place. "Now this is something we can use." I placed the pearl-handled, pocketknife inside my remaining dress pocket.

Finding that knife had been a miracle, and it helped in our escape. Finding out Caleb had used it to carve his ID into the cabinet, and then escaped weeks before we arrived at the house, had given us hope. My focus returned to the knife in my palm, confident that the memories had exhausted themselves for now.

Two small rusty screws on either end secured the pearl handle in place. A hairline crack ran through the centre between the fasteners. Apart from the fracture and rust, it looked like it had the day my father had shown it to me. The relic belonged to my grandfather, and how Caleb had ended up with it was a mystery, but I was glad he had. I closed my fingers around the warm and weighty object.

"Are you cooking that, or should I?" Caia said to Marcus. She tugged on one of the remaining long chunks of her hair.

"No, I got it." Marcus sat on the ground and picked up the stick he'd sharpened earlier and threaded the skinned and cleaned legs.

"How about some help?" I held up the pocketknife and jutted my chin at the chunk of hair Caia weaved between her fingers.

She shook her head. "That knife blade is not coming near my neck."

With some effort, I released the small scissors from one end. I raised my eyebrows and squeezed the rusted blades together. The old tool emitted a faint squeak of complaint. "What about tiny scissors?" It was the first real opportunity to check her hairline since she'd arrived.

"Fine, I guess, but careful, I don't need a case of tetanus from those rusty things," she said and sat beside Marcus.

The tired blades took work to use, but they were sharp enough to trim her hair. I started at the front and worked around to the back, lopping off the long, awkward tendrils. A knotted piece hung from her nape, and I swept it up as Caia bent her head forward and snipped it. The small, black butterfly emerged as the pieces fell away.

"Look, she has one, too," I said to Marcus, laying a finger against her hot, damp skin.

"One what?" Caia pushed away my hand and probed the back of her neck with her nail-chewed fingers.

"A tattoo." Marcus rested the roasting stick against a rock. The meat sizzled over the low burning flames. Large fingers pushed Caia's out of the way and Marcus swept the fine hairs from her hairline to show the mark. "Yup, it's the same."

"Would one of you tell me what the fuck you're looking at?" Caia shoved Marcus' hand from her neck and covered the tattoo with hers.

Beth had pulled her gaze from her book at Caia's swearing. She narrowed her eyes.

"Same as us," I said to my sister.

Beth nodded and went back to reading to Shaun; his head still rested on her shoulder.

"There's a tattoo," I said, seating myself by Caia and

169

sweeping up the strands of hair that had loosened from my twist. "Like this."

Caia's warm fingers probed my hairline, goosebumps rose on my arms.

"Why?" she said.

Brown, damp locks fell on the tops of my shoulders as I pulled the stick free from my hair. I gathered them again and twisted them into a new bun, securing it once again with the stick. I shrugged. "You're special."

"Shit, I know that." Caia smiled.

My eyes widened. "What can you do?" I said.

Caia scrunched her face. "Do?"

"What's your talent or gift?" Marcus joined in as he turned the skewer with the frogs' legs. Steam rose from the cooking meat.

A sudden clap of thunder made me jump as the storm drew closer.

Caia turned away from me and rested her hand on Marcus' arm. "I think you know what that is," she said in a manner that told me more than I wanted to know.

Marcus flashed his white teeth in a wide grin. The orange glow of flames reflected from his eyes. "Besides that." His tone mimicked Caia's.

I gave an indistinguishable shake of my head, and muttered a word of disdain under my breath.

"What April means is can you do anything, you know, weird, special... different."

"Not weird," I corrected, "exceptional." I squeezed the folded knife still in my hand and placed it in my pocket, reminding myself to put it away later.

Lightening flashed. Caia's back straightened, my eyes narrowed as they took in her stiff body language.

"What can *you* do?" She emphasized as she turned to look at me.

I shrugged. The gift I had was not remarkable, at least not to me. Other people could do what I did. "I remember things."

"And..."

"That's it."

"What's so special about that? I remember things, too," Caia said.

"It's not a big deal," I said, voicing my thoughts.

"Sure it is." Beth pulled her face from her book long enough to interject. "Sh-she doesn't just remember some things. She remembers everything... or did. What did you s-say it was called?"

"Hyperthymesia." I'd remembered the name for my gift days earlier.

"Huh! Sounds like a disease, but I guess that's something. What about you?" Caia turned to Marcus.

He winked. "Nope, I'm not a part of the butterfly tattoo gang. The only thing I did was not get sick."

"Shaun?" Caia stared across the fire toward the young man who would not, could not, answer.

"He has a tattoo but..." my voice trailed.

"And you?" Caia addressed Beth.

Beth looked away from her book. "You first."

"I asked first," Caia countered.

"Show her," Marcus spoke to Beth.

I turned my attention on him. *What is he talking about?* "Beth?" I looked at my sister.

"Urgh!" She grunted in frustration. "Fine!" She lifted Shaun's head from her shoulder and rose to her feet. With her book in her hands she sat beside me and folded her legs.

Beth rested the open book in her lap and sat back with her hands behind her for support. She fixed her gaze on her field guide. Thunder rolled, and I slapped at a mosquito gnawing on my thigh. A few seconds passed, and then in slow motion, one by one, the pages flipped in one direction and then the other.

"That!" She smiled at me.

"How the hell–" Caia stared at Beth.

"There's a storm coming, it was just wind." No air moved, but I had to be sure Beth caused the pages to turn. The rattling picture frames on Cecil's apartment walls and the chair leg sprang to mind. *Had Beth been behind those too?*

"It wasn't the *wind*." She said in a calm voice.

I shrugged. "Convince me." *I want that one, Daddy.* The whisper of the past echoed in my head as I watched a younger Beth point to a telekinetic toy on the computer screen in front of her. The new memory formed in my head.

"Fine!" Beth stood and dropped her book in my lap then stared at the glowing fire. After several seconds the flames jumped higher as if she'd fanned them.

Caia yelped and scooted over.

"Watch it, Beth!" Marcus pushed himself back and pulled the cooking meat from the fire. "I'm trying not to burn these."

"Wind, again!" My intent was to frustrate her; I had an inexplicable feeling that would help.

"AARGH!" Beth yelled. A stick lifted from a pile of wood and dropped into the fire. "There, happy now!" She folded her arms, a smug smile on her face.

"Holly, Shit!" Caia said.

"Impressed," I said, and held out her book, "but not happy."

Beth took the guide. "Why?"

"Because you showed him first." I pointed to Marcus.

Marcus put up his hands in defence. "Leave me out of this. I found out by accident, and it was just the book, no freakin' flames or sticks, which by the way, that was awesome."

Beth smiled at Marcus. "It's true," she said to me. "I was

practising by f-flipping the pages in my book. I told Marcus it was the wind, but he didn't believe me."

The black sky lit up as though fireworks had exploded overhead and with the brilliant light came the deafening boom of thunder.

"BETH!" A strange, frightened voice yelled. The four of us stared at each other wide eyed, trying to decipher who had spoken. Under the dark, electric, and angry clouds, we arrived at the same conclusion as gazes shifted from each other and landed on Shaun.

Shaun had drawn his bare legs to his chest and wrapped his arms around them. Lightening flashed again and lit up his face. In that second his eyes widened with a hint of awareness.

"Beth!" He called again.

The eye of the storm had arrived and like Frankenstein it brought Shaun to life.

26

RESURRECTION

WE TRUDGED IN THE EARLY MORNING LIGHT, HOT AND tired. Marcus and Caia out front as they knew the path well; having followed it before we'd met. Beth and Shaun trailed several strides behind while I plodded along at the end another several strides back. The night's storm had done little to ease the humidity, but it had prevented us from sleeping. The only positive effect from the heat was that after a short while, our rain soaked clothing had dried.

"Carcass coming up!" Caia called back and exaggerated a long stride as she stepped over the remains. "Just so no one gets surprised." She looked behind her, and I could just make out the amusement on her face even with the distance between us.

"Careful." Beth led Shaun around the obstacle.

Despite his panicked calls the evening before, he reverted to mutism; the blank stare returned to his eyes. Beth had spent the entire night with her arm draped over his shoulders, comforting him as the storm raged. I couldn't help but chuckle at the irony as I remembered the girl who had once cowered from storms herself. And I was proud. Beth hadn't needed me to count with her between the flashes and booms. Instead, it was her unwavering voice that counted for us as we waited out the sky's tantrum. The two couples had clung to each other while I sat alone.

Carrion beetles scuttled out from the squirrel remains as I reached the body and walked around it. If anything, it was the insects that devoured corpses I found more unsettling. I quickened my pace to catch up to the rest. "Caia, you said you've seen a lot of dead things."

"Yup." Caia kept walking ahead.

"Do you think it's the virus?" Marcus stopped and turned.

Beth and Shaun stopped when they reached Marcus and turned to face me as I approached.

I shrugged. "Maybe."

Caia walked back to Marcus. "What virus? You know you never explained how I got this tattoo." She rubbed a hand over the back of her neck.

Marcus sighed. "I remembered some more stuff after we separated. One of those things was how I came to C.E.C.I.L. and a virus.

I looked at Caia. "What do you remember?"

"Besides roaming these woods?" she said.

I nodded.

"Nothing. Stuff from when I was little. That's it. Are you going to explain this virus?"

"I'll tell her." Marcus took her hand, and they walked again. Beth and Shaun followed.

"Now?" Caia's voice floated back to my ears.

"Later," Marcus said.

I waited until they were out of my sight and turned, facing in the direction we'd just walked. The desire to flee plagued my every step, and I stared back down the trail.

"Are you coming?" Beth snuck up behind me and touched

my shoulder. Her words spun me around and spurred me to follow. Perhaps the subliminal message had worked on me; it didn't take much to make me change my mind.

The hike took us on winding trails, up and down hills, through fields and back into the forest. We met no one and any signs we found of others having been there before were small and old. We walked until our feet hurt, until we grew hungry, until we were tired, and then we rested.

For three days we did the same—walk, eat, rest and then walk some more. The forest walls trapped us, encircled us, and once again I felt as though the trees were like the bars of a prison cell. Its winding path, a long corridor within, although no one else seemed to notice but me. The others content to march along in futility as each day began and ended the same.

A strange feeling hung in the atmosphere and woke me before anyone else. Overnight, the heaviness of humidity had lifted and cooler, thinner air took its place, but there was something more than the change in weather that alerted me. I inhaled, enjoying the freshness as it sucked in through my nostrils. A gust of wind rattled the leaves and tickled my skin. I welcomed and revelled in the sensation, knowing soon the sun's heat would return.

The small cooking fire burned out hours earlier. I wiped a finger along the length of a charred log and transferred soot and ash to my skin. It would not be long before the heavy quiet disappeared as birds sang the sleeping world awake. My eyelids fell, and I bathed in the serenity, and for a moment it was as though time stopped.

A loud snap returned me to reality. Narrowed eyes

searched the darkened forest around the camp. Adrenaline-filled blood pulsed through my carotid. A deep inhale through my nose and exhale from my lips steadied the erratic beating. My hand instinctively went to my pocket. At the moment my fingers slipped into the soft fabric, my brain flashed to the image of the knife lying inside the front pouch of my pack.

The skin on my neck crawled, and my arms prickled. The intrusive camera with its watchful red eye invaded my thoughts. *Were we being watched?* My heart skipped at the thought.

"Marcus!" I whispered to the sleeping body on the other side of the burned-out fire. Another snap sounded closer. "Marcus!" I repeated louder than the last time. The slumbering form shifted and then settled.

My hand rubbed over the ground beside me and found a small, hard object. Without a second thought, I tossed the projectile at the sleeping figures and cringed at the dull thunk as the rock hit its mark.

"What the fuck!" Caia's sleepy voice cried out, and she sat up in a hurry. In the dim, pre-dawn light I could just make out her hand as it rubbed the top of her head.

"Sh!" I hushed, laying a finger over my lips. "Wake up, Marcus; I think we're being watched."

Caia's whispered words to her sleeping partner roused Marcus from his sleep. "Whatsamatter?" he said, his speech slurred.

"Someone's out there."

"Who?" His mouth uttered a more coherent sound.

"I don't know." My voice was above a whisper as his question ignited annoyance. "The Collector, maybe."

"Who?"

I sighed. "Truck Man."

Another loud snap and the three of us quieted, waited,

listened, but it was difficult to hear anything more than our collective breaths.

"Where's your knife?" Marcus whispered low.

"In my pack." I pointed in the direction where Shaun rested, his head on the backpack.

"Shit!" Marcus said.

The snapping of branches and rustling of leaves grew louder as someone or something approached. It crossed my mind it might not be human. *What if it's a bear or a wolf?* We'd been lucky so far. Our travels had only scared up small creatures like squirrels and chipmunks, though we'd seen the tracks and scat of other animals, we had not come across any.

I stood up and walked over toward Marcus and Caia who had also risen.

Beth rolled over and sat upright, rubbing at her eyes. She yawned and stretched her arms over her head. "What's going on?" She spoke in a rough morning voice. A moment after asking she jumped to her feet as she heard the commotion.

Seconds passed and a dark shadow emerged from the bush. The obscure figure moved closer toward us in the faint light. Marcus picked up a cooking stick, sharpened to a point, and held it in front of him.

It was The Collector, I was sure. Several scenarios raced through my head, jumbled and nonsensical. The only clear idea was there was no time to search for the knife.

The four of us stood paralyzed as the figure edged along the trees. He used the shadows as cover as he approached. Mutual fear mounted with every step.

I wanted to yell out, but my tongue froze as did the rest of my body. My eyes strained to see weapons he might carry, but I saw nothing. The silhouette continued to creep in the darkness.

"What do you want?" Marcus yelled with threat in his voice.

The unexpected shout made me jump. The figure paused, and I held my breath. Seconds passed, and the pause lengthened, giving us hope, and then the intruder stepped out from the cover of the trees. The morning sky had brightened in the few minutes that passed. My eyes landed on his face, and my throat squeezed. I blinked hard, and my stomach fluttered as the person I thought dead came into view.

27

ZOMBIES

HE WAS OLDER, TALLER THAN WHAT I LAST RECALLED, NO longer a child, but on the verge of adolescence.

"Caleb," I whispered and moved forward with cautious steps.

"April, what are you doing?"

I ignored Marcus' voice and walked until I stood in front of my brother. He stared. Clear blue eyes examined mine. Facial muscles twitched and tensed as his jaw set. Hollow cheeks replaced the fuller ones he once had, but he did not look starved. A long, straight nose reminded me of our father's, with eyes like our mother's but not as piercing and framed by thick, dark lashes. Brown, wavy hair, hung in knots above the tops of narrow shoulders, the same length as Marcus and Shaun's.

Tanned and dirty arms poked out from ripped sleeves, his chest covered by a tattered and worn green shirt which showed more skin than it should. Crudely ripped matching pants fell at the knee or higher, depending on which leg you looked at.

My gaze returned to his oval face, and my stomach

tightened. Tears stung and pooled in the corners of my eyes. "Beth!" I kept my focus on Caleb. "Come here."

Beth's footfalls stopped, and she stepped up beside me. Caleb shifted his attention.

"Beth, this is our brother, Caleb." Emotion filled my voice, and it took all I had not to pull him into my arms. But I had no idea what his mental state was, if he even knew who we were, and I did not want to scare him away. That he stood in front of us, alive, when if I was being true to myself, I had given up hope, was unbelievable. I didn't want to blink, for fear he'd disappear.

Beth sucked in a sharp breath. "Holly crap!"

"Caleb, do you remember Benny?"

Caleb's expression changed from mistrust to one of recognition. The hard angles of his jaw softened and eyes shone. The relaxed look reminded me of the ten-year-old boy I remembered sleeping in the back of a strange vehicle. "Benny?" He whispered then cleared his throat. His focus shifted, and his brow creased in concentration. His eyes brightened. "Av?"

No longer able to hold back, I released everything I had kept to myself. Caleb stretched out his arms and wrapped Beth and me into an embrace. Together we shed tears of happiness, relief, and reunion.

After a moment we pulled away. Beth wiped her cheeks with the back of her dirty hand, leaving behind a fine streak of dirt. "Great to see you, Caleb, but man, you st-stink." She pinched her nose.

"Beth!" I scowled at my sister.

"What? It's true!" She glowered. "Anyway, he's my little brother. I'm supposed to bug him." She smiled.

Caleb laughed. "Well you don't smell any better, Ben."

Beth lifted an arm and sniffed. "No," she coughed and shook her head, "you're right about th-that."

Beth's humour eased the emotion charged atmosphere. When our nervous giggling settled, I began the debriefing. "How have you managed?"

Caleb narrowed his gaze. "Managed? Managed what?"

I waved my arms at the surroundings. "All of this after escaping?"

"How do you know about that?"

"Because we were there too, at the house. Saw the carving inside the wardrobe. They tested the last vaccine they created on you first, then you escaped. Jasper told us." And he had written it in his journal. The entry repeated in my head.

"Who's Jasper? What vaccine? What carving?" Caleb said.

"A friend, I'll tell you about him and the vaccine later. You don't remember carving your ID and the cryptic warning inside the wardrobe?" GOB42L8 floated in front of my eyes.

Caleb looked up and scratched his head. "Ya, I do, vaguely. A long time after I left, I remembered I had a knife and must have left it there. Could have used that thing so many times."

"It's okay, Caleb, we found it," I told him.

"Really?"

I nodded. "Do you remember where you hid after you escaped?"

Caleb smiled. "The best hiding places are the ones in plain sight. At night I stayed in a shed in the woods behind the house. When they slept, I snuck inside the kitchen and stole food and water, they never locked doors. If they looked for me—they didn't try very hard." Caleb scratched the top of his head. "Heck," he laughed, "I even watched them digging a grave when I was halfway up a tree. Overheard one goof say the hole was for me when they caught me. A few days later the morons disappeared, and I stayed and ate whatever they left behind. I wanted to leave but didn't know where to go. But then someone came back, so I got out of there and took food and an old blanket." His hand slipped to the nape of his neck. The corners of his lips lifted into a proud smile.

"Wonder if that's when we showed up at the house," I said to Beth. Caleb had escaped from there just before we arrived.

"Could be," she agreed then changed the subject and pointed at Caleb. "We sh-should check for one."

Caleb's eyes darted between us. "Check for what?"

"A tattoo, in the hairline at the back of your neck. Beth has one, so do I."

Caleb turned without complaint and swept up a handful of matted hair. The morning light was bright enough to make out the dark shape of a butterfly.

"So?" His knotted locks tumbled into place.

"Like ours. Come on, we'll introduce you to the others. That is unless your paths have already crossed?" I raised my eyebrows.

Caleb peered around me toward the camp and squinted. "No. Never saw them."

"But you saw others, right?" I said.

Caleb shrugged. "Not many."

"How is that possible? There were more people that fled that night. There had to be."

My brother looked at me. "Oh, I believe you. But there are lots of trails that connect with each other like a giant maze. Anyway, I watched from a distance whenever anyone was around."

"You didn't approach? Ask for help?" Beth said.

"From who? Those kids were..." Caleb paused and picked at a scab on his chin, "zombies."

Beth narrowed her eyes. "There's no such th-thing."

"Well they stumbled along the trail, and never spoke to each other, just walked, and ate, and slept. Nothing more."

"How did they eat?" I glanced at Caia and Marcus, their

heads close together, lips moving with whispered words. Shaun dozed beside them.

"Same way you do, with their mouths." Caleb folded his thin arms.

"Smart ass," Beth whispered. Brother and sister stared at each other. At equal height their piercing, blue gazes locked in battle.

"My God, you two have only just reunited and you're already at each other. I guess nothing changes."

Beth and Caleb broke their staring contest and fixed their eyes on me. I shrugged.

Caleb dropped his arms to his sides. "The zombies ate what they scavenged, berries, leaves, bugs—whatever."

"They had enough sense to hunt and gather?"

"I guess human instinct; will of survival—that kinda stuff."

"Huh!" *Had the brain-washing at C.E.C.I.L. included survival training?* I thought of Beth's field guide.

"Oh, and sometimes there was food, real food, left behind."

The information snapped me out of my thoughts. "By who?"

Caleb shrugged. "Never saw who. Only saw open cans of food and ate some of the grub myself."

Was it The Collector? Was he leaving food? Is that how he lures, I used Caleb's term, *the zombies. And if he finds them where does he take them? What does he do with them?*

My skin prickled and though there was a chill to the early morning air, it wasn't the temperature that had brought on the sudden case of goosebumps. I closed my eyes; my head hurt.

"So, who are your friends?" Caleb gave a slight flick of his head and folded his tanned arms again. Sunlight highlighted the faint white scar on his chin, awarded to him when he fell off his bike the summer before everything turned into a haze.

I sighed and turned toward the camp; Beth and Caleb

followed, I had introductions to make. "Marcus, Caia," the three of us stood in front of them, "this is Caleb, our brother."

Both Marcus and Caia's faces morphed into surprise as their eyebrows shot up and their jaws hung open. Narrowed eyes and pressed lips of skepticism followed.

"You sure about that?" Marcus stood and tapped his finger on the point of a sharpened branch.

"Of..." I began but Beth interrupted.

"Who the hell do you th-think he is?" Beth moved closer.

Caia picked up a small twig from the ground and rose to her feet. She pushed it through the gap between her teeth and closed her lips around it. "Maybe, he works for Truck Man," she said, the stick remained wedged in the space as she spoke.

"Av says he's our brother, so he is."

My jaw dropped. "You don't remember?" my voice was much louder than I'd planned.

Beth stared at me wide-eyed. "I do. He even called you Av, it's just he looks different. Not the same from my memories."

"He's older."

"I know that. But my memory isn't as good as yours, only bits and pieces. I recall a brat. Not this," she jutted her thumb over her shoulder at Caleb, "soon-going-to-be-taller-than-me s-skinny guy with the beginnings of a dirt s-stache."

"Hey!" Caleb interjected. "I can hear you, you know." He brushed the tips of his fingers over the faint shadow above his lip.

With an idea in mind I walked toward my backpack next to Shaun, who had just sat upright. He stretched his arms above his head as I crouched beside the pack and searched inside the main compartment. My hands pushed aside the remaining food ration packets, the extra t-shirt, and sweatpants-turned-into-shorts in search of the journal. My fingertips swept over the metal lid of the strange box we'd found at the compound then brushed against a soft leather cover. With the object of my quest in hand, I flipped the diary open and pulled out the folded drawing before replacing the book back in the bag.

I unfolded the paper and held the sketch beside Caleb. "He might be taller and older, but it's still the same face."

Caleb craned his neck and looked at the image. "Like looking into a mirror."

"Really?" I glanced at my rendering. Illustration was something at which I excelled.

He shrugged. "Kidding. I haven't seen a mirror in a long time, and I don't remember what I even look like." He smiled and straightened, his blue gaze fixed straight ahead on Marcus and Caia.

I shook my head and chuckled.

"Hang on," Caia reached over and took the paper from my hand. She rubbed a finger over it. "There." She turned the illustration. "Now it resembles him." The twig protruded between her lips.

I stared at the drawing in her hands. Between the nose and mouth she'd smudged the pencil lines with her fingertip.

"Complete with dirt stache," Caia said.

The four of them spoke low as I returned the picture to the journal. Lost in my thoughts, I paid no attention to their words. Once again my fingers touched the metal coffer and for a moment I had the notion to show it to Caleb. In the same instant, I thought better. Marcus and Caia didn't need to know the container existed. I envisioned the gold hearts nestled inside and the indent for the missing piece, the item shaped like an infinity symbol or something similar. I rearranged the contents of the pack, hiding the box at the bottom, and then rejoined everyone. Beth had brought Shaun into the group, and he sat close by her, his head rested on her shoulder.

"You didn't tell me you had a zombie, Av," Caleb said. The

others passed around berries gathered the day before and took their share.

"No such thing," Beth said, giving Shaun a handful.

Caleb popped one of the small, dark fruits into his mouth. "Whatever."

I took a sip from a water bottle and handed it to Caleb.

"We should finish up and get going," Marcus said then he took the bottle from Caleb's outstretched hand, "before it gets hot."

My head shaking went unnoticed. It was futile to argue them out of a pointless hike. An iridescent, green beetle crawled across the ground and then onto my leg. Antennae twitched spastically as it crawled over me. A dirty palm slapped at the bug but missed, leaving behind a red mark above my knee. "Ow!"

Caleb shrugged. "Breakfast escaped," he said.

"Ew!" The thought made my nose wrinkle.

"Trust me, when you're hungry enough, you will." Caleb stood, cracking his knuckles. "Let's go." He walked away.

The rest of us followed. I fetched my pack and slung it over my shoulders, my bedroll fastened at the bottom.

"Come on, Shaun." Beth stuck her hand out toward Shaun who had yet to rise to his feet.

He sat still. His gaze fixed on the remains of last night's campfire while Marcus and Caia stomped the charred bits of wood into the ground and spread the ash. Dust floated into the air, appearing like smoke. I fastened the pack's belt around my waist. The click made him jump.

"Shaun," Beth said again in a lilting tone, and she wiggled her fingers in front of him. Poor Shaun, he was a zombie.

"Caleb!" I called, seeing he'd headed down the trail. "Wait there." I would not lose my brother again. Caleb stopped.

"Come on," I said to my sister and strode away with Marcus and Caia.

"Shaun!" Beth's voice tinged with impatience as it reached my ears.

Marcus and Caia held hands as they strolled ahead of me. I hung back, not wanting to leave Beth and Shaun behind, but I didn't want the others to get too far ahead either.

"Shaun!" Beth called louder. "They're leaving without us."

"Hold up!" I called out and walked back over to Beth. Neither of them had moved. "I'll help you." We each took a hold of one of Shaun's arms, but he shook us free.

"Shaun?" Beth touched his shoulder.

Shaun turned his head and his eyes darted between hers and mine. "I can do it myself." His voice cracked as he rose to his feet. Beth and I stared in wide-eyed disbelief. "And I am not a zombie." We watched him join the others.

28

BREADCRUMBS

L<small>USH</small> <small>GREEN TREE TOPS STRETCHED UPWARD TOWARD THE</small> cyan sky, their leafy tips brightened with the rising sun. Colourful birds flitted among the branches; their daybreak harmonies pleasant to the ears. The fresh morning air soothed my sunburn. An occasional breeze disturbed the loose hairs at my neck and they fluttered against my skin, the light touches a constant reminder of the tattoo. The beauty and marvels of nature surrounded us, arousing our every sense—and I grew tired of it.

Caleb lead the group with Marcus and Caia close behind. Beth and Shaun trailed them by several paces while I once again held the place of caboose in our hiking train. The position was one I was happy to take as a large blister had formed on the back of my left heel causing me to limp. But the last member of the group had its advantages, one of which was catching bits of conversation as they floated on air currents back to my ears. Though much of the discussion among those out front was inaudible, I heard some of the words spoken between Beth and Shaun. His recent awakening had him asking several questions, and Beth obliged with a great deal of patience. I couldn't help but smile as most of his queries revolved around my sister. Shaun may have just come out of his trance-like state but his attentiveness to Beth showed he'd paid close attention to her. Another advantage, was no one took notice of the trail I left behind as I limped along.

I dropped a piece of material onto the path, cut late at night from the legs of my sweatpants and kept in my pockets, then paused for a moment. The single, grey square blended with the ground, lost to the brown and grey tones of the path. A sprinkling of a few more improved its visibility, and I continued walking.

Is it really worth the risk? My mind argued and for the moment I stopped dropping the bits of cloth. *Am I risking our lives by leading him to us? But what if he wants to help?* I argued back and sprinkled the ground again. *He's already killed someone, maybe even more.* My hand closed over the pieces and prevented any others from falling. I bit my lip and looked behind me, noting the evidence I left of our presence was obscure. It would take a keen eye to notice the trail.

Beth's giggle interrupted my thoughts, and I glanced at the couple ahead of me. But it wasn't long before the conflict in my head continued. *We can do this. We can catch him instead and end this game of hide and seek. If we don't end it, we'll always be on the run. Stuck forever on these damn trails.* My fingers unfurled and let a few more bits fall to the ground.

Or he'll get us first. I looked back again at the indistinct trail. *He'll find us, regardless of anything I leave behind, sooner or later.*

. . .

The whine would have gone unnoticed had I not stopped to separate a bunch of stuck together fabric squares. I stood quiet as the others tromped ahead, unaware I no longer followed.

Again, the faint whimper caught my attention. "Hey! Come back!" I didn't want to yell any louder than I had to, afraid the sound would scare whatever cried in the nearby bush.

Beth turned around first, and she mumbled something to Shaun, before walking toward me. A few seconds later, the rest of the group followed.

"What's the matter?" Beth said, standing by my side.

"Sh! Listen!" Moments later a faint moan piqued everyone's curiosity. "The sound's coming from over there, I think."

Bravery in numbers, I heard my father's voice whisper in my head as the five of us left the trail and headed into the trees.

The black wolf lay on his side; his chest rose and fell with laboured breaths. He lifted his head and gave a feeble growl. A dark eye glared at me before closing.

"Poor thing!" Beth knelt beside the emaciated animal, the wolf too sick to care.

"Wait, what if it has rabies?" Marcus said

Beth shook her head. "No. It's not foaming at the mouth."

"You can't be sure," Caia said. "I wouldn't touch it."

Caleb crouched. "What's wrong with it then?"

"We've seen him before. Right Caia?" Marcus said.

Caia looked at Marcus and nodded. "That's the black one from that pack of four. Sure of it. They all looked healthy back then. I still say it's rabies."

I sat on the ground by the beast's head. The subtle tilt of his muzzle in my direction was almost unnoticeable. A loud breath escaped from his open mouth. "Give me your canteen." I thrust my hand toward Marcus. Without asking why, he pulled it from around his neck and handed it over.

The wolf blinked as I unscrewed the cap.

"What are you doing?" Caia said.

"We can't save him, but I'm at least going to make his last few moments a little better." I tilted the canteen and let some water drip into the wolf's open mouth. His almost grey tongue lapped with weak enthusiasm.

"There, that proves he doesn't have rabies, he wouldn't be able to swallow at this point,"

Beth said.

"Poor puppy." Without thought, I reached over and let my fingers sink into the thick fur of

the dying animal. Caleb and Beth did the same.

The wolf's breathing eased and slowed as we comforted the creature. His eye opened again, the black pupil stared into mine as I stroked his neck. And just as I had seen awareness illuminate in Beth's and Shaun's eyes, I saw the light extinguish in the wolf's as he took his final breath.

As the morning turned to midday, the cool air that had spurred us forward warmed and slowed our movements, and we spent more time resting. Hiding among the trees we slept and restored our energy on the few remaining rations. Caleb savoured every bit of his measly portion with eyes closed, and he hummed as he chewed. Once finished he curled into a ball and within minutes snored, oblivious to anyone around him. Apart from our exchange earlier that day, he hadn't spoken but a few words. I supposed having been alone for so long, conversation was not a priority. Marcus and Caia, however, never stopped talking, at least not to each other. Their constant whispering and flirting irritated me, and it was a relief when they moved further from the group and disappeared behind a more secluded stand of trees.

The three of us rested in silence, our thoughts kept to ourselves. Shaun stared at a mosquito feeding on his arm. After a moment he squished the annoying pest when before he would have ignored it, unconcerned by the bug or the resulting itch. He licked his thumb and washed away the remains; his nose wrinkled in disgust.

"Beth," he said.

His voice, still unfamiliar, startled me. Like Caleb, he had spoken little during the hike or when we found the wolf.

Beth smiled and touched his arm. "What is it?" She waited with utmost patience for him to answer.

Shaun's brow furrowed in deep concentration; his eyes dimmed. His absent gaze made me wonder if his lucidity was fleeting but then the brightness returned. "Mosquito!" He grinned, teeth in a perfect row. He'd had to have worn braces.

"Yes!" Beth beamed with pride and patted his hand.

Shaun wrapped his arms around her and hugged. Beth and I gasped at this show of affection. "Thank you," he whispered and kissed her on the cheek.

Beth placed her hand to Shaun's cheek and looked at him with adoration.

I leaned my head against a tree and drew my legs toward my chest. Eyelids heavy with exhaustion closed to bird songs, and the hushed broken conversation between Beth and Shaun lulled me to sleep.

Dreams had not interrupted my slumber. I slept and then I woke sometime later. Beth and Shaun lay on the ground, curled together; Caleb slept under a maple across from where I rested. I scratched at a new, red welt on my arm and rose to my feet. The heat penetrated the trees, and I ran a hand over the back of my neck. More hairs had loosened from my bun and they were damp with sweat. I readjusted my locks, hot skin cooled as I gathered them on the top of my head. For a moment I considered sporting Caia's hairstyle but decided against it, at least for now.

The feeling that something changed was undeniable. My senses took in the details of our surroundings. Heaviness settled in my gut. The forest grew quiet as though its inhabitants sensed the change. The pull to investigate was irresistible, and I stepped further into the woods.

Every step through the trees and undergrowth was loud to my ears with the crunching of leaves and snapping of twigs despite trying to move with stealth. When I neared the clump of trees behind which Marcus and Caia had rested, I looked back at my starting place where my companions still slept.

A loud snap spun me around. I scanned the forest, looking for whatever made the noise. My eyes narrowed as The Collector came to mind, and I searched for his form skulking through the trees. A light gust rustled the leaves and carried a strong musky sent to my nose, like a mixture of skunk and wet dog. A tall tree in the distance swayed back and forth while the others around stood still. I kept my focus on the forest looking for another dark shape, one that could be as dangerous as The Collector.

I envisioned the page in Beth's field guide explaining what to look for if there's a bear in the area. The undeniable odour was one and a smell I remembered from years ago on a family camping trip. The swaying tree was another.

Abdominal muscles clenched, and my heart raced as I approached the clump of trees with quiet steps. I stopped and placed my hand on the nearest tree, its grey bark rough against my palm and scarred with large claw marks. They looked old, but it unnerved me. I had no intentions of surprising the lovers nor did I want them to accuse me of spying. But I needed to warn them without alerting the bear.

I called to them in a low voice and listened for a moment before taking a hesitant step forward. A twig snapped, startled me, and sent my heart into another round of quickened beats. I closed my eyes, let out a steadying breath, and expected Caia to utter some expletive for having disturbed her. But the silence that followed made me brave, and I stepped with purpose around the clump of trees.

In the time it takes to inhale and exhale my face contorted in surprise, disappointment, anger, fear, and worry. They had disappeared.

29

A SYMBOL OF CHANGE

THE BEAR DID NOT STAY IN THE AREA FOR LONG. ONCE WE were sure it had moved on, we searched for our missing companions for what seemed hours, our senses on high alert for dangerous intruders, man or beast.

After finding no sign of either Marcus or Caia, Caleb led us toward a nearby lake. We trudged along the trail, and while I lagged behind, I left no breadcrumbs.

The body of water shimmered in the afternoon sun and despite the lukewarm temperature it refreshed as we washed the dirt from our skin and the stink from our bodies.

"Any idea what happened to them?" Beth picked up a small, flat rock and threw it. The shale skipped along the surface three times before sinking.

I shook my head, bouncing a flattened stone in my palm, eyes fixed to the spot where Beth's had disappeared. A quick flick of my wrist and it skimmed the top then sank. "Maybe nowhere. Maybe The Collector got them." I imagined the little squares of material dropped on the path, and my stomach rolled with guilt.

"Do you believe that?" Beth hurled another rock, and it soared, silent and innocuous until impact. First the gurgling plop as surface tension broke then the violent rush of disturbed water expelled into the air. The lasting effect of ripples moved in slow and widening circles until each one hit the shore. A surge of tepid liquid lapped at my feet.

"No, not really." I sank to the rocky beach and stretched out my legs. As I did my left heel rubbed against the broad flat rock. A sharp breath sucked in between my teeth, and I drew back my leg. Skin hung from the opened blister.

"Here, let me fix that." Beth grabbed her backpack and sat with my foot across her lap as she tended to my injury. Her knack for science had emerged as more of her personality showed. If it ended in ology, she excelled. Beth bandaged my foot with the adeptness of any well-trained medical practitioner. "There, that should help. What do you s-suppose Caia can do? If she remembers, she never said." Beth packed away the first aid kit.

I shrugged. "Your guess is as good as mine."

"She's good at s-swearing." Beth stretched out her legs and lay on the hard surface, a carpet of lichen beneath her head. The broad flat rock was the only shaded spot near the water's edge and would make a great place for a campfire. It stretched from the shore and back toward the forest edge.

"Somehow I don't think that's a talent." A gurgle rolled through my stomach. "Besides, so are you."

"Pfft, I hardly ever s-swear."

"Ha, you hardly ever do NOT swear," I corrected.

"Who the fuck cares, anyway?" Beth sat upright. A piece of wet hair pasted to her cheek, and she unglued the lock with a finger. "Do you think they'll come out s-soon?" She motioned with a thrust of her chin towards Shaun and Caleb standing chest deep a little further down the waterfront.

"When they do, they'll look like raisins."

At that moment Shaun and Caleb waded toward us and closer to shore. When the water came up to their waists, they stopped and waved. "Okay, we're coming out," Caleb yelled with his hands cupped around his mouth.

I gave him the thumbs-up, and we turned our backs to them. The sound of sloshing grew louder as the bathers made their way out of the water. Wet feet slapped on the ground; a spray of water hit the back of my neck and arms.

"Wish I had something clean to wear." Caleb said.

The t-shirts and cut-offs Beth and I had worn draped over tree branches, drying from a quick wash in the lake. We had changed into our cleaner spare clothing after our swim.

"So do we!" My nose wrinkled as I caught a whiff of Caleb's dirty shirt.

"Dressed?" Beth said.

"Yes," Shaun replied, and we turned and faced the guys.

Drained of energy and the want for any hiking, we stayed by the lake sheltered from the late day heat. Banal conversation floated between us but it wasn't long before we recounted our ordeal to Caleb. We told how we came to the house and how we escaped. We shared our experiences at C.E.C.I.L., before we left and when we returned, and the things we'd discovered. I summarized Jasper's journal and reiterated the need to leave the trails; they ignored my pleas. The only information we did not discuss were the gold hearts that nestled inside the strange silver-toned box with the butterfly etching.

When the dialogue waned, we began the tasks of making camp. Shaun searched the nearby trees for sticks and chunks of wood while Caleb and Beth prepared longer branches for fishing. The rusted fishhook tied to a small piece of line hung from one pole. While my green shoelace and a length of stiff wire shaped into a crude hook fastened to the other.

I held up a single wooden match. "Are there more?"

Beth glanced in my direction. "In my pack," she said and returned to bait hunting with Caleb. I chuckled at them as they scrambled over the ground and through nearby tufts of wild grasses, their hands grappled with grasshoppers and other creepy crawlies.

I gathered dead leaves and twigs and piled them on a level spot on the rock. Reaching into my pack, I pulled out the journal. There were several blank pages at the back and they came in handy for fire starting. I tore out a remaining half page and tucked the diary into the bag.

When Shaun returned with an armful of wood, I built a fire. The match I struck against the rock erupted. The tinder ignited, and I fed the small flames with larger pieces of fuel. When it was a decent size, my stomach growled, my sibling's promise of fish on my mind.

Shaun sat across the campfire and flipped through the pages of Beth's book. "Beth can do this without using her hands." He held the field guide toward me as though he waited for my confirmation.

"When she was little, magic fascinated her. She watched a magician bend a spoon with his thoughts and that trick convinced her she could do the same, so she practiced every day. I never saw it work, not until..." The picture frames and chair leg rattled in my head. "Did she tell you?"

"No, I remember her doing it the other night. It's amazing. And she's..." he paused, "amazing." He spoke low, his ears turned red, and a blush tinged his cheeks. He cast his eyes onto the book he held and ran a hand through his blonde hair.

"Anyway," he said, the redness in his face fading. "Do you have a super memory?" A beam of late afternoon sunlight shone over his head highlighting flecks of gold and copper.

"I don't know that it's such a big deal."

"Before, when I couldn't speak, it was like... ah... being locked inside my head. I understood—seeing, hearing, feeling—but I couldn't reach out." He shifted again, shadows of leaves danced over his face.

The campfire crackled as I tossed another stick into the flames, small sparks shot upward and extinguished.

Shaun continued. "I don't remember much."

"Don't worry, it'll come." I smiled, hoping my words reassured the uncertainty I detected in his voice.

"Beth said Shaun is not my real name, that Marcus gave it to me."

"Yes, though I'm sure you'll remember soon. Even I took a while... and Beth."

Shaun nodded. "Hmph, ya, and then there's this tattoo." He rubbed a hand over the nape of his neck.

An excited and happy shout interrupted as Caleb whooped. The trees and vegetation surrounding the shoreline blocked our view of him but his voice echoed in the still air. I scanned the nearby trees, worried the unexpected and loud noise would draw unwanted attention. *Hypocrite*, I thought of the pieces of cloth and regretted having ever dropped them. A few moments later my siblings returned to camp with three, decent-sized fish, each almost a foot long.

I pulled the knife from my pocket and handed it to my brother. "Your job tonight."

He bounced the multi-tool pocketknife in his palm and turned it over, inspecting every angle. He pulled out one tool then folded it back into place before moving on to the next. "There's something about this thing."

I raised my eyebrows. "You don't recognize it?"

"Oh no, I do, it's mine. There's just something else." He narrowed his gaze. "Oh well, it'll come back to me." He flipped open the blade and stabbed it into a fish.

"Stop!" I said.

"What?" The point buried into the belly of our dinner. A small stream of blood oozed from the cut.

"Do that over there." I pointed toward the water.

Caleb rolled his eyes. "Come on Shaun, you can help."

Shaun jumped to his feet and followed Caleb. Though he had several years on my little brother it was as if his stupor stunted him. But over the last couple of days, as his awareness and memory improved, he matured. With time his behaviour would agree with his age and not Caleb's almost thirteen years. Beth studied Shaun's retreating figure. She sighed and smiled as though she were alone.

"You really like him, don't you?" I was sure I knew the answer but wanted to hear it from Beth.

She shrugged. "He's okay."

"Just okay?"

Beth shrugged again.

"He likes you too."

Beth's eyes brightened. "Ya?"

I nodded. "Just be careful."

Beth chuckled. "Yes, mom."

When the boys returned with the fillets, the coals burned hot and Beth had found the perfect branches with which to cook our dinner. Caleb gave her the knife, and she sharpened the points of the forked sticks.

The fish sizzled, tiny wisps of smoke curled from the

cooking meat, and I licked my lips in anticipation. We sat and waited, our eyes glued to our meal.

"Enough for two more?" The sudden question surprised me. I startled and almost dropped the skewer I held into the flames. Two smiling faces gazed upon us, one wide and brilliant white, the other gap toothed.

"Where the hell have you been?" Beth focused her attention on the fire and not the returning members to the group.

"Nice to see you, too," Caia said.

"Well?" I peered up at Marcus and waited for their explanation.

"Well," he said seating himself between Beth and Shaun. Shaun shifted over to give him room. Caia settled herself on the other side of Shaun next to Caleb. It was the first time since she'd joined our group she wasn't sitting near, or on, Marcus.

"Short story," Marcus began, "Caia, and I woke from our nap, thought we saw someone in the distance, tried to follow."

"The Collector?" The pitch of my voice rose, and my body tensed.

Marcus narrowed his eyes.

"I meant—"

"I know who you meant. No. Someone from our group before," Marcus said.

"Maybe it was the bear." I scanned the edge of the forest again. Goosebumps rose as I imagined shadows prowling through the woods, and I had to look away.

Marcus glanced at Caia. "What bear?"

"There was a bear skulking around where you two disappeared."

"You saw it?" Caia's eyes widened.

"No. But I smelled it."

"And I found fresh bear crap and a track or two," Caleb added, and all eyes fell on him.

"You did!" Beth and I said in unison.

"You didn't tell us that," Beth said.

Caleb shrugged. "Meant to, I guess I forgot."

A loud snap in the woods refocused our attention on the trees, and we sat quiet and waited.

Maybe I didn't imagine the shadows. I looked at the knife sitting on the ground in front of Beth. After several tense minutes I relaxed a little though I listened intently for any further disturbing sounds. "So, you didn't find him? Whoever you thought you saw?" I said to Marcus.

"Her," Caia corrected, "and no, she disappeared."

"How d'you find us?" Caleb said.

"We heard a yell." Marcus slapped at a mosquito.

I glared at Caleb as we pulled the cooked fish from the fire. The food quieted further conversation, and the only sound came from the crackling campfire. My eyes constantly scanned the trees between each bite, and I could not enjoy the late afternoon meal.

The sun began its descent and hung just above the treetops brightening the leaves and casting the rest of the forest in shadow. Soon the cyan sky would turn orange and red before succumbing to the dark.

And what will the night bring? I couldn't help but wonder as I stared up at the eastern sky.

"Hello there!" Beth's greeting pulled my attention away from the heavens. A dainty blue dragonfly landed on the top of her knee. Its segmented body was like a thin twig with translucent, paper wings. It sat still while its tiny head swiveled and large compound eyes took in the surrounding sights. "Did you know a dragonfly is a s-symbol for change?" Beth moved her finger toward the small creature, one leg after the other climbed aboard, and she held it up at eye level. The delicate insect wiped its front legs over its face and cleaned its bulging eyes. Then with a flutter of four wings, the bug lifted, hovering for a moment. The blue critter blended with the sky, and I lost sight of it as it flew away.

Beth's snippet of dragonfly knowledge burrowed into my brain. I hoped a change came soon.

30

PREPARING FOR GOODBYE

WHILE THE BROAD FLAT ROCK CREATED THE PERFECT SPOT to build a campfire, it was not the same for sleeping arrangements. I sat upright and rubbed my lower back. The pre-dawn morning air chilled my skin; I shivered and draped my grey blanket over my shoulders. Thoughts of the bear entered my mind but disappeared. Other than my worries the night had been uneventful.

Heat emanated from a charred piece of wood; fissures emitted an orange glow. I covered the burned remains with tinder and blew life into the smouldering log. Flames erupted with a hiss and a plume of smoke. No one stirred as I placed another piece of wood on the rekindled fire.

I pushed my feet into my shoes and tiptoed away from camp enveloped in my warm covering. It was my favourite time of the morning, right before the sunlight touched the sky and woke the creatures of the day. A rocky knoll with a smattering of juniper bushes and other shrubs overlooked the reedy shoreline and made for the perfect spot to watch the day begin. I sat and observed the edges of darkness change from deep blue to a greenish hue as the sun rose behind the trees. In the dim light a heavy fog hovered above the lake and blurred the landscape. The atmosphere was eerie, and my imagination conjured a multitude of animals lurking under the vaporous cover; the bear once again entered my thoughts for a moment. But every passing minute treated my eyes to another delight as dawn broke and I forgot my worries.

A dark shape emerged from the shadows a few metres away below my position and meandered through the undergrowth. The odd snapping of sticks punctuated the quiet rustle of vegetation in its wake. My heart skipped and my body prepared to flee, but then decided I was far enough away to watch the moose. Considering its size, the creature's grace and agility surprised me.

The huge horse-like animal foraged on plants and grasses. Broad and flat antlers splayed from the skull like two enormous hands. The increasing daylight highlighted the muscular frame of the beast, and I gasped. The majestic bull moose was the biggest herbivore I had ever seen in the wild.

I shifted to get a better view and dislodged a stone. The brute lifted its massive head, ears flicked; the powerful jaw mashed a mouthful of grass into pulp. Flared nostrils emitted a low snort, and he continued his trek across the shallow, marshy water and disappeared into the trees on the other side.

With the moose gone, I was no longer distracted, and the rambling in my brain started again. The quarrels had kept me from a good night's rest as much as the hard ground. I tangled with my conscience the whole night, the back-and-forth debate of leaving, and the pro and con arguments for staying. The list of disadvantages for following the others outweighed the advantages, and despite the dangers I could face, I made up my mind. But my decision tore me apart. In twenty-four hours, I would slip away and leave the others behind. We needed help, and I hoped it wasn't too late.

As per our daily ritual, we packed up camp after a sampling of berries and the rationing of one packet of food. Three rations remained, and we'd resolved the night before to save them and instead live on what nature provided.

The hike was an obvious climb, and I took up my usual spot at the end of the line as my feet carried me over an obstacle-covered uphill path. Every so often the toe of my shoe caught a root, and my foot landed with a hollow thump. A break in the trees showed us the lake below as we ascended.

Just ahead of me, Shaun and Beth held hands, and their whispered words drifted to my ears. Beth giggled and leaned against his shoulder; the match couldn't be more perfect. While he softened her brusque manner, she gave him the confidence to regain himself. And though his memory had not returned in its entirety, there was no trace of dazed behaviour any more than the rest of us.

Caia walked just behind Caleb and several steps ahead of Marcus. Either they'd grown apart or were beyond the constant need to be with each other. Whatever the case, I no longer cared, more important issues occupied my mind.

The day was hot despite the break in humidity, and we welcomed the persistent company of a gentle breeze. Leaves rustled in the trees as the wind blew through the branches but there was no concern of approaching storms. The sky was clear except for one solitary cloud.

My mind wandered and revisited memories, pulling forth thoughts I tucked away with the promise to explore. The hour had arrived to solve *the why* and I called up a memory I'd had before. If it helped ease the perpetual boredom than it served a dual purpose.

"Hello, you must be April. Such a pretty dress you're wearing." Grey eyes glinted as he scowled at me.

I looked at my green dress and wondered if that's what he meant. Pretty was not my description. "Thank you." The words were empty.

"Thank yoouuu...." He drew out the last word as he waited for me to finish the phrase.

Beth fidgeted with her collar and ignored my gaze. My eyes darted between Daddy and Mommy as I sought their guidance, but soothing a distraught Caleb kept them occupied. "Uncle," I whispered.

"Uncle...." Again his speech trailed.

"Cecil." We were not family, and I didn't understand why we had to call him Uncle.

Dark eyebrows rose high, and 'Uncle' smiled. He patted me on the head, and my body tensed under his cold hand. A negative energy surrounded him and instinct told me not to trust this man.

"Hello, young lady, Beth, is it?" Cecil's attention turned to my sister.

"Yup." Beth, still fixated on her blue dress, wriggled. "stupid dress," she said in frustration.

"Beth!" Our mother warned.

"But it's itchy," she whined.

"Oh, I'm sure it's not that bad," Cecil said.

"Is so!" Beth complained louder, small hands balled into fists, and she stomped her foot. Beth eyed him for the first time, and her icy gaze challenged his narrow one. "Sorry.... Uncle.... Cecil." Her tone was insincere.

Cecil snickered and then turned to fuss over Caleb in our

mother's arms. Daddy stepped between Beth and me and laid a comforting hand on each of our shoulders.

I recalled a more recent memory of introductions to Cecil.

"That's right—Bethany." He turned his cold gaze to me. *"And you are..."*

"April."

Why had he pretended not to remember our names back at the house? Another *why.* My foot snagged a tree root, and I tumbled forward. Shaun spun and caught me before I toppled into him.

"Are you okay?" He said; his eyes showed as much concern as his voice.

"Yes, thank you. Sorry."

"That's okay. No harm done." He reached for Beth's hand again, and she leaned into him the second he touched her. A small giggle escaped from my lips, but they were oblivious.

"Now, I have a special song for you girls."

The first introduction to Cecil returned to my head, and it thrust me into the past, though my eyes concentrated on my footing.

After he recited a verse, we sang it back. Sang the words until we knew the song as well as he did and then we sang it again. We sang it so many times it was the only tune I heard for days whether I was awake or asleep, a never-ending earworm. 'Come to Me my Children' had become etched in our brains, and we sang it whenever Uncle Cecil came to visit.

The familiar melody played through my mind, and I shook my head as though to turn it off or at the least reduce the volume.

From the beginning, Cecil had manipulated us and our parents. What I couldn't understand was how he'd gotten away with it.

The pair ahead of me giggled, and I returned to the present.

Shaun pulled my sister closer to his side and kissed her forehead. My eyes wandered from the couple and up toward the trees. The sudden, creepy sensation of close observation caused me to squeeze my eyelids shut for a moment. The memory of the ever-watchful cameras returned.

Beth passed me the water canteen, and I took a sip. The liquid trickled down my throat, leaving behind a cold trail as it pooled in my stomach. When I finished, I gave the bottle to Shaun.

After several minutes, the slope levelled under my feet, and the increasing burn in my thighs eased. I wiped the sweat from my forehead with the back of my hand and looked over my shoulder. The hill behind us was steep, and I didn't look forward to my solo descent before dawn, but I had to take my leave. My throat tightened and eyes stung. I blinked hard and pushed away my intentions and the threat of emotion. I had to be brave.

When we stopped, the sun was above our heads. Random sunbeams streamed through the trees, highlighting the forest floor. The constant breeze kept the biting insects from bothering us too much.

The trail wound its way out onto a high outcropping of rocks. We tread with careful steps toward the edge and peered out at the trees and the water below though Beth stayed back behind everyone else. Saplings and larger fir trees grew out from crevices in the outcropping. They blocked a part of the view, and it was difficult to see how far the cliff hung out over the lake.

I found a spot with a good vantage point. "You're kidding me!" I whispered to myself. Across from the bluff was a large, flat rock near the water's edge. We had walked around the lake and were opposite from our camp the night before.

"Just exactly where are we heading?" I spun and said to no one in particular; hands clenched at my side.

"What do you mean?" Caleb scratched his head.

"Where are we going?"

Marcus, Caleb, Shaun, and Caia took turns peering at each other. My peripheral vision caught Beth staring at me.

"We're walking," Marcus spoke.

I closed my eyes and exhaled through pursed lips. Inside I seethed.

"No need to worry," Marcus said. He winked and smiled at me, flashing perfect teeth.

"The point to walking is to get somewhere—A to B. Think about that." I folded my arms. A large gust of wind fluttered my hair, and the stick fell, setting my piled locks free to tumble to my shoulders.

"Not always," Beth said, "s-sometimes it's just for exercise." She shrugged.

My fists clenched tighter; fingernails dug into my palms. "We don't need exercise; we need to find our way out of here, to find help, to get back to civilization. We need to know what happened and to know if we're the only ones left alive on this damn planet!" I gasped, my rant finished.

"Okay, okay." Beth took my hand. "Let's sit."

Together, we rested on a soft carpet of emerald moss. Everyone gazed upon my face.

"We'll stay here for the night," Marcus announced.

"Yeah," Caleb seconded, "we can stop for today and stay here."

The rest nodded. Tears burned, but I didn't prevent them from falling. I let Beth wrap an arm around me while Caleb sat on the other side and rested his head on my shoulder. They didn't know, but I wept for them, for our parents, and from exhaustion.

"And tomorrow?" I whispered to the group when my crying ceased, my throat raw with emotion. "What happens tomorrow? More of the same?" I stared into the depths of blue, green, brown, and amber but no one answered.

A lock of hair whipped into my eye and stung. The wind had grown stronger, and we retreated to the forest edge. Trees squeaked and groaned as their trunks rubbed against each other under the forceful gusts, branches clacked overhead, and we made a collective decision not to have a campfire. We would eat whatever edible vegetation we gathered and could wait till tomorrow for more sustenance.

I sat on my own, studying each person, storing every characteristic and moment with them into my memory banks.

Caia stared at Marcus with soft green eyes. Her cropped hair stuck out in a random mess. She wedged a small twig in the gap between her front teeth. Her fingernails painfully short from constant chewing. A rough girl, yes, but she wasn't without charm, though she didn't show it often. An invisible and impenetrable wall surrounded her, and Marcus was the only one she trusted to an extent. She had revealed little of her life and remained a mystery. I would miss her least.

In unison our heads tilted back as the trilling rattle from a red squirrel echoed in the tall pines. When the racket ended, I returned to my observations.

Marcus intrigued me the moment he had stepped into our camp. His rich brown eyes mesmerized, and it was easy to get lost in his gaze. Add to that his brilliant, perfect smile and he could make anyone swoon, though he no longer had that effect on me.

A mass of dark curls framed his face, and I often wondered how he managed the heat under that mane. Muscles rippled and flexed with every movement under smooth brown skin. Unlike everyone else no ink marked him for special abilities or talents, yet he was no less important, if anything, he was more. Marcus had survived whatever illness inflicted the world and decimated the population. And his survival had provided the answer for a vaccination and maybe a future cure. Without Marcus, the liberation we experienced would not be possible, although it was hardly freedom. While concrete or wood walls did not imprison us, our surroundings did. Unmarked, yes, but he deserved his own butterfly tattoo.

Shaun's laughter drew my attention. As his personality and memories made their slow return, he evolved from a boy into the young man he was. My sister's heart claimed him, and he more than earned her affection. Whether his name was Shaun didn't matter to us, and people would love and admire him even if he was nameless, but he struggled with his identity.

Strong, yet mild mannered, his ability to safeguard the well-being of others became clear with each passing day. Amber eyes as warm as the sun sparkled with light and emotion. Selflessness showed in everything he did. If his special gift wasn't of great empathy, then he had other hidden talents. The care and concern he exhibited for Beth made my decision to leave more palatable.

A strong gust shook loose a dead branch, and it fell at my feet, breaking into three pieces.

"You okay?" Shaun said.

I nodded and smiled. Shaun gave me a *thumbs up* and returned to devoting his attention to Beth.

Caleb sat nearby but apart from the others, and I couldn't help but think it was because he'd spent weeks in the woods by himself. Not quite thirteen he'd survived living in the forest longer than we had. His strength of character, mind, and body was a big part of his success.

While Beth favoured Mom, and I resembled Dad, Caleb's features were an equal representation of both our parents. But the shade of his blue eyes fell somewhere between Beth's and mine.

My little brother had matured in the last five years despite not having the daily guidance from our parents or any he remembered. A strange part of me was thankful for the hypno-drug we received during our captivity. The stupor had kept us from worrying and missing each other. My gaze concentrated on Caleb, committing every bit of him to memory, unable to pull away, unable to look at Beth.

My throat pained, and I blinked away my sudden blurred vision. When I was ready, I drew in a deep breath and focused on my sister. Beth rested beside Shaun, and she leaned against him; his arm wrapped around her. They whispered to each other. She smiled, and I saw in her eyes how much she cared for him. That glare could chill your blood if she were angry with you or warm your heart if she wasn't. As on most days wavy brown locks sat atop her shoulders. An unruly piece hung across her cheek and Shaun swept it back with a gentle brush of his hand.

I recalled the moment Jasper moved her into my room and told me she was my sibling. When I realized it was the truth, I couldn't wait for her to become aware. We had reunited, and I needed her to be my sister. The fire Jasper deliberately set at C.E.C.I.L. almost caused our separation. In the seconds before losing consciousness, I feared Jasper would not free Beth. It wasn't until I'd read his journal that I realized I'd thought wrong. I summoned the entry and read the words from memory.

It is late. Midnight soon, I think. We made it out through the tunnel and are at the house. My heart has yet to return to normal. The girls are upstairs, sleeping off their sedation. I had time to place April's locket around her neck before sending them down the chute but not Beth's. I did not count on her calling out for her sister and having to place her inside the chute with April. The plan was to send them down the laundry chute one at a time but Beth's sudden awakening caused me to free both girls at once. I was lucky I had brought sedation for her as well. I will give her the necklace later, for now it will be safe, hidden inside this journal.

It was because of Beth that we'd survived our imprisonment. Her stubborn resolve and her urging me to not give up spurred me on, even on the worst days. It's what pushed me now, though she was as reluctant to leaving the trails as the others. Once again, I wondered why the subliminal suggestion hadn't worked on me, but I was glad it hadn't.

Ben, Benny, Beth—she was more than a determined girl who spoke what was on her mind. She was a teacher, a healer, and a force. She was younger than me, but so much wiser.

I turned away. Unable to keep myself together any longer, I focused my attention across the cliff. Somewhere beyond the woods was home, was our family. And tomorrow I would set out to find them.

31

BLOOD AND WATER

WE NEVER HEARD HIM. HE SNUCK THROUGH THE PINES under the cover of the wind. By the time we noticed him in camp it was too late.

Marcus and Caia stood together, mouths open and eyes wide with surprise. Shaun wrapped an arm around Beth's waist and drew her closer, protecting her from harm. I scrambled to my feet. In one smooth and calculated move my hand dipped into my pocket and pulled out the knife. The blade sprang forward as I had practiced.

Caleb gripped the strong forearm across his neck with both hands. The blood drained from his face and in that moment he looked like the eight-year-old boy I remembered.

The Collector sneered and pressed a gun to Caleb's temple. "This boy's comin' with me."

"Why didn't you tell us about the gun?" I glared at Marcus, angered that he'd hidden that fact.

Marcus shook his head and stepped forward. "'Cause I didn't know."

"Don't come any closer." The Collector waved the pistol around then moved back a step, dragging Caleb.

Marcus raised his hands in acquiescence. "Okay, okay, calm down. Listen, take me instead?"

Caia reached out and stopped Marcus as he took another step. "No!" Her knuckles whitened with her tightened grip.

The Collector laughed. "I don't want you." He pulled Caleb along as they neared the edge.

"Stop! What do you want?" Mouth formed words, lips moved, but I did not recognize the voice.

The Collector's wild eyes darted from Marcus' face to mine. "Told you already—him." The barrel of the gun pressed tight to Caleb's head.

The muscles in my stomach contracted, and I gripped the knife, pressing the handle into my palm.

"Why?" Beth cried. Shaun pulled her closer.

"'Cause I've been looking for him for a long time." The Collector waved his weapon at us and took another step back.

"What are you going to do with him?" Stalling was all I thought to do.

"Nothin' you need to know about, but I'll tell you a little something. This punk escaped and Cecil sent me out to find him, said he was important. I've been searchin' ever since for this brat." Muscles flexed as he squeezed Caleb tighter. "So he's comin' with me, he's caused me enough trouble." He stepped back and twisted the barrel against Caleb's head.

Caleb winced. "Let me go!" He shouted and tried to wiggle out from under the arm holding him. But Caleb was no match for the biceps pressing him against The Collector's body.

"Shut up, or I'll squeeze the life out of you." He tightened his hold around Caleb's neck while their feet scuffed and stumbled with another backward step.

"Stop!" Beth yelled.

"Cecil's dead!" I blurted. My eyes flickered to the cliff.

The Collector seemed to think about what I said for a moment before speaking again. "True or not, I have a job to do. And if he was important to him, then there's a reason. I want to know why." An uncaring glare fell on me, and a flash of something familiar crossed his emotionless face.

"Wait, I have something better. Something I think Cecil was looking for, you could take that instead." The silver box and infinity key came to mind. Though I didn't want to part with either, it was all I could think to trade for my brother's life.

The Collector's eyebrows rose "Really, and what's that?" His glare intensified, and I didn't think he could appear anymore callous.

"It's true, she'll sh-show you," Beth said from the safety of Shaun's embrace.

I stared at my sister and wondered if she knew what I planned or if she played along.

"Enough of this nonsense." The Collector stepped back again. "Time to go." Sweat dripped from his nose.

Caleb's eyes grew wide, another misstep, and they'd both fall.

My heart raced as a multitude of outcomes swirled in my head, and I envisioned each horrible one. "Wait! It's true. Cecil was looking for something, and I have it now," I said and moved toward the pack.

"STOP!"

The Collector's shout riveted me to the ground.

"Look, if she has something for you then let her get it." Marcus stepped forward.

The Collector narrowed his gaze and pointed the weapon at Marcus. "Stay. There!" Spit dripped from the corner of his mouth and cheeks reddened.

Caia grabbed Marcus' arm. "Stay still," she pleaded and stepped up beside him.

"Stay. There." The gun shifted from Marcus and trained on Caia. She gasped; her hands trembled. The tough exterior she displayed disappeared.

"Let me get my pack, and I'll show you." I drew The Collector's attention in desperation.

"Nothin' funny or I shoot you then him." The pistol turned on me. "And drop the knife."

The pearl handled pocketknife slipped from my grip and landed without a sound on a patch of thick, green moss.

Locked in his gaze, I moved backward with slow and careful steps toward the backpack. His head rotated as he tracked my every move. If he'd had red eyes, he'd resemble the cameras at the compound. *Did he ever watch us?* The thought flickered. Prickles trailed from my feet to the top of my head. The pack sat out of the way, closer to the forest edge, and I hoped he'd step away from the ledge.

The Collector watched my steps and from the corner of my eye, I saw a flash of blond hair rush forward.

"Shaun!" Beth yelled.

The Collector yanked his left arm away from Caleb and pushed him back as Shaun slammed into him. A shot rang out and the two of them disappeared over the ledge. Caia's eyes widened. She gasped as though she had the breath knocked from her, and she slumped to the ground. Marcus ran to her side. Caleb lay on the ground; his legs dangled below the ledge.

"NO!" Beth screamed and ran where Shaun fell. She dropped to her hands and knees and peered over the edge screaming his name between gasping cries. I rushed forward to help Caleb and glanced at Marcus kneeling by Caia. His hands covered her chest. But when I saw the blood gushing between his fingers and a puddle growing beneath her, I knew nothing would save her.

I rushed to Caleb and sat in front of him with my legs stretched out and one foot braced against a gnarled cedar growing along the rocky ledge. We clasped arms. Sweat trickled from my temples, and my breaths came in quick pants as he pulled the rest of himself back onto the plateau.

Caleb lay on his back, ashen and chest heaving, an arm draped over his face. My stomach knotted, and tears streamed down my cheeks. I turned to look at Beth still on her knees but her body curled forward. Her elbows pressed to her ears and hands clasped behind her head. She trembled with breathless sobs as the forest looked down on her impassively.

I rested my cheek against Caleb's. "Stay here," I whispered to him, and he nodded.

Creeping over to Beth, I laid a shaking hand on her shoulder and tried to coax her from the ledge. But she ignored my plea and swatted my hand away. "I'm going down there." She struggled to her feet and turned defiant, tear-filled eyes on me, daring me to say different.

"Okay, Beth," I conceded.

Beth's eyes left my face and looked past me. She gasped. "Oh my God."

I turned around and saw Marcus. He cradled Caia's head in his lap and stroked her chopped hair with blood-stained hands. Her unseeing green eyes stared at him. He looked at me, his handsome face stricken with grief. "I tried to stop the flow," he said, "but the blood kept gushing." He rubbed her lifeless hand.

"It's okay." The inappropriate words tumbled from my mouth, and I regretted speaking. I glanced back Beth who had turned away and walked toward the trees.

"No, it's not," Marcus whispered, "I should have stopped it."

"Stopped what?" The heavy scent of copper stung my nostrils. With the amount of blood loss it was certain Caia died before she'd even hit the ground.

"The bullet."

"Oh, Marcus." My throat tightened. "Things happened too quickly for anyone to react. No one could have predicted Shaun's reaction." The image of him saving my brother's life at the cost of his own overwhelmed me, and fresh tears welled.

"Shaun?" Marcus said and looked toward Beth as if he suddenly realized his surroundings and circumstances.

I shook my head. A tear tracked down his cheek.

"Music," he said, and with a gentle hand he closed Caia's eyelids.

"What?" I wiped my running nose with the back of my hand.

"She told me she was a musical prodigy. Piano mostly, but she could play pretty much any instrument you put in front of her. Did you know she could sing, too?" He smiled. Brown eyes glinted with a memory as though he heard her singing in his head. "She always sang to me," he whispered.

I remembered the day she sang 'Come to me my Children' with Beth. Her voice better trained. "Yes, her voice was lovely." My vision blurred. I hated the tune that had invaded Beth's mind, causing her to hum it even in her sleep. And yet, the one moment I had thought the song beautiful was when it came from Caia's lips.

"Where are you going?" Caleb's voice broke into my thoughts and drew my attention toward him. He sat upright, the colour returned to his face.

Beth worked her way through the grasses and shrubs along the far side of the rocky plateau. She mumbled something.

"What?" Caleb said.

Beth turned and glared at her brother. "I'm going down there."

"Beth! Wait!" I called.

"No. Now."

"Beth, just hang on."

"No!" she yelled and shifted her gaze to a golf ball sized rock lying next to Caleb. It rose just above the ground and flung itself over the cliff. Beth sunk to her knees and wept again.

I rushed to her side and gathered her in my arms, rocking her until her sobs eased and her body gave in to exhaustion. She went limp and laid her head in my lap. I stroked her hair and studied Caleb and Marcus, neither of them had moved.

"I couldn't s-stop him." Beth whispered.

"Who? Shaun?"

Beth exhaled a shaky breath. "I tried to get the gun from his hand, but I couldn't."

"Oh, Beth." I squeezed her shoulder.

"What's the use of telekinesis if it doesn't work when you want it to?"

Locks of wavy, brown hair slipped between my fingers as I withdrew my hand from Beth's head. The image of Beth and her field guide played in my mind. I sat in silence, unable to answer her question, not knowing how.

"The book pages, they're easy, but it's not important. This was important." Her voice cracked.

"Some things just take time." I shrugged, not knowing what else to say.

"I practice all the time, every day. Easy, is all I can do."

"You threw the rock, and before that, a piece of wood. Those aren't easy." My words were trivial.

Beth rose to her feet. I followed her gaze as she stared out over the space where Shaun fell.

"I have to make sure," she whispered.

It took Beth and me a few minutes as we hiked a rugged and steep path to the lake. The ledge above jutted out further than the rest of the rock face making it appear as though the cliff hung out over the water. From our new point of view, there was plenty of shore below the bluff. While it was possible to hit the lake from the ridge, one would have to launch themselves from the precipice.

I stared up, noting that our once blue sky had filled in with grey clouds in the late afternoon. My attention wandered back to the base of the cliff. Shrubs, trees, and rocks made it impossible to see. Neither of us moved.

I sighed. "You stay, I'll go look." Since our escape we'd come across more dead bodies than I would have liked. Just thinking about them and the pungent smell of rotting flesh made bile rise in my throat. But it was Beth who was squeamish. A fact I found strange as she didn't mind bandaging wounds.

"No." She grabbed my arm. "I'll go."

"Are you–"

"By myself." She inhaled a full breath, pulled her shoulders back, and thrust her chin forward as she picked her way over small boulders and brushed away the vegetation with her hands.

She disappeared behind the shrubs and rocks. I waited for a scream; a sob; any loud noise that showed she'd found either body. My pulse quickened as seconds and minutes passed and silence followed. A cool rush of air blew in off the lake and fluttered the wisps of hair that framed my face.

"Beth!" I called. My voice gave in to impatience.

The leaves on the surrounding bushes rustled and branches

snapped, but it was not from the wind. Beth trudged toward me, her eyes puffy once again as sweat, dirt, and tears ran over pale cheeks, a streak of blood across her chin. I didn't have to ask if she'd found Shaun, I read it in her expression.

"And what about...?" There was no need to clarify.

Beth stiffened, and she clenched her jaw. "Saw his feet poking out from behind a bush, blood, no movement, no sound. Dead. I didn't care to look at that bastard any more than that."

We took twice as long hiking up the steep incline to Marcus and Caleb. When we reached them, they laid the last of the rocks and downed branches they had gathered to cover Caia's body. When they finished, the four of us sat in a row facing the open ledge.

I tipped my head; grey puffs filled the once blue sky. The three-dimensional formations churned as smaller bits broke away and hung like shredded cotton balls from invisible strings. My hair let loose and fell down my back. A single drop splashed on my nose.

We didn't take cover when the clouds burst. Instead, we sat in quiet as the rain pelted the ground and us. The rhythm hypnotized as the water cleansed the dirt from our bodies, eased the pain from our souls, and washed the blood from the rock.

My father's face flashed before me. *'You can't get blood from a stone.'*

"You can from here," I whispered back. Rivulets of blood and water rushed forward and fell from the cliff.

32

DRONE

After the quick downpour we left the rock plateau in the fading daylight and headed back down the sloping muddy trail. The hike back was slippery and more than once I reached for a nearby tree to steady myself. The hike back was faster than our ascent, and the usual banter between us silenced by the tragedy that had befallen our little group. The hike back was more crowded than I had intended as I'd planned leaving the others behind in search of help. Yet despite the company I was alone with my thoughts. The guilt and sadness I carried down the trail weighed more than any load in my backpack.

By the time the path leveled off, the black night engulfed us. A small stand of maple trees to the left of the trail appeared as a perfect spot to rest. "Let's stop here." My voice was brittle. No one argued with my suggestion, and we huddled together, drained. Chirping crickets and whining mosquitoes lulled me into a restless sleep. Dreams of Shaun and Caia interrupted, and I woke several times from my own cries and that of the others. I wanted nothing more than to go home.

. . .

Dawn woke me with a start, and my mind instantly replayed the tragedies. Tears welled, but I wiped them away. The musty scent of wet leaves and dirt filled my nose. While the others slept, I scanned the forest, searching for the eyes I sensed. Goosebumps rose on my arms as my lungs drew in heavy air instead of the refreshing coolness I'd enjoyed on other mornings. I pulled the knife from my pocket and flipped open the scissor tool. "Beth," I whispered.

Her red and puffy eyes popped open at the mention of her name and she sat up. "What." She killed a mosquito on her arm and left it there.

My stomach knotted, and I swallowed the ache in my throat. "Never mind. It's stupid. Sorry I woke you."

"Wasn't asleep. I don't th-think I slept at all. Not really."

"Well, sorry anyway. Try to sleep, okay?" My voice cracked.

Beth shook her head. "What?" Her eyes flickered toward the pocketknife in my hand, and I looked down at the scissor tool and squeezed the blade.

"Nothing, I... Nothing." I pushed the small scissors back inside the knife.

"Do you want me to cut it?" She chucked her chin toward me.

"No, it's okay."

She moved closer to my side. "I could use the distraction," she said and took the pocketknife from my hand.

Small rusty blades squeaked as Beth snipped the ponytail gathered in my fist one small piece at a time. The clipped locks brushed against my neck when they fell.

"Okay," Beth said, and I removed my hand. Gentle fingers combed through the shorter pieces; tiny scissors shaped the cut.

"Done," she announced several seconds later. Bits of hair clung to her skin as she reached over my shoulder and handed back the knife.

"Thanks." I slipped the knife into my pocket then ran my hands over my head. The hot morning made me glad for my new do.

I led the way along the trail, having told the group my intentions to return to the road, and they followed me without complaint. No one seemed to care any more about anything. Several times I checked behind me as Marcus, Beth, and Caleb kept to themselves. Beth wiped at her eyes when a moment of grief came over her every so often. Then she'd find her strength again and forge ahead. More than once I caught Marcus punching a tree he walked past. He winced once when a landed punch resulted in scraping the skin from a knuckle. Caleb tried to lighten the mood with a lame joke he remembered from when he was a little but he gave up after a short while. Guilt and shame filled my head again. *Was it my fault?* I had stopped tossing out pieces of cloth way before the trail that led to the plateau and yet perhaps it was what had led The Collector there.

Heavy feet trudged over the still damp ground as the sense someone or something observed us wouldn't leave me, and I remained vigilant. My eyes scanned the trees ahead and behind, fingers ached, and I loosened my grip on the knife in my pocket. Paranoia replaced logic. Even my ears joined the insanity, believing they heard the familiar whirring of cameras.

The sun was high overhead as we arrived at the lake where we had spent four days. When we'd first arrived there back then, my thoughts of Caleb having survived after escaping the house had been doubtful. The hike back to that spot had taken half the time, but I had a goal, and my determination kept us walking longer and further each day. We were closer to the way out now and as much as I wanted to continue; we needed to rest.

"Let's stay here for the night," I said, dropping the much lighter pack from my shoulder.

"Why? There's plenty of daylight left, we can keep walking," Beth said.

"No. We need to rest, and I need to figure things out."

She folded her arms. "Like what?"

"Like where do we go when we get off these trails? Maybe I should read the journal again, make sure I got it all."

"Don't you remember everything?" Marcus' snide comment was the most he'd said since leaving the rocky plateau.

"There were pages I only skimmed." I grabbed my pack and poked through its contents. "Do you have spare batteries for this, Beth?" I pulled out the old flashlight we hadn't used in a while and pressed the button. Nothing happened, and I tapped it against my hand.

Beth lay on the ground beside me with her backpack behind her for support. She shook her head and sniffed from her persistently runny nose.

"Are you sure?"

She sighed and sat upright, unzipped her bag and searched. "Here," she said and threw the small stuffed bear at Caleb.

"Hey! That's mine!" He held up the bear and poked his finger in the space left by the missing eye.

"The button eye is in Beth's pack, too," I said to Caleb.

"Oh Yeah?" Caleb looked at Beth.

She ran the back of her hand across her nose. "Yup."

Caleb tossed the toy animal back to Beth, and she stuck it inside her pack.

"Like I said, no battery." Beth zipped the backpack.

"Don't close it, I need the matches."

Beth huffed and opened the bag again. She dug her hand inside and searched, unzipped and zipped interior and exterior pockets, then she pulled out individual items and placed them in front of her. "Ah, I can't find them."

"Last night you said there were more when I struck my last match."

"That's 'cause I thought there was, but..."

"Does that book of yours show how to start a fire with sticks?" I half-joked.

"Yup, it does." Beth said.

Sweat trickled down my back as I gripped the stick and rubbed the other end against a larger and flatter piece. The smell of burning wood stung my nose but there were no signs of fire. I touched the spot on the wood and withdrew my finger. The friction caused heat but not enough for smoke. A small pile of dried grass and other bits sat waiting to feed flames that had yet to ignite. While we had all taken turns, we were unsuccessful despite the smouldering wood scent. Even the bow and drill method failed as our shoelaces proved too stretchy and the stick slipped too many times.

"Beth, please search your pack again." I said somewhat out of breath, and ran my fingers through my short, damp hair.

"Nope," Beth said after a few minutes, "What about this?" She pulled a small magnifying glass out. "This could work."

"We don't have much time." I held out a blistered palm and looked up at the late afternoon sky. It wouldn't be long before the sun sank below the treetops.

"Let's go fishing." Caleb jumped to his feet, and Marcus followed.

I looked up at my brother. "This might not work."

"Sure, it will, I have faith in you." Caleb smiled and then he and Marcus headed to the lake.

I piled dry grass onto the bare rock and concentrated a tiny point of bright sunlight through the magnifying glass onto the tinder. Within seconds a thin wisp of smoke curled from the tuft. I shifted, and the smoke disappeared. "Damn it!" I said and readjusted the angle.

"The slightest change will make it go out," Beth said.

"No kidding." With the glass held in place, the concentrated sunlight once again ignited the grass. I added dried leaves and the tiniest bits of wood, blowing gently until a small piece glowed. I laid the magnifier beside me and continued to build on the ember. Beth handed me larger pieces of wood as embers turned to flame. When Marcus and Caleb returned with the evening catch, there was a campfire.

Paranoia returned while we ate as I heard the whirring once again.

"What the hell is that?" Beth said.

I looked at my sister mid-chew. "You hear that?"

She stared at me with knitted brows. "Of course."

"I thought... never mind."

"There!" Caleb pointed at the trees to our left.

"What?" Marcus said.

"I don't know, a flash of something silvery-white, maybe some blinking lights. The trees got in the way." Caleb explained what he'd seen.

We sat in silence, our attention focused on the early evening sky. The whirring interrupted as the object appeared again and hovered above us. Tiny lights flashed orange and red.

"Drone!" Caleb whispered.

Marcus scratched his head. "Shit!"

My heart skipped. *How long had it followed us and who*

watched? I stood up, stepped forward, and stared at the drone. It hung for a few seconds longer before rising and disappearing above the trees.

"We should go," I said.

Beth jumped to her feet. "It'll be dark soon. We sh-should wait till then."

"Beth's right," Caleb added, "it won't follow us in the dark."

"Where did it come from?" Marcus wiped his mouth with the back of his hand and tossed a handful of fish bones into the fire.

I shook my head. *Will we ever be free from watchful eyes?*

33

NOT SO LOST

I wound a pair of socks around the ends of the two longest branches we could find and then dipped them into the dying fire. Once lit, Marcus dumped a contained of lake water onto the remaining embers. A column of white steam rose into the darkening sky as the coals hissed and screamed in protest to their dousing.

We stepped with caution through the dark forest. Caleb and Beth held the sticks as the burning socks showed the way. Marcus and I followed close behind and stomped out the flaming bits that fell to the ground.

The homemade torches burned bright and quick. Black wisps of smoke curled and blended into the night bringing with it the awful, pungent smell of melting plastic as the nylon fibers in the socks burned. Before long all that remained was a fading orange glow to break the dark. We trudged in a close pack; our bodies moved as one, our eight legs carrying us over the forest floor like a giant spider. When the remaining flames snuffed out, we stopped.

"Maybe we should s-stay here," Beth whispered, and we

sunk to the damp and earthy ground. The cooler night air kept us huddled close together.

"Do you think the drone belongs to someone else from C.E.C.I.L.? Another collector? Someone we don't want to find us?" My skin erupted into goosebumps as I voiced a worry that wouldn't leave me alone.

Beth shuffled closer to me. "God, I hope not."

"No!" Marcus' emphatic answer startled me. "He was the only one. We never saw anyone else. Ever!" An owl's hoot punctuated his words and ended the conversation.

Mosquitoes buzzed my ears and the tiny feet of invisible insects tickled my skin. But as a heavy drowsiness took over, I no longer worried about what crawled on me or who followed us.

"I was eaten alive last night." Caleb said, his voice breaking through the remains of my disturbing, early morning dream. The faces of tens of collectors with maniacal grins floated behind my closed eyelids. Their laughter echoing in my head as they flew their drones through the trees and hunted us down.

I sat upright and rubbed my eyes open to my first look of our surroundings. Tall pines, maples, birch and other nameless trees stretched out as far as I could see in every direction of the mixed forest. "It'll be a miracle if that drone finds us now." While we may have lost the drone, we also may have lost ourselves. I stretched my arms over my head and yawned. "We should go."

"Where to? I may have roamed some of these woods, but never in the dark and mostly I stuck to the trails. Don't recognize this place." Marcus scrubbed his hair; bits of forest floor fell from the tangled mess. His bloodshot, puffy eyes darted from my face to the trees.

"Aargh!" Caleb yelled. Tiny tracks of blood stained both of his forearms as he scratched ferociously at his many bites.

"Will you all shut up!" Beth, curled up on the ground with eyelids squeezed closed, hissed through clenched teeth.

"Beth," I warned.

"Urgh!" she grunted.

"Come on, Ben, I can't stay here any longer," Caleb whined.

Beth narrowed her sleepy eyes at him. "Fine. And don't call me Ben."

"No problem—Benny." Caleb cocked his head to the side and smiled before rising to his feet.

Beth pressed her lips together and pulled herself up from the ground.

"So, Which way?" Marcus waved a hand toward the surrounding trees.

I turned a small circle. Every direction looked the same. "Um!"

"Aren't you three supposed to be all smart and stuff?" Marcus studied us with skepticism.

"This way," Caleb chirped and headed out in the direction he pointed.

Beth sighed and nodded. "Yes, it is," she agreed and pursued our brother.

Marcus focused his dark brown gaze onto me, and I nodded. "Let's go," I said and trotted after my siblings. Behind me Marcus groaned, and his footsteps followed.

"So, who do you think's flying that drone?" Caleb stopped after several minutes of walking and waited for the rest of us.

"Does it matter?" Marcus yanked a maple leaf from a sapling and twirled it between his fingers. "Whoever it is knows we're out here. They'll either leave us alone or they won't, right?" He dropped the leaf to the ground.

Caleb shrugged. "What if they wanna help?"

Beth glared at our brother. "And what if they don't?"

He glared back. "Always so positive, Beth."

"Shut up! Idiot." Beth stomped off.

"Think I'll take her side," Marcus said and followed. "Hey, wait up!" He called to Beth.

"You don't even know if you're going the right way," Caleb called after our sister.

Beth responded by holding her arm above her head and pointing her middle finger to the sky.

I shook my head. "Just like home."

"What?" Caleb looked at me.

"Nothing. Come on," I said, hurrying to catch up.

Caleb whistled no unrecognizable tune as we trekked four abreast through the woods. Beth and Marcus stayed quiet and there was an odd sense of confidence in my steps like my feet instinctively knew where they were going.

"Is this it?" The trail lay in front of us, but we stayed hidden under the cover of trees, uncertain if we'd found the right path.

"There!" Caleb pointed after a few minutes. On the far side was a small, faded blue tag pinned to a large tree. It was the only tag I had seen on any trail, and I remembered it from when I'd first seen it. When Marcus led us out of the woods and on to the trail many weeks ago. And it signaled our release from these trees.

My heart skipped, and I couldn't help but smile.

I tipped the last ration pouch and swallowed the measly bites of my share. The pitiful mouthful would do little to satisfy my hunger. We had a long enough walk ahead and needed as much energy as possible.

"So we agree then?" Marcus chewed on a twig; the end of it protruded from the corner of his lips. The action reminded me of Caia.

A round of head nods and affirmations answered his question. The discussion to stay hidden while following the trail had been the only conversation while we ate and rested.

We picked our way over fallen trees, through bramble bushes and other tangled shrubs as we followed the path from inside the forest edge. Though the trail with its somewhat even ground and despite the overgrowth in some places, looked enticing, we couldn't risk the drone finding us, regardless of what we thought. So, we continued battling through the underbrush.

This aimless hike now had a purpose, and visions of camping trips filled my head. Our family had camped at many campsites throughout North America, but we always came back to our favourite spot—Algonquin Park. We had spent weeks tenting in the park and even went on overnight backpacking adventures on much longer trails after Caleb turned six.

My feet stopped and my body jarred as though I'd walked into a wall and in truth, I had—a wall of memories. The unusual shaped tree in front of us jogged my memory. "Does this place remind you of anything?" I called ahead to Beth and Caleb. Marcus was a few steps behind them. They spun around and stared.

Beth folded her arms. "Are you okay? You have a weird expression on your face."

I nodded.

"What do you mean?" Caleb said.

"Look at that tree." I pointed to the American beech. While

most grew tall and straight this one had two large branches growing out from the trunk about a metre from the ground. They looked like a pair of arms bent at the elbows. After the bend the branches stretched up to join the rest of the tree in the canopy. Think!" I tapped my head. "I know where we are."

Caleb and Beth walked back to me leaving poor Marcus, once again, looking lost.

My sister and brother stood in front of me. Their faces showed the depth of their concentration. My eyes darted between them as I waited to see who would remember first.

Just like when her awareness returned, Beth's eyes lit up as though someone turned lights on inside her head, and she gazed at Caleb.

"You do too, don't you?" Caleb said as he examined her expression.

Beth nodded.

Caleb squeezed his eyes shut. Beth tapped her foot, and I rubbed the crease in my forehead.

"What's happening here?" Marcus joined our little session.

I put my finger to my lips. "Sh!"

Caleb's eyes sprung open. "Holy crap!" He stepped closer to the tree.

Beth and I followed.

"Would someone let me in on what's going on?" Marcus huffed.

"We know where we're going!" Our three voices came together and echoed through the trees in unison.

34

THE ROAD TO FREEDOM

WE COULDN'T MOVE FAST ENOUGH AS OUR FEET CARRIED us over territory that suddenly became familiar. Whenever I thought all my memories had returned another surfaced. And this time I shared the return with my siblings.

"Aren't we following alongside the trail?" Marcus said. A tree root tripped him up, but he maintained his balance.

"This way's faster," Beth answered his question as she and Caleb took the lead.

"Trust us." I smiled at Marcus, holding back a branch so it wouldn't slap him in the face. Sweat dampened my shirt, and it clung.

While time had altered parts of the land, there were things that remained unchanged and one of those was Caleb's natural sense of direction. Like my memory, Caleb's intuitive ability made him special. His internal compass meant he never stayed lost for long. And that talent grew stronger with the return of his past.

Caleb pushed away a low-hanging branch. "Remember the first time we saw that tree?"

"Yup, Av had a panic attack 'cause she thought we were lost," Beth said.

"Well, we were. Mom and Dad were setting up the tents and we went exploring. Mom said not to go too far. Dad said stick to the trail. As soon as we were out of their sight, you two took off through the woods."

"And?" Beth said.

I scratched a new mosquito bite on my arm. "And you wouldn't listen to me telling you to stop. When you did, the time marked on my red watch showed half an hour had gone by."

"What happened?" Marcus said.

"Beth boosted me up to one of the tree's arms and she climbed the other, and we waited for April to catch up," Caleb said.

Beth looked back at Marcus. "April was mad."

I nodded. "And scared. It was getting dark, and I thought we'd be lost forever." I pointed to the middle of the path ahead of Marcus. "Careful."

Marcus stepped over the skeletal remains of a small creature. "Obviously you weren't lost."

"Well, we were. Then when Caleb saw that I was worried. He led us out to the trail and back to camp. It was like he'd just walked down a couple of halls in his school. No big deal."

Beth and Caleb's remaining bonds to C.E.C.I.L. appeared to break as we continued to hike. Their voices floated back to me with recounted memories of camping trips and home life. Despite Caleb's young age on many of our adventures he remembered a lot. But the excursions before our permanent imprisonment at C.E.C.I.L. stood out the most. My siblings' wish to find our parents was now as strong as mine, and the pull of the trail faded.

Rays of sunlight poked through the canopy and dotted the

forest floor like spotlights leading the way to freedom. The trees seemed to part as we moved through the bush and the trails gave up on keeping us trapped.

In single file, we emerged from the timbers, the bars of our prison, strode onto the dirt road, and we stopped.

The whirring came to my ears first then the bright sunlight glinted off the silver drone. The flying robot had found us again, and I caught my breath.

"Shit!" Beth whispered by my side.

Caleb wrapped his hand around my forearm. "What do we do?"

My heart skipped and for a moment the desire to run back into the woods was all I could think of doing.

"Let's go!" Marcus urged, "back to the woods."

The drone hovered, watching and waiting for us to make the first move. I shook my head, not caring who watched or followed. "No." I'd had enough, and I was going home. I walked ahead leaving the others, but it was only for a moment.

"Fine," Marcus said.

I looked over my shoulder and saw Marcus, Caleb, and Beth following.

After several minutes the drone disappeared, and I could only guess it returned to whoever operated the machine. The knife bounced in my pocket. Nothing would keep me from finding our family. No one would ever hold me captive again, I would die first.

Pebbles flew off the toes of my worn and dirty shoes as I kicked them out of my way. The frayed blue and green laces were no less enthusiastic as they flopped with every energetic step. My legs grew weary, but determination kept me going.

The sudden and familiar sound of a distant rumble

reverberated in the pit of my stomach, and my resolve came to an abrupt halt. Waves of anxiety coursed through my body.

I looked up at the blue sky though it wasn't thunder. My shaky hand dipped into my pocket.

The ground beneath my feet vibrated, and I stared at the road ahead, waiting for the vehicle to appear from around the blind corner. The knife rested in my palm as Cecil's truck drove towards us. My jaw fell open and bile rose from my gut, burning my throat.

"What the hell?" Beth whispered beside me.

I grabbed a hold of her hand. Like bookends, Marcus and Caleb stood at our sides—Marcus to my right and Caleb to Beth's left. We gathered in solidarity in the centre of the road.

The rusty red truck rumbled to a stop. The sunlight reflecting off the windshield and the distance made it impossible to see who sat behind the wheel.

I pulled the pocketknife free and flipped out the blade. The click rang in my ears.

The driver's door opened. A foot clad in a brown shoe appeared on the gravel road and a hand on the edge of the doorframe. The driver emerged from the vehicle.

I gasped and swallowed back the burning bile. The knife fell from my grip, and I heard it hit the ground with a crack. My feet pounded the dirt road; the sound of other shoes scraping the road beside me fell on my ears. Stones pressed into the bottom of my shoes, naked heels and toes felt each one. The warm air swept over my face, fluttering the short pieces of my lopped off hair against my forehead; my eyes focused straight ahead.

Legs wobbled as the bones that held them strong for so long seemed to disappear. And as I entered his outstretched arms they crumbled, and I fell into him. My whole body dissolved into safety.

"Sh! It's okay, you're safe now. Sh!" my father whispered in my ear.

My sobs eased, and I pulled away and looked into blue, familiar eyes. Tiny wrinkles stretched out from the corners when he smiled. I took in his brown hair dusted with grey at his temples. The blue t-shirt paired with khakis made me smile. This was my dad, no matter how hot it was, he wouldn't wear shorts, unless we were camping. Sounds of joy interrupted my observations, and I turned to see my mother holding Beth and Caleb in her embrace.

"Mom!" My voice cracked with emotion, and I switched places with my siblings as another round of crying racked my body, and I dissolved once again. Her purple cotton t-shirt was soft against my cheek and unlike Dad, she had on a pair of black shorts.

I shuddered as the last sob left me, and I regained control. The remaining tears blurred my vision, and I wiped them away.

Mom handed me a tissue. My fingertips rubbed over its softness, and I pressed it to my face, sniffing in the faint pleasant scent. Finally, I blew my runny nose. A simple action that pleased.

"How did you find us?" I crumpled the tissue and stuck it inside my empty pocket.

Mom looked over her shoulder. Sunlight caught silver threads weaving through her long dark hair gathered in a loose ponytail as she waved at the truck. A young man in blue jeans and wearing a red t-shirt stepped out and waved his free hand, the other held the drone.

"Who's he?"

"Another survivor, like Marcus," Dad said.

Marcus had not left his place on the road, and I motioned for him to come forward. A sudden rush of emotion welled up inside me again, but I pushed it away. I had too many questions to contend with let alone overwhelming feelings. Marcus bent and picked something up off the ground then joined us.

"So, you met him when he was at C.E.C.I.L.?" I said to my father.

Dad cocked his head. "Yes, honey. How much do you remember? Do any of you remember?"

A sense of unease floated among us as we waited for someone to speak. Most, if not all my memories before C.E.C.I.L. had returned. But the past five years were hazy with no memory of the first three and the strongest memories coming from when I started waking from the hypno-drug. As for everyone else I couldn't manage a guess.

"Let's discuss this later, Ian." Mom put her hand on Dad's arm.

Questions blurted from my mouth; Beth and Caleb joined in with their barrage. Voices brimmed with excitement and desperation as we searched for understanding and clarity.

Dad held up his hands. "Sh! Hold on. I understand you have a lot of questions but I can't make heads or tails of what you're saying all at once. Why don't we do what your mom says? We will tell you everything we know. But first, let's get out of here."

Tears pooled in my eyes, and I nodded.

"Here," Marcus, who had kept quiet, stepped up beside me. "The plastic covering on the handle broke when it hit the ground. I think it hit a rock." The pocketknife lay across his palm.

The pearl coloured plastic had cracked across the middle but the small screws on each end kept it in place.

"Let me see that," Caleb said.

Marcus placed the old knife into my brother's waiting hand. Caleb inspected it and plucked at the broken piece.

"What are you doing?" I narrowed my eyes and reached to grab the knife.

"Hang on." Caleb pulled back from my reach and continued to work at separating the cracked handle. A snap made my stomach sink. "Huh, I had this funny feeling." Underneath the pearl covering was a hollow space and inside was a small, flattened infinity symbol.

"How did you know it was there? Did you remember something?" I said.

"Nope. It was just a weird feeling I got, no real memory." Caleb plucked the golden piece of metal from the interior. "What is this? How come I have it?"

There was a silent exchange of unspoken words between our parents.

"We could always go back and search again," Mom said to Dad, keeping her gaze on his face.

Dad closed his eyes and shook his head. "Maggie, it's gone. Somehow Cecil, or someone else, found it."

Mom sighed with resignation. "Without the other components, that is useless." She pointed to the item pinched between Caleb's fingers.

"Hang on." I yanked on the pack on Marcus' back.

"Wait a minute," he said, and the click told me he'd unbuckled the belt at his waist, and the backpack freed.

I set the bag on the ground and rummaged through the items. "Is this what you're looking for?" I said and held the silver box out to my parents. Once again, they spoke to each other without words.

Dad took the box from me and traced a finger over the etching of the butterfly. "Where did you find this? Never mind, tell us later." He pushed on the lid with his thumbs. "It's locked." He stared at Mom.

"We'll get it open at home." She forced a smile.

"Wait!" My fingers uncurled. The metal cylinder lay in my palm. "We found this taped to the underside of Cecil's desk."

Dad smiled when I dropped the key into his hand.

We huddled as he opened the box. Mom's eyes grew wide. She gasped and covered her mouth. Her loving gaze fell on me and then Beth as she poked at the tiny hearts.

"Jasper gave them to us."

Mom nodded, her eyes filled with tears. "Poor Jasper," she whispered.

"We found him back at the cabin," Dad said.

"You were at the cabin?" The question was dumb, it was obvious; I glanced at the old truck. "So, you knew about the cabin?"

"No, not at first." Mom rubbed the creases in her forehead.

"Not even when they took me there?" Caleb kicked a stone, and it bounced off the front tire.

Mom sighed. "By the time we found out they had taken you out of the facility four days had passed. All we were told was you were alive. As much as Cecil imprisoned you in your rooms, he and his goons confined us to the labs and the apartment in the basement. And they limited our visitation with all of you."

"Cecil had grown more unstable. Your mother and I were sick with worry for your safety." Dad patted Caleb's shoulder as Mom pulled Caleb close and kissed his forehead.

"Why not you? Why didn't you get us out?" Something akin to betrayal surfaced and made me question my parents.

"Because Jasper had to, honey. We went over all the possible scenarios and escape routes several times. And while it meant our separation it was the only option that gave all of us the best chance for survival. Once we got out we took a vehicle from the compound and headed toward Kearney where we hoped to find help."

"Is th-that where you've been all along?" Beth stammered.

Mom and Dad looked at each other. "Beth, honey, are you okay?" Mom said.

Beth scratched her head. "Yes, why?"

"It's just... well, you stuttered." Mom reached out and touched her arm.

Beth looked at me and then back at our parents. "I..." she stopped. "What do you mean?"

"I thought it was just the excitement before but now... it's just you never did."

Beth's eyes widened. "I didn't?"

Dad shook his head. "No, honey, you didn't."

Beth turned and looked at me. "Didn't we have this conversation?"

My thoughts returned to the night we woke in the strange house, and I replayed the dialogue in my head.

"Have you always done that?" I said.

"What?"

"Stutter."

There was another long pause before B2 spoke again. "I don't know... I th-think so.

The memory faded, and I nodded. "We did. You believed you always stuttered, and I didn't question or think about it after that. I'm used to it now and don't notice anymore, but they're right."

Beth's eyes rolled upward as she thought about what we said. "It's not as bad though. Is it?"

"No, it's much better," I said.

"Could be a side effect from the drug." Dad looked at Mom.

Mom nodded. "Yes, it could be. There are some pharmacological agents which, while rare, have proven to cause stuttering. And if you say it's better..." Mom looked at us.

Beth nodded. "It is."

"Then you should be back to your old self soon." Mom smiled.

Having not forgotten her original question Beth looked at Dad, folded her arms, and asked it again. "Is Kearney where you've been all this time?"

Dad nodded. "When we weren't out searching for you, yes. You see, we secretly gave Jasper the vaccine a week before the fire. The night he got you out, we gave him some booster to use on himself within a day or two, and he–"

"But he got sick!" The echo of Jasper's final words whispered in my ear and the entry in his journal floated in front of my eyes.

"Because he didn't take the booster. We found the vial in the nightstand drawer."

I nodded my head. "It was Cecil."

Mom rubbed her forehead. "What do you mean?"

"Cecil found him and injected him with the virus." My chin quivered.

Dad shook his head. "He wouldn't have wasted the booster then, knowing it wouldn't have done any good. Did you see this happen?"

I shook my head. "No. Jasper kept a journal. It's in my backpack."

Dad's eyes widened and then looked at the green pack. "I'll need to read that."

I nodded.

"And if Cecil hadn't found him, us, and he'd taken the booster?" Beth continued the interrogation.

"Then he was to wait two weeks after the booster and bring you to us. When Jasper failed to show up after three, we knew something had gone wrong and have been searching for you ever since. Jasper knew of our location but as for his, we had no idea." Dad's gaze fell to the contents in the box. "I guess it didn't go quite as planned, but we've got you back now."

"Here, honey." Mom held out her hand to Caleb.

Caleb placed the golden symbol into her palm. Mom pressed the infinity sign into the empty impression in the tray inside the silver container. There was a low mechanical noise as four thin pieces of metal, one on each side of the golden hearts, slid into the fine grooves along the edges.

"Remember I told you the lockets keep secrets? Of course, this isn't what I had in mind." The hearts popped open.

"I knew they opened." Beth folded her arms. Inside each golden heart was a micro SD card.

"And these," Dad pointed to them, "hold information on the virus, well all we discovered, plus a few other things." He smiled.

"Like what?" I said.

Mom wrapped one arm around my waist and the other around Beth's. "Let's go home and we'll tell you all about it."

Dad draped his arm over Caleb and rested his hand on Marcus' shoulder as he guided them toward the truck. "We've got a lot of work ahead of us."

Caleb and Marcus sat in the back of the old, extended-cab pickup along with our backpacks and the quiet stranger with his drone. Mom and Beth climbed into the cab, and Dad sat behind the steering wheel.

A warm breeze lifted the hairs on my head as I stared down the dirt road. The leaves rustled, and the tree tops waved as though to say goodbye.

"You coming?" Dad called through the open window.

The forest held my focus, and I couldn't shake the hunch we'd be back, then I climbed into the truck on the road to freedom.

35

CATCHING BUTTERFLIES

MOM AND DAD HAD TAKEN UP RESIDENCE IN A VACANT house in a town devastated by the virus. Others from the compound followed and moved in to neighbouring homes. It was there where they encountered Noah, the only survivor in Kearney and whose drone they'd used to locate us. Together, they worked on making do in the small community with no electricity or running water. In recent days, the new residents had installed a few solar panels, which made their daily life easier.

We cleaned up, we ate, and then we talked. Mom and Dad told us what they learned of Cecil and his plans, and I shared with them information in Jasper's journal and what we had suffered. We chatted late into the night, and while there were many unanswered questions we stopped when no one could keep their eyes open any longer. With heavy eyelids and weary legs, I stumbled my way down a hallway and climbed into a bed. My body sunk into softness and fell into a deep sleep.

. . .

Eyelids fluttered open to lilac walls. The sun shone through the window and gave me my first glimpse of the bedroom where I'd spent the night.

I sat up against the headboard and rubbed away the sleep that blurred my vision. *Is this real?* I questioned in my hazy, post-slumber state.

Aside from the white furnishings everything else was a shade of purple. The bedroom had once belonged to a child who had perished from the virus. Apart for a violet teddy bear sitting on the dresser at the foot of the bed, the room was empty. The bear stared at me with sad, brown eyes. Goosebumps rose on my arms as I thought of the child that had slept and played in the room I now occupied.

"Come in!" I called in response to the light rap at the door. Soon I would find out if my surroundings and the hundred thoughts and unanswered questions that swarmed in my head were real—if what had happened had.

Mom stepped inside the bedroom and grinned. "Did you sleep well?" she said and sat on the edge of the bed. The motion transferred along the mattress, and my body jostled then settled into the soft cushion. Every muscle, bone, and organ sighed in comfort and pleasure.

"Considering the overwhelming abundance of information gained last night, yes, I did." If it were a dream, there would be that look. The one that said 'what do you mean' mixed with a hint of pity for being so confused.

Mom patted my arm, and I trembled under her warm touch. "There was a lot to take in."

A held breath escaped in a loud sigh. It had not been a horrible dream but a terrible reality. "Can I summarize, make sure I have it straight?" Some things needed clarity.

"Of course," she said.

"You met Cecil years ago," I began, counting the points of

my summary on my fingers. "He worked on the man-made avian flu project before its shutdown in 2011."

Mom nodded. "Along with your father and I."

"You never explained why."

"Why the shutdown?"

"Yes," I said.

"Because there was fear someone would steal the results and use it for untoward reasons."

"Well they were sort of right. Anyway, after that and before another battle with avian flu and some unknown...," I made air quotation marks, "... virus in 2023, Cecil visited us often." I pressed down on the tip of my third finger.

Mom squeezed my leg. "And for that, I am very sorry."

"It's okay." I smiled and continued my list. "As a renowned virologist, he, Cecil, was asked to head up a research and rescue facility."

"So, he said, but we still haven't figured out how he garnered so much trust. He was a private person, and we knew nothing of his personal life, any of his life." A distant look came over her for a moment then she focused on me again.

For the next fifteen minutes I pinpointed the timeline. Cecil had asked my parents to join him as they prepared for another battle with the avian flu, and they'd agreed. More human cases developed each year, and we were on the verge of a true pandemic resulting in a great loss of life. The facility was near one of their favourite places. They had no qualms with moving further north for an important cause though it was still a distance from our new home.

"Avian flu was just a cover then." The sleepy haze cleared, and I recalled every detail of last night's conversation.

"Seems it was. WHO reported fewer cases, and it looked like we had averted yet another potential disaster. Then this unknown virus showed up on the virology radar."

"The Butterfly Flu, so called because it keeps mutating, making it hard to develop the right vaccine, but it's not a flu," I said.

"Yes. And without getting technical, no, it's not."

"And it started in birds then jumped to mammals." Visions of dead animal carcases in varying stages of decay played in my head, and the poor wolf.

"Yes."

I scratched an old mosquito bite. "Mosquitoes carry and spread it faster."

Mom nodded. "After three years working at the facility and no vaccine, Cecil expressed his desire to house those he deemed more fitting as a devastating pandemic was inevitable. Your father and I disagreed, quit, and returned home. Before we could inform anyone, Cecil and his goons abducted all of us in the middle of the night." Mom rubbed the creases in her forehead.

Move them out! Cecil's voice yelled inside my head, and I startled. "A manipulating narcissist?"

"Yes, but until that night, we never realized how dangerous he was. Eccentric, yes. Egotist, okay. But dangerous?" She shook her head. "Afterward we did what he asked, but we saved and stored everything about our work." She shifted her weight on the bed, and I bounced a little. "And did I mention paranoid? When the death toll rose in those last two years, he sealed us inside and cut off all communications. By then it didn't matter; no one would care. We were in the throes of human extinction."

"Catastrophic pandemic, taking people and animals. What about now? Has it stopped? And his goons, where are they?" The Collectors face flashed in front of my eyes, and my pulse raced.

"For now, maybe, I don't know. As for his thugs? We found

two bodies at the compound and by a process of elimination they were part of his team."

Images of the burned body in what remained of the simulation room and the decomposing one lying just inside a room with his foot blocking the door, came to mind.

Mom continued, "One was burned beyond recognition and the other... well he was found in his room. The rest escaped. Some with us. The others... well."

"Here!" My eyes widened.

"It's okay. They weren't loyal to him. They had no choice."

"How many?"

"All together? Cecil had ten guards. Five of which were armed and followed him like he was God. The other five operated under duress. Those five are here in Kearney."

"With three being dead," I thought of The Collector again, "that leaves two of them wandering around out there. Somewhere." My hand waved toward the window.

"If it helps any, we haven't seen any signs of them. We don't consider them a threat. Enough about that, I want to know about you. How are you doing? You have all been through so much."

I shrugged. "Physically, I'm fine. But I barely remember anything from the last five years. Only bits and pieces. And anything that really stands out comes after I started to become aware. That drug he gave us..."

"Mind control drugs." Dad walked into the bedroom with Beth, Caleb, and Marcus trailing behind him. He held up a large black book in his hands. The word History imprinted in silver on the spine. My eyes darted toward Beth.

"What's that, Ian?"

"This," Dad yawned, dark circles rimmed his eyes, "is Cecil's manifesto."

"What?" Mom and I said in unison.

"It's all here; his entire plan, the names of the children—everything. He called them his butterflies. Did you know he had a brother? I'm not sure why he mentioned him yet. I still have more to read."

"Butterflies? I never heard him say that. And no, I didn't know he had a brother. Where did you get that?" Mom said.

"I did, once. He mumbled something like 'I have to check on a couple of butterflies.' I thought I'd misheard but..." Dad said.

"And the book?" Mom asked again.

"Beth gave it to me after everyone went to bed last night. I didn't expect to find what I did." Dad yawned; its contagious effect spread around the room.

I glared at my sister; my mouth open. She stared back and shrugged. "I th-thought it was the same history book like yours and had no idea it wasn't, otherwise I would have read it. I kept it in the big inside pocket of my backpack," she said as if she'd read my mind.

"Why did you take it though?"

"I wanted someone to see how the history was written. I think Cecil had them printed with only what he wanted included. You said yours excluded all the history up until the late twentieth century. Anyway," she pointed to the book Dad held "this is more important than any history book."

"Important? That's an understatement." Dad squeezed Beth's shoulder. "The hypno-drug, in high concentrations, can erase short-term memory, in even higher doses, long-term. Just like Jasper wrote in his journal. Cecil created it though it seems it was for something entirely different from what he used it for. The drawbacks were its daily administration and its volatility, too much and you could be a permanent..." Dad paused, "zombie. Oh, and did I mention some of this is cryptic? Might take me a while to decipher." He scratched his head.

Caleb looked at me. "See, told you there were zombies."

Dad tapped the book. "Cecil had it all figured out."

"If he wanted a race of exceptional people, why did he sacrifice some?" The cabinet filled with the clothing and other items of twenty-nine residents came to mind.

"Not everyone living at the compound was as remarkable as he hoped. And there were the employees in the greenhouses, maintenance, office—they had families, and he sacrificed their children too.

My hands clenched into fists.

"It's why he had you tattooed, so there wouldn't be any mistakes," Dad said.

"Tattooed?" Mom's eyes widened.

Dad nodded. "Beth and Caleb showed me theirs, a tiny butterfly on the nape of their necks. I'm told April has one too."

I rubbed my hand over the back of my neck. "Bastard."

"And the song?" Beth said.

"Also mind control. From what I gather, an experiment before the drug." Dad held up the book again.

I told them of the subliminal message within the nature recording played in the simulated forest at C.E.C.I.L. about sticking to the trails. And how it hadn't worked on me as well as the others.

"At least now we know why you stayed in the woods as long as you did, and why there are others still out there." Mom glanced at the window in the bedroom.

"I tried to convince them," I said.

Mom squeezed my leg again.

"That doesn't explain why they brought me to the cabin." Caleb said.

"We don't know, son, but we think it might have to do with what we didn't tell Cecil." Dad rubbed his stubbly cheek.

"Huh! What do you mean?" Caleb said.

Mom explained not only had they created a viable vaccine using Marcus' blood, but they were on the verge of a cure, and that information they kept from Cecil. She massaged her forehead. "We told him we only had the vaccine and showed him the formula, but he insisted we were hiding something from him."

Dad rubbed his eyes. "And we were, we hid a lot of things. But at that time, we had given Jasper the lockets with the micro SD cards, the golden infinity key, and the key to the silver box. The container itself, I hid in our room, so technically your mother told the truth." He stifled a yawn and looked at Mom.

"Ian, why don't you sit down on the bed before you fall down?" Mom turned her attention to Dad, who stood with his eyes closed and swayed a little.

He held up his hand. "I'm fine."

"And the box? The keys? The way the hearts open? Lockets don't require mechanical intervention to open them." I looked to my parents for the answer.

Dad winked. "No, they don't, but I may know a thing or two about mechanics, operating a soldering gun, stuff like that. The compound had a lot of useful equipment at my disposal. It was just a matter of redesigning and crafting objects we already had."

"We asked Jasper to keep everything safe. Then Cecil became wary of Jasper, and he was no longer allowed in the labs. Jasper had to hide the items. We rarely saw him after that, but we found a means to communicate. There were ways around the cameras." Mom's gaze softened as she looked at Caleb. "Then they took you from the compound, but we were confident you'd survive exposure to the virus. Cecil said you were alive, but it was Jasper who confirmed it. He'd overheard a conversation and though he wasn't sure where you were, he had an idea." Mom turned her body and patted a space beside her on the bed; Caleb joined her, and she continued. "We gave grandpa's old pocketknife to Jasper to–"

"Wait! How did you have the knife, they kidnapped us?" Beth interrupted.

Dad ran a hand through his bed-head hair. "Two or three days after our abduction, Cecil and one of his guards, accompanied your mother back to the house. She had an hour to gather personal effects, and she grabbed the silver box containing Beth's locket and a few other possessions. The pocketknife was in a jacket of mine."

Mom shook her head. "Anyway, Jasper took a hazmat suit and respirator and snuck out to wherever it was he thought you were. And as he wrote in his journal, he found you in the unguarded cabin, gave you the knife, the golden infinity key, and left the door open." Mom wrapped an arm around Caleb and pulled him close.

Caleb rubbed his temples. "I don't remember hiding the key under the plastic handle or escaping through the unlocked door."

"He was a brave man," Mom said.

The image of Jasper's deathbed flashed in front of me.

"But you remember carving in the cabinet?" Beth moved over to the dresser at the foot of the bed and sat on it. The purple bear rested in her lap.

Caleb shrugged. "A little, it's hazy."

"And we already know you left the knife behind," I said and smiled.

Dad's eyes glistened with tears of exhaustion. "Unless there are more questions I'm going back to bed." He focused on Marcus. "You've been quiet."

Marcus shrugged. "Just taking it all in, you know?"

Dad patted Marcus on the shoulder.

"Hang on!" Beth jumped from the dresser and tossed the

violet bear. I caught it and stared into its brown eyes. Tied around its neck was a light purple ribbon, a small silver medallion hung from it with the letter J engraved in its centre. I hugged it to my chest.

"You said th-there are names in the book?" Beth asked our father.

"Everyone with a butterfly tattoo."

"Why the butterfly?" It seemed I still had questions.

"The butterfly is a symbol of hope, change, endurance—life. Cecil believed all of your talents would only grow and improve as you age," Dad explained.

"Hmph! Well th-that explains it. More practice it is then." Beth twisted a piece of hair around her finger. "About the names?" She questioned as her eyebrows rose to meet her hairline.

Dad flipped the book open to a marked page. He pulled something out and handed it to Beth. "Is this him?"

Beth held the photo to her chest. Her eyes closed but tears leaked out from under her lids.

Dad glanced at Marcus. "Well Marcus, it seems your intuition about that young man was right. His name really was Shaun." Dad wrapped an arm around Beth and kissed her on the top of her head.

"What now?" I asked my dad as another question came to mind.

"We rest."

"And then what?" Still another question spilled. I gazed into mom's gentle eyes. Caleb's head rested on her shoulder, and it reminded me of the little boy she once carried on her hip. My sleepy father's arm draped over Beth's shoulder. She stared at the picture he'd given her and smiled. Marcus stood behind her, whispered something, and grinned. I could only imagine they reminisced of the young man who had touched our lives, but theirs in particular. I ran a hand through my lopped off hair; Caia's gap-toothed grin flashed in front of my eyes, and her beautiful voice whispered in my ears.

"Then we start over." Mom smiled.

"How?" I thought of the others that still roamed the trails as I ran my hand down the back of my neck. More questions tumbled from my lips.

Mom leaned forward and kissed my forehead. "By catching butterflies."

ABOUT THE AUTHOR

Sandra J. Jackson has two books published with Creativia, *Promised Soul* and *Playing in the Rain - Book 1 of the Escape Series*. Both novels have received 5-star review awards from **Readers' Favorite** and *Playing in the Rain* won the **Golden Quill Book Award** for Sci-Fi in August 2018. A short story, *Not Worth Saving*, was published in New Zenith Magazine's 2016 fall issue. And in October 2017 her short story China Doll won second prize in the Prescott Journal short story contest. She holds a professional membership with the Canadian Author Association and is a member of Writers' Ink.

Sandra lives with her family in a rural setting in Eastern, Ontario. She is currently working on editing Book 3 of the *Escape Series*.

Website: www.sandrajjackson.com

BOOKS BY SANDRA J. JACKSON
AVAILABLE ON AMAZON

Promised Soul

Playing in the Rain – When all that Matters is Freedom – Book 1
Escape Series

Catching Butterflies
ISBN: 978-4-86751-779-6

Published by
Next Chapter
1-60-20 Minami-Otsuka
170-0005 Toshima-Ku, Tokyo
+818035793528

9th July 2021